The banioxle wandered in front of the beast. The mighty bull-thing roared. The banioxle froze in fright. It had yet to move when the minotaur picked it up and ripped it in two.

Blood splashed freely from the minotaur's hand.

"Let's not play, Es. Fold it up. Kill the illusion. All of it. Now!"

But the world didn't begin to fade. It didn't tremble or waver. The minotaur remained real.

The minotaur rubbed its wet hands dry on its sides. The bull-man was about thirty meters away. The damn thing was nearly four meters high. It was moving toward them.

"There's something interfering with my control, Charley. Something's reinforcing the illusion against my will. I'm not strong enough."

Scratching the illusion would normally be easier than erasing a single part of it—but this was Esmerelda's dream. Doyle didn't know how much he could help.

PARADISE

BY DAN HENDERSON

# PARADISE

**TOR**

A TOM DOHERTY ASSOCIATES BOOK

PARADISE

Copyright © 1983 by Dan Henderson

A TOR Book

Published by Tom Doherty Associates, Inc. 8-10 West 36th Street, New York, New York 10018

First TOR printing, April 1983

ISBN: 48-549-2

Cover art by Tom Kidd

Printed in the United States of America

Distributed by:
Pinnacle Books
1430 Broadway
New York, New York 10018

"Would you ascend to Heaven and bodiless dwell?
Or take your bodies honorless to hell?"

from "The Equilibrists,"
by John Crowe Ransom

"Once a nigger, a nigger the universe over."

Answar Meriwether

# PARADISE

A JIM BAEN PRESENTATION

The three of them were sailing. They were doves. Charley Doyle had spent weeks on this illusion, and he was pleased. The flaws were weeded out: The sun burned yellow, not pastel green as it had the last time. For the moment, then, he was without fear. His concentration was perfect and his imagination had made for them a world in which to play.

Inside the illusion, he turned hunger loose —not aching hunger, but the soft nagging kind that is sweet because it is soon to be fulfilled.

The trio shifted direction.

Cool air brushed against Doyle's feathers as he savored the rich blue sky and the autumn landscape below. Esmerelda swooped. Even as a bird she managed somehow to exude a perfectly human sensuality, Doyle thought. Max was different: The German glided elegantly, but cautiously—something hawkish in him even as a dove.

They came in together over a wooded rise. Clinging to the branches below were tatters of orange and yellow. In the Y's of the trunks appeared the swollen darkness of squirrel nests. A cornfield spread out in the approaching valley. It was ripe. There was the sweetness of spilled grain in the air, a smell that mingled with the mellow scent of decay that had grasped the papery stalks.

Gentle cooing erupted: admiration from Doyle's two friends.

"At last," he thought. "At last I've put my anger behind. I've accepted." He did not think of Earth or Janet, his lost home and his lost wife. Those things were far away, unreal. They were less real than this illusion.

In Paradise, the illusion only was real.

Toward the enormous banquet they raced, wheeled once over it, and then began to drift down through the golden air to the feast. And then it happened:

BOOM! BOOM! BOOM!

Pain flared at the side of Doyle's head. One of his eyes went blind. Gunshots echoed in the valley.

"Damn you, Doyle!"

"He's hit."

The single bird fluttered lower, winged. It was all dove now as it filled with the fear of the ground, the dangers there. The bird see-sawed as it failed in flight. Instinctively, it angled toward the thickest of the corn rows. It sought refuge as its single wide-lensed eye caught the dog already loping across the brown broad earth.

"Stop it, Charley. Stop it!"

Esmerelda's words were outside and didn't make sense to Doyle. Vaguely, he knew he had once again betrayed his friends—but that didn't matter. This mattered. The fear matter-ed. The fear was real. He needed something real.

His tiny heart hammered as he hit ground. The ground was cool and rich and it smelled like a nest, a grave. The dove saw three rough red spots on its sleek gray wing. It smelled the copper of its own blood. Now it heard the panting of the dog, loud and then soft, soft and then loud, as the animal paced back and forth hunting for the dove's scent. Doyle heard the padding, padding, padding as the furred feet touched the ground in search.

The dove shivered, murmured, prepared to die. Its remaining eye shined through the grass like a piece of buckshot. Only at the last did Doyle remember he had not always been a dove, but had once been a man. The man could no longer die—but the dove could. Doyle waited for the killing teeth to appear.

Doyle did not believe in Paradise—although he was well acquainted with several kinds of hell. Neither did he fly. He walked. As he walked, he wheezed.

"You know, Charley, a little exercise would help you climb these stairs," Gentry said. Gentry was a square-built and muscular man whose appearance disguised his intelligence. The two of them were taking the stairs up to the U.S. Attorney's office. The steps were cracked and the walls were painted gray. Air in the shaft stank with heat and sweat, poisoned by August in Memphis.

"A little more exercise would kill me," Doyle said. He counted to himself. Three flights to go. "And I could give up cigarettes and get some sun, right?"

"Right."

"And divorce Janet and forget Meriwether? You want me to give up all my fun things?"

"I just want to be able to climb the stairs in less than an hour," Gentry said.

"Why? Speed only means we have to face Cole that much sooner."

The bodyguard grunted in agreement.

Ernest Cole was the U.S. Attorney. He was Doyle's boss. Cole was an excellent politician and a lousy DA. He was one of the hells Doyle acknowledged.

"You going to tell him about your car?"

"No."

"He'll find out on the news."

"He doesn't watch the news. His lips move

when he watches TV," Doyle said.

"Have it your way. If somebody blew up my car, I'd want my boss to know about it."

"If I had me for a boss, it'd be okay too—but I've got Cole. He'd have the FBI called in if he heard Meriwether had boobytrapped my car. It'd ruin everything. Everything. You know Meriwether was just playing a little joke."

"Damn funny joke."

"I kind of liked it," Doyle said. "It means we're getting close. It's the first good sign we've had."

When he was able to breathe normally again, Doyle attacked the steps. *Damn the elevator operators*, he thought. *Damn the elevator mechanics. Damn high-rise architects. Damn the inventor of the step.* If he nailed Meriwether, he wouldn't have to climb these steps anymore. He could quit. And—after ten years, going back, going way back to when he was a cop—it seemed to be ending. Finally, it was ending.

As the two of them passed through the carpeted reception area—thick carpet Cole had installed, even while there wasn't enough money to hire investigators—the receptionist stopped him.

"Bad news, Mr. Doyle. Congress still hasn't acted on the budget."

"Meaning still no check?"

"Yes, sir."

Doyle turned to Gentry and said, "Can you believe one reason I grabbed hold of the

government teat was job security? I should
have gone into honest work like pimping."

"There's more," Sam the receptionist said.
"Cole wants to see you. Pronto."

Doyle shook his head in mock dismay. "Oh
Lord, this world and one more. You're a bodyguard, Jack. Guard me."

"Sorry," Gentry said. "I'd need a plumber's
union card to help."

"At least come along and keep me from
tearing his tongue out," Doyle said.

Cole was at his telescope when Gentry and
Doyle entered. The telescope was for watching women. Cole had put up the telescope
even before his law books were on the shelf
—and he'd refused to take the U.S. Attorney
post until the offices were shifted so he had a
better view of the Civic Plaza. Doyle watched
the fat of the man's haunches ooze inside their
polyester cage.

Finally, Cole turned from his telescope and
sighed. "There's so much flesh in the world
and I can't chase it. You know why? Because
I'm locked into this office running flack for
you. It's not fair."

"Life isn't fair," Doyle said.

"It ought to be."

"Ought has nothing to do with it," Doyle
said. "Reality—mean, ugly, stinky old reality
—is what counts."

"You're hard-core, Doyle."

"I'm wise."

Cole arched, his eyebrows and shook his

head for Gentry's benefit. "Wise? Would a wise man badger upstanding citizens? Would even a moderate fool?"

"I don't follow you."

"It's Meriwether. Friends of his have been on the phone all morning. I think you need to lay off."

"Why?"

"It's called 'harassment,' Charley. That's against the law. We don't do that. We enforce the law. We don't break the law."

"Just paid him a little visit is all," Doyle said. He shifted slightly in his seat. He had known this was coming. Meriwether had made too many connections since he turned from cop into rogue. He was on the side with power now.

"What's this bunk about a killing, anyway? Meriwether hasn't killed anybody."

"Not that we can prove. And I think he's tried to kill me. Anyhow, I didn't accuse him of murder. I just sort of implied it."

"Charley, dammit, Charley. You're supposed to be a professional. Up to now, you've been aces. If you know so much, why haven't you brought it to me to take to the Grand Jury?"

"We can't get an indictment yet. When we can, I'll let you know."

"When?"

"Soon."

Cole rolled his eyes. "Soon isn't good enough. I'll give you till Friday."

"Friday? Are you crazy? Do you know what we're up against?"

"No—and I don't know because my hotshot assistant won't tell me."

Doyle swallowed. He saw that Gentry was tense; the bodyguard's eyes were pleading. Doyle hadn't even told Gentry the whole story, or even the reason he really wanted Meriwether. He found it hard, even now, to mention what happened to the little girl named Charlotte. Doyle knew that Gentry thought he was on a fantasy goose chase—and that, if Doyle talked now, they would blow the little they had.

But if Doyle didn't talk, the investigation was over. Friday was impossible. He would have to talk, or at least pretend to talk. He had no choice.

"One big problem is we have to find Meriwether."

"What?" Cole said. "You just talked to him."

"I talked to his body. It wasn't him."

Cole blinked. Doyle imagined the U.S. Attorney's gray matter puffing and wheezing the way Doyle's lungs worked on the stairs. He would have to be careful not to blow Cole's fuses.

He started slowly. He pieced together the recent changes in Meriwether's life. In the last two weeks, Meriwether had shut down the Mississippi farm where he'd run his porno mill. He had cut loose from his black-market gasoline operation. There were other, minor things.

"He's quit smoking. He used to smoke a pack a day of French cigarettes. And he's redecorating his office. He used to have a dozen pictures up of young white girls. They're coming down."

"So what?"

And Doyle realized he couldn't say. There was no proof—only his intuition, supported by street talk. There was no evidence that Meriwether even knew of the raped, murdered children. None. Except in Doyle's mind.

"It's just a hunch: the pictures, the smoking," he said. "But I've known Meriwether for years, and I'm telling you that the man I talked to isn't him. You know my record. I don't have hunches; I have facts that no one else has seen yet. I'm telling you Meriwether is more than just crooked. He's evil—and he knows I'm tracking him. When he found out, he hid. I'm sure of it."

Cole blinked some more. "What about it, Jack. You buy it?"

"Meriwether's fingerprints are the same. His voiceprint's the same. All the evidence says Charley's wrong—but I've seen him turn the evidence upside down before. Until now, I've never thought he was crazy, either. I just don't know."

"Hardly an enthusiastic endorsement, I'd say. You're still certain though?"

"As sure as I breathe," Doyle said. He lit a

cigarette. He was almost trembling with anger at what he couldn't say about Meriwether. About how Meriwether had stolen his libertarian ideas and turned them into a rationale for crime. About how the two of them had been friends and Doyle had been betrayed. Even about how a black man, Meriwether, could rise out of the ghetto and begin making his mark—only to sell himself out when he already had it made.

"Christ," Doyle said. "How can I be sure? It even sounds crazy to me. I just know something's happened to the man, and the man we got ain't the man we want. Maybe it's something else. Maybe he's converted, or gone into est, or his hemorrhoids have cleared up. All kinds of possibilities. Until I have the answer, though, I can't take this in good faith to a jury."

Cole scratched himself under the right arm. He yawned. For a moment, he closed his eyes. When they opened again, Doyle saw there a brightness he didn't recall seeing before. "You know what it sounds like, don't you?"

"No. Do you?"

"It sounds like what that Australian said happened to him, or almost happened to him," Cole said.

"What Australian?"

"The one who's been on all the talk shows. The one who says UFOs tried to steal his soul."

"I don't get it," Doyle said.

"His soul, Charley. They tried to steal his soul. Like what you're saying happened to Meriwether."

"Ernest, every day I'm gladder I don't watch TV news. I'm gladder I don't watch TV at all, because the things people tell me they've seen absolutely boggle my mind. How an adult at the dawn of the Twenty-First Century can believe little green men are crossing interstellar space to steal the souls of kangaroo cowboys and porno dealers from Memphis, Tennessee, astonishes me. I mean, of the millions and millions of people on Earth, why them?"

Defensively, Cole said, "I don't know about Meriwether—but the Australian was a judge."

"I get it. Sure," Doyle said. "The little green men—realizing how corrupt and inefficient our justice system is—have come here from the edge of the Universe to set it right. After searching all the benches in the world, they miraculously found a judge who had honor, humanity and intelligence. Having found this miracle, they took his soul. Now they're gathering up all the souls of the unpunished crooks, so his soul can judge theirs. That explains Meriwether."

Cole's face lighted up like a Jack-o'-Lantern. "Hey, great. That may be it. This time you're really on to something."

"Ernest?"

"Yeah, Charley?"

"Grow the hell up."

Cole reddened. He sputtered something, but Doyle was already on his way out of the office. Before Doyle was through the door, however, Cole managed to speak English.

"Charley?"

"What now?"

"You have until Thursday to finish with Meriwether."

Orion swims in a sea of poison. The electromagnetic ball surrounding the green planet is one hundred light-years in diameter. The poison ball has spread and spread until finally it has brought plague to the weaker of the Nothing Makers. The plague must be stilled.

Physical being annoys Orion. He has existed outside matter for most of the lifetime of this galaxy, assuming only a skeleton of light when Council convenes. He finds the skeleton stiff, an encumbrance. Physical shape is a crutch for the weak, for the newly gathered of the Nothing Makers, or for those whose thoughts are too dirty to ever be pure and free. Yet—yet—Orion is become physical again. Duty demands it; Council has called. In order to combat the plague, he must continue to drag about a physical shape.

Earth is purely physical, as is its culture.
From experience of star-lives before, Orion
knows that such cultures need radio for communication. They need television, briefly.

But those things, while not the crime, are
the evidence of the crime.

Their crime is different, more subtle and
abstract.

The signals poisoning space are not mere
communication. They seem to be an entertainment, however unlikely. Cubans, their
red-haired wives, talking mice, pointy-eared
"aliens" and poems about detergents are
found in the signals.

For their own amusement, the Earth people
are poisoning space.

But that is not the crime, either.

"They defy thought. They eat reason and it
makes them ill," huffs Interharg. Interharg,
the brutal thinker, is also not happy about
being called into shape. "Shut down their sun
and happily we may applaud their death."

"Ignorance demands death," other voices
agree.

"No," says Orion, although he does not like
what he must say. "The Rules of Reason say
this is a clean ignorance, a young ignorance. It
is not for the sternest judgment. They only
now begin to approach an understanding of
matter, of the problems of light, of nothingness."

From his study of Earth, Orion knows they
have just begun to name the innermost soul-

parts of the atom. The people are at the edge, but they will not look beyond. Some of them understand that the quanta carry not only energy, but information. Some understand that the very laziness, the disorganization, of electrons is all that keeps the sub-atomic world together. Some even begin to understand, but not yet to comprehend, the probability waves tick-tick-ticking out from the soul particles.

And what none know, what none have apparently even thought about, is how marshalling those bits into radiation waves—the longer waves of radio and television, especially—by itself imparts information which the electrons "learn."

By learning, they become more orderly and less lazy. Instead of proceeding purely at random, they acquire "purpose." And—ten years, fifty years, a hundred years later—they transfer that purpose into an atom where they make their new home.

And here, and there, only occasionally but with increasing frequency, an atom collapses because of it. And another. And another.

And given time, the collapses will make a thunder and the thunder is the sound of the fabric of the Universe giving way.

Orion, who is not easily amused, finds it interesting that a low form of entertainment has accidentally started all things down the road to collapse.

He chuckles, a pinkish light.

Unlikely as it seems, Orion has also found

hints of maturity among a few individuals in the Earth's population. By the Rules of Reason, those few must be saved.

"I propose an Egg," he says. "It is not pleasant, but it is our duty."

"What a prismatic piece of diffracted magenta," Interharg grumbles. He calls Orion a bleeding light—and he refuses to help Orion with the dirty work ahead.

Orion feels the weight of his long life upon him. He is as close as any among the Nothing Makers to achieving pure being. His advanced state protects him against the poison; could, indeed, protect him against the eventual winding down of the Universe. But his duty to those that have graduated from the Egg, but have not become pure, calls him back. He must become more deeply physical.

He must again see, and touch, and taste, and hear. And feel. He has not done these things in star-lives. To do so will cost him years in his struggle to become pure.

Scarcely two million individuals from the planet's billions will be saved.

Orion fully forms his body of light.

He side-skips across fifty years of poison.

Reports of UFOs circle the globe.

Orion seeks a mind barely flickering with the possibility of future maturity. He eases himself inside the bone and flesh dome-case of the hull. He maps the neural pattern of this pitiful, young mind. He forms a template of the mind, and the template will be microed and microed again. It will enter a chip fired in the heart of a black hole.

Orion calls the chip the "Egg." Interharg calls this one "Council's Folly." Others call it "Paradise."

Orion works. He fills with second-hand emotions from the minds he screens. He weeps for loves he has never known. For dead children he did not bear. For wars he does not understand and could not prevent.

The alien learns pain again. He hurts with loneliness, disgust and misunderstood beauty. He cries. He screams. He hurts deeply, but it is not the hurt that bothers him. What bothers him is he enjoys the hurt.

He knows, as he works, that he is being seduced into reality. Pureness, reason, wisdom, duty: Those exist only apart from, outside of, in contradiction to reality. The more pure he has become, the less real he becomes.

And now this.

Orion justifies his good feeling by thinking he does a kindness to the hulls whose minds he steals. He is stripping from them their neurotic, powerful drives—the drives that make them special. In Paradise, those special minds will exist again—and there they should heal. They should learn to deal with the life on the other side of physical reality.

This particular hull, named Max Gunther, will stop bleeding for the ideal of a world at peace. The ulcers in the hull will heal and its blood pressure will drop. It will begin drinking beer in Hamburg without fearing that nearby strangers may be KGB or CIA. The hull will become normal.

And its mind will be set free in Paradise.

Soon, Orion thinks, this planet will see its civilization collapse as the dreams of those like Gunther are taken from it. Or else—unlikely, but always a possibility—the civilization itself will fully mature to replace the stolen dreams from the absent minds.

Either way, the poison signals will soon stop.

Orion gently places the template of Gunther's mind into the Egg.

He rests, he lovingly remembers Gunther's pain, and then he descends again into the poison ball for the next mind. Around him, hundreds of others from Council descend.

The lights in Earth's sky are beautiful.

Answar Meriwether had almost put the attack out of his mind. When it happened, he thought it might be a brain aneurysm by the way the pain happened, by how it it seemed to alter his way of thinking. He'd had trouble breathing, too, but he blamed that on the French cigarettes he smoked. His doctor

checked him and found nothing. And, since
the attack, Meriwether had found himself
more alert, more happy, than he could remember.

He'd also decided his life needed wholesale
change.

Within a year, he thought, he should be
completely legitimate. Let two years pass, he
might even enter politics. There was no reason to be in crime anymore—not even the
good reasons he used to have. There was no
need for him to lie awake and wonder when
his old buddy, Doyle, would nail him.

*How come it took me so long to decide?* he
wondered. *Foolish. It was foolish. Thought I
had some duty to help fight the Man. Crazy—
'bout time I outgrew that.*

Meriwether's Afro was aristocratically
short; the hair stopped at a razor-line two
inches above the silk collar of his white shirt.
He had light chocolate skin and, when he
smiled, he smiled with teeth of ice. Behind his
back, he was called "Obsidian"—and that
pleased him very much.

The reputation would help as he entered
legitimate business.

He put his fingers together in a tent and
waited for the men to assemble. Lew was
missing; Lew would be following Doyle and
his bodyguard. Three men, three hulks,
moved into Meriwether's office like shadows.

"You did well," he said.

The one called "Tiny" smirked. "But he

don't scare easy. It was like he was expecting it."

"He was."

That morning, Doyle's car had blown up. Of course, by now, Gentry was starting the car remotely—which Meriwether expected. Doyle would know that it was not a serious threat, just part of the game. *At least I hope he knows. He's changed, soured*, he thought. *But that, too, is past.*

"What next?"

"We drop it," Meriwether said. "I would have called it off before now, but it was too late. Plans have changed."

"But we just rolling," Tiny protested.

Meriwether stared at the man. His head was too small for his two hundred pounds. He was a stupid man, and careless. And the present troubles were all his fault.

"I'm thinking of turning you in to him," Meriwether said.

Tiny stiffened. His hands touched his crotch and he made a plaintive mewing sound. Sweat—he always sweat too much—made shiny lights on his forehead. The thick features took on an expression of pleading.

"But I won't. You've been punished, and I have to take the heat. You understand that?"

Tiny nodded.

"Good. We lay off Doyle from here on out. That game's over. Anybody still playing the game after midnight answers to me—and if the word doesn't get out by midnight, you answer to me. Clear?"

There were three nods in unison.

"New business?"

"Acey's been bustin' in houses over in the Smith development. You want SOP?"

Meriwether considered. Standard operating procedure would be to bring Acey in, make him sweat, and then see that he repaid whatever he stole—at double its value. Funny, that approach didn't make sense anymore. It was a joke, really, his doing the Man's work.

"No. It's not our problem."

"But you've always—"

"This isn't always," Meriwether said. "This is today, and today is a new beginning."

Again, three nods—but there were questions in the eyes.

The youngest of the three fished a cigarette out from a belt pouch and started to light it.

"Don't do that," Meriwether said. "We don't smoke in here anymore.

"Anything else? All right. Hit the streets."

When the door closed, Meriwether dimmed the lights. He keyed on a tape by Vivaldi. Slowly, delicately, his thin fingers moved in circles on his temples.

He would have to turn Tiny in, he decided. It wasn't exactly fair, and he would never have done it before—but before was past, and the past was dead. *I promised him I would take the heat, but he shouldn't have raped those girls. I know he paid; thanks to me, he pees like a girl. But that's not enough. I got to get Doyle off my back if I'm going straight, and Tiny's the only way.*

He picked up the telephone to call the U.S. Attorney's office, then stopped. He knew he should feel guilty, but he didn't. It was something else that bothered him.

Something had changed in him, and the change was for the better. He was out for Number One, now. It was the only game that made sense. The only one.

*Of course it does. So what's the problem?*

He looked at the pictures on the wall of his office. He was happy to be rid of those white girls. He tried to remember what had attracted him to them, but he couldn't. Now, the idea filled him with distaste.

*Maybe I had a stroke, one of those little ones. But I'm too young for that.* He paused, smiled to himself. *And I'm too old to let adolescent ideals stop me from what I must do.*

He picked up the 'phone again. This time he dialed and the ringing at the other end didn't bother him.

When he asked for Doyle, he was told Doyle hadn't come in yet. No, he hadn't checked in either.

Meriwether hung up the 'phone gently. "Doyle late for work? Strange things are going on. Compared to that, my personality hasn't changed at all." He turned to his Video Display Terminal and logged on to get the latest stock reports.

What Doyle had in mind, after Gentry brought him home, was to drink a bottle of the best whiskey in the world and then seduce the most beautiful woman in the world. He bought a bottle of Jack Daniels and planned to seduce his wife—confident that he would succeed in both his quests.

Doyle lived in Midtown. Midtown was an arc surrounding downtown Memphis. It was a doppelganger of the real city, now that the rich and well off had returned to downtown —leaving the poor to move east. Now the poor were made poorer since they had to buy the gasoline to make the long trips into town that the rich had forced on them.

Janet and Charley Doyle lived in a ramshackle house cooled by two aging air conditioners. They could barely afford to operate the two, and the house needed four. On nights like this, the deep nights of August, the whole world seemed to wilt in Memphis. There was a heaviness in the air that led inevitably to depression—and Doyle sensed himself falling into the pit.

If Janet was happy, his mood would lift. Doyle really had little use for his own happiness. He thought it was a stupid thing to be concerned with: happiness. His, anyway. Useless, too. But for Janet, for Janet he wanted

happiness. He had always felt hollow before
her; he had sometimes wondered if the fanati-
cal way he pursued his goals was a reflection
of that. He could only be still, could only be
calm, when she was near.

As he entered through the back door, Uriah,
his black cat with the battered features of
many nights in the alleys, appeared from the
quickening dark. "How goes it, old buddy?
Raised enough hell for one day?" The cat
scooted in as Doyle opened the door and
heard the radio chattering from up front. The
news was on. He could hear a chalky-voiced
man describing a spaceship: more UFO reports: Christ. But it would please Janet, he
figured. She seemed to think the UFOs held
salvation for the world.

Doyle had quit arguing with her about the
good reasons why UFOs couldn't represent
alien visitors. The physics of the problem
escaped her; the pointlessness of it didn't
offend her.

"Charley? Is that you?"

"Me, hon."

There was music in her voice. She appeared
in the long hall. She was slim, slight-chested,
her face delicate and floating in the semi-
darkness. They hugged. He smelled her hair.
Marvelous hair: blonde and smelling of apricot. He felt the wounds of his day begin to
heal.

"What's happening in the world?"

"New 'FO reports. There's been a rash of

them in Italy. A woman there—you should see her, she's beautiful—says she was attacked by something in her sleep. She said it felt like a wool blanket was being pushed down on her face, like she was being suffocated. It sounded awful."

"See her?" Doyle asked.

Janet pulled away slightly. "I was next door at Sue's. I saw her on TV there."

"Mmmmmmmm," he said. He would have to give in and buy a television sooner or later, he realized. He hoped it would be later. But he knew, when Janet asked him straight out, he would agree to buy her one.

Janet talked on. Doyle half listened.

"And the Northern lights are acting up. They're brilliant. They say it's because of sunspots—but there're not supposed to be sunspots right now."

"No? Odd." He wondered: Is it possible for the physical world to catch human madness? What was the link between mind and matter anyway? What if gravity went bonkers tomorrow? It could happen, he decided. It probably would.

"I smell something that smells almost as good as you do," he said.

"Eggplant Parmesan. There was a special at Montesi's."

"Fantastic. Ready soon?"

"After some wine," she said.

Ho ho, I'm being suckered, he thought. Tonight she asks for the TV. Fine, wonderful . . . as long as there's tonight.

Later, after wine, after dinner, after sex, Doyle's worries returned. He lay in the heat and darkness, sheets damp beneath him and Janet's breathing beside him. He smoked cigarette after cigarette, and sleep would not come.

Outside, Memphis was at its infernal worst. Hot, thick air became a blanket in the ninety-degree night. Even the neighborhood dogs were silent, become soggy lumps of fur curled beneath shrubs. Defiantly, the hall air conditioner continued its losing struggle. The sheets grew damper.

Doyle's eyes blurred slightly. He felt a kind of numbness in his brain. He stubbed out his cigarette.

"Overwork," he said to himself. "Too much strain."

But he could not shut out thoughts of Meriwether, and of blood, and of the frightening increase in UFO reports. *What the hell is happening to the world*? UFOs, oil companies, sinners and Commies: Everyone had their favorite villain, and the villain was everyone.

"Including me."

The room became wavy. Doyle suddenly felt short of breath. "Jesus," he said aloud.

He felt a bright hot pain, like the flash of a migraine. "Janet, I—Janet . . ."

His words stopped. He felt something like a wool blanket forced down on his face. He tried to cry out, and he couldn't, and he felt fear.

And then he felt nothing.

The morning came and Doyle felt well rested. He felt good, cheery—unworried. He felt like he was a kid again, waking up to a new world. He playfully grabbed for Janet as she moved from the bathroom past the bed.

"In my life, what's got into you?"

"Lust," he said.

She squinted at him. Her contacts weren't in, and their absence gave her a peculiar glassy stare. "This isn't like you," she said. "Nothing but nights with the lights out: that's you."

"Things change," he said. "I just feel so damn good today. I don't think I've felt this good in ten years."

"Not even when we married?" She backed off to study him.

"That's almost how good I feel."

Uriah leaped onto the bed and stopped. His back raised. He hissed and fled the room.

"What's wrong with Uriah?"

"Don't know," he said. "Cats are dumb. Come here."

Doyle pulled his wife close and held her. She was tense for a moment, then nestled against him.

"You'll be late for work," she said.

"I plan to be," he said.

*   *   *

And the other Doyle was nowhere. Doyle
No. 1, the Doyle with burning memories of
strangled children, with fears for the world
and with a desperate desire to clean up one
small corner of his world, was nowhere. Was
gone.

It was strangely peaceful, this nothing. "I
have gone mad," Doyle told himself. He didn't
hear the words. He saw them. The words were
green and appeared in the grayness, then disappeared. The attorney scraped through his
memory, trying to think of a madness or a
condition that resembled this. He came up
with . . . nothing. *Maybe a nerve disease of
some sort, in which something has cut off
communication between the body and the
brain.* That didn't help: He could remember
nothing like that, either.

"What a flaming mess."

He watched the words appear, glow, and
then fade away.

The only thing that he could imagine that
resembled this would be to be stuck in a sen-
sory deprivation chamber. That's where you'd
feel this. Something like this. *Except you
could still try real hard and hear your heart-
beat; you could feel your pulse, maybe. But
here there's not even that.*

He floated in the nothingness. He was perfectly comfortable. The twinges from his ul-
cer, the slight pain from his back: both were
gone.

"Janet kept telling me I needed a vacation,"
he thought.

The words appeared. He wondered what he
was watching *with*. "I haven't got eyes, not
that I can feel—not that I have anything to feel
with. But I feel normal, somehow. Like when
I've been concentrating on a brief, and I forget
everything and there's nothing between me
and my thoughts."

*That's how I feel.*

*It feels good.*

*... BUT WHAT'S HAPPENED?*

He must be sick. He'd been meaning to get
to a doctor, but kept putting it off. *Doctors are
quacks anyway*, he thought. *Almost as bad as
lawyers*. He chuckled.

And he knew why he hadn't had a physical
in ten years. He could still remember his last
visit: He'd gotten an inflamed cyst on his
neck, and it hurt. Finally, he could put off an
office visit no longer.

*And the guy was an idiot!*

He remembered:

"Well, I could cut it out, but that would be
messy," and then nothing.

"Well, what else can you do?"

"What do you want?" the doctor said.

Anger flashed up in Doyle. Suddenly, he
could "see." The doctor, pale-faced but in rich
clothes, was leaning back in front of him. The
antiseptic smell, the cold of the examination
bench, the lingering taste of the glass thermom-
eter, were real to him. His thoughts: "I'm

paying good money, to take my own advice.
I—"

He realized that he had, for a moment, been
back in some sort of reality. Grayness swirled
around him again. His thoughts again glowed
green. The illusion of being in the doctor's
office disappeared.

"Well, I'm damned. What did I do?"

Doyle chewed on the experience. *It was a
memory, just a memory—but it was like I was
there again. It was perfect. And it started . . .*

"When I got mad."

*Yes.*

He tried to think of Janet, to think of his
love for her. Nothing happened.

He thought of the curved blonde line of her,
and his want, and he wondered, "Is this love?"
Sensations washed over him as his mind focused on his feelings for his wife. He remembered the way the feel of her skin changed below the ribs and moving toward the fur-
row; he remembered the shine of the downy
hairs on the back of her neck, and the always
present smell of apricot. He could feel himself
becoming aroused, but still nothing happened.

"Aroused with what?"

The feeling vanished.

He started again.

Hair, warmth, smell. He let them build.

He remembered making love on a Sunday
while rain fell soothingly on the roof. He
added detail to detail, fine-honing what it had

been like.

The smell of musk and her touch captured him again. He was in her arms, feeling how tight she pulled. He felt the hotness and smoothness of her skin. Sweat rolled from him. He was with her. He whispered her their private joke:

"This isn't love: It's terminal lust."

And they laughed together. Their voices laughed as one.

It was funny; it must have been.

Others were laughing, too.

The survey is completed; the dirtiness is done.

Orion flashes in the night sky.

Interharg, despite his refusal to join with the Egg-making, heads a task force that surrounds the green planet's sun. His teammates hold hands around it; they drink of the star. Sunspots swarm at its surface—and the guts of the star itself spews forth its own radiation, shattering the dangerous patterns sent out from Earth. Radio communications there will become impossible. Space will become clean. By the time the sunspots have ended, Earth will have cured itself—or its culture will have died.

*All very satisfactory*, Orion thinks.

Yet he has worries. He has picked up copies of his own feelings from the younger members of his own task force. They, too, are dwelling dangerously on the physical. Such is madness; such threatens all that is pure and wise, the foundations of the Nothing Makers and their society. Only by discarding reality have they been able to survive: Bodiless, they are one. With bodies, they become different from each other and the Rules of Reason cease to govern.

And deeper, deeper, Orion realized the fragility of their existence compared to full-bloodedness he has witnessed. He is all browned.

Thinking these things, Orion side-skips toward M31. The point of focus for Council is in that direction, at the edge of the Milky Way. And he is as suddenly there.

He glides in to a hero's welcome. He ripples; he does a little dance in ultraviolet; infrared smears in pleasure. Throughout his spectrum, he is pleased.

He flutters. Light, his chosen method of speaking, is edged in humility. He has pride in an honest time's work. Some who were sick and are now returning to wellness are here. Orion feels their joy. He knows the why: He himself risks sickness, that others might be well.

Before he can return to Thought, he must have say.

Colors speak.

"Some of them are good, and some of them are great. None are ready." He flickers, bringing himself up to full brightness. Dreams he shows: of men struggling up a mountain face, winds biting and cold eating: their courage. Ambitions he shows: floods tamed and fires contained. Wisdom, honor, duty: Orion bleeds color to show a man beaten and not responding, in the name of freedom.

The deep green of awe oozes from his hearers.

Then Orion displays other scenes in a bubbling of brown. He shows swarms of the hulls, feasting on the broadcast dreams of others. He shows the fat ones unmindful of the hungry; the warm unthinking of the cold, and the sated ignoring those who thirst. Suddenly, he brews an image: Thousands and thousands are primed with a liquid intoxicant. These thousands make noise inside a concrete bowl. These hulls, these trap-minded, vent emotion without purpose at other hulls who collide, fall down, and chase an air-filled ellipsoid of leather.

"?"

Orion switches focus. He sprays the feel of those people onto the audience. The hearers mute gray.

A flicker of yellow comes from one who had been ill: What is its meaning?

Orion: I cannot say.

Yellow again: Is there hope?

Orion flashes back: For the chosen, yes. For the others, wisdom cannot say.

Mauve streaked with green: How long?

Orange tinted with red: The time it takes for
light to reach from me to you; the time it takes
a thousand stars to live. I know not.

No longer does he fill flushed, but drained.
Orion joins the others by muting himself to
gray. There is stillness. Light goes out and
presences return to where they wish.

"COUNCIL IS PLEASED."

Orion responds: Your pleasure honors me.

Council dissipates.

Orion hangs by himself, reluctant to turn
loose light. He is uncertain. He needs to let go
of all things physical. This, he knows. Yet he
is reluctant.

He has not told all to Council. While he is
happy with the choices he made for the Egg,
the hulls-not-chosen do not seem to him likely
to merely fade away. They are unreasoned;
they are ugly—but they are vital.

They are alive with reality.

And even those chosen do not seem at all
ready to give up physical being. Even in their
unhappiness, they seem to appreciate physical pain. Pain means for them.

Orion is disturbed. "I have been poisoned
by feeling," he thinks. "They still have no
power. Cleansed, my doubts too will be
cleansed. I must wash in a star. I must burn."

But burning is no answer, he knows. He
must reason and think. He must forget hurt.

He must forget desire.

He burns.

"Hello," Doyle said.

There was no answer.

Doyle tinkered with his thoughts, trying to replay what happened to his mind when the laughter came:

"Terminal lust."

He "sees" a flash of tightly curled hair, damp; he "smells" the rich, slick scent of woman; he knows apricot and longing/

Seeing himself as a Dirty Old Man/

Laughter/

HELLO/HELLO/HELLO/

And there was answer. Hello, a thought like stroking a cat's back; hello, an autumn afternoon with leaves crunched in great piles; hello, diving into a brilliant clear pool and the cold water comes aching down his sides.

Images swirl around Doyle. The real and unreal mix together. He exists, for a moment, in a kaleidosope of his memories and feelings. He begins to understand: Only with strong emotions can he "see." And, obviously, what he "sees" can be seen by others. What others, he does not know. But they are out there. He feels them. To reach them again, he must "see."

And he sees.

And he gets answers.

Hello! A flash of a dusky man with sideburns like wolf paws. The man faded.

Hello! Not a memory, that voice. The voice

is rich with the world and knowledge, and it is softer than skin. The woman appeared in a scarlet evening dress. She was lighted from inside, like one of those round candles that has nearly burned itself out. Doyle could see her clearly—but he could not tell how.

He tried to turn and see the man.

"But what am I turning?"

Green words flash up.

There is more laughter.

"Pictures, my friend, pictures. Let pictures talk." It was the man who spoke. He spoke in a gruff tone, but Doyle could feel the friendship behind the words.

The man appeared. He became solid. The man floated in the blackness, above and to the right of the woman's exposed shoulder. His legs were crossed in mid-air. He smoked a cigar.

"I am Max," he said. "This floozy here is Esmerelda."

The woman extended her hand. "Now don't be shy," she said. "Give me your hand."

"But I don't have a hand," Doyle said. Green letters again. "I don't have—"

"Nonsense," Esmerelda said. "I'll help, but you must help me. You must *want* to meet me. Need it. Now, imagine you're reaching out. Like this."

Doyle suddenly saw his hand. His body began to form. The two hands met. He had a sensation of velvet, of polished wood, and then their two hands passed through each other.

She sighed. "You've still got some work to do. Meanwhile, you can introduce the parts of you that have arrived."

"I'm Charles Doyle. I'm a lawyer."

Max snorted. "A shyster. That explains why he's such a slow learner. Perhaps he's afraid of being overexposed?"

Esmerelda studied Doyle. "Thank heavens for that. I was wondering why we needed a nudist."

For a moment, Doyle did not follow them. He was trying to make himself more substantial. And then he glanced down.

"Good Lord!"

He had been in bed. He had been naked, as always. And that was how he appeared here. Naked. Before two strangers.

He was run over by a remembrance, a shame. It was a time in a boys' locker room, years before, when he had also been naked. Doyle had been a fourteen-year-old late for puberty among the strutting cruelties of the normal arrivals.

And anger came over him—part of the anger that had shaped him. He had a sudden desire to out-do and out-be the pimply bastards in their idiotic maleness.

A tingling swept over him. He felt all his body now. Fire burned in every pore of his skin. He felt as if he were being twisted, reshaped. His joints were tearing. And then, as suddenly as the agony began, it was over.

"He has arrived," said Max.

"Arrived?" said Esmerelda. "Rather, he has premiered."

Said Max: "Not to be critical, Mr. Doyle—but you still haven't corrected the original problem."

Doyle again looked down and gasped. He was still naked. Big-time naked. "It has to be me, but . . ." His hands, the general proportions of his body, were still the same—but the excess weight was gone. The skin was evenly tanned. His chest was broader and hairy. Furthermore, his sexual apparatus was such that he could have become an overnight smash in the porn-theater world.

"Whoops," said Max, as Doyle panicked for the second time in as many minutes.

Doyle was suddenly wearing three shirts, five pairs of pants, scarves and boots and ties and gloves, and an evening jacket—all under what appeared to be a pup tent.

"He has power, all right—but his sense of proportion is lousy," Max said.

"Perhaps we should let him get his bearings," said Esmerelda. "Goodbye," she said to Doyle. "Until later."

She disappeared.

Max lingered. "Don't take us too seriously: You're coming along fine. If you're like the rest of us, I want to congratulate you. As best I can figure, we're in Paradise."

"Paradise?"

"Yes. Heaven, Valhalla, the Happy Hunting Grounds. I didn't believe in those things be-

fore, but . . ." He shrugged. He shrugged like a
man used to carrying a great burden, but the
burden had been removed. It was the exag-
gerated shrug of a lion. "I'll tell you this: You
now have the power to make your dreams
come true."

Doyle reluctantly asked, "So you think
we've died?"

"Me? No. Some of us do, but not me."

"What do you think?"

"I think . . . we've been freed."

"Freed?"

Max nodded. "You'll figure it out soon
enough," he said. He began to fade, then he became solid again. "One more thing: New-
comers have to use their most powerful feelings to generate anything at all—as you have.
You'll learn to use all your feelings, but until
then, I'd be careful. Especially in your case.
You and your wife make a XXX dirty movie."

The German winked, then he winked out.

"Ever been caught in a rainstorm?" she
asked.

"Yes," he said.

"Was it good or bad?"

"Good. It was real good," Doyle said.

"Remember it for me. Use words, if you

have to—but feel the rain again. What does it smell like?"

"It smells like laundry. No. More like a beach, a clean beach. It smells like the sound rain makes. Can you smell the patter of rain?"

She laughed gently. Doyle knew, by now, he did not hear the river-running sound of her laugh, but was hearing her feelings and then making up images to fit.

"Oh, I can. Smell."

He sniffed. There was the suddenly released freshness from the trees. Bird calls were muted, but somehow they added to the smell. It was cold outside him, but inside he felt warm.

*Why is that?*

*Because I'm remembering being caught with Janet in Overton Park. We were friends, just friends then. I think it was the first time I knew I was in love.*

"I'm getting you now," she said. "Keep going."

It was March, early spring. There had been a traveling exhibition from China in the Brooks Memorial Art Gallery that they had come to see. Every sensation was precise: the feel of the rough pavement under his soft-soled shoes, the cool smoothness of the concrete where they sat while he smoked, the dry smooth echoing of the linoleum in the gallery itself.

"Wonderful," Esmerelda said. "You see her clearly now?"

"Oh yes."

They are walking on the curved drive between the gallery and the concerts shell when the first splatters hit. The beads of rain are hard and small, like B-Bs. She grabs his hand and they begin to run down the graveled aisles of the shell. The sky darkens and darkens. They climb up onto the stage and scoot back where even the wind doesn't blow the rain. From inside, they watch the rain fall. It is warm and dark where they are, while outside the rain is like white plastic curtains. Little rivers begin to run down the aisles; a Coke cup is picked up and runs the rapids down to the foot of the stage.

"I'm there," Esmerelda said. "Can you see me?"

The scene wavers, grows indistinct. "No."

"Can you remove her from the scene?"

"I don't want to."

*I don't. I want Janet back, and this is as close as I've been in months. I don't need dreams; I had my dream, and she was all the dream I needed.*

Gently, he leans forward. Her blonde hair touches his nose. He smells the warmth and apricot. She leans back against him. He is happy. He closes his eyes and listens to the rain.

When he opens his eyes, her hair is red.

"What?"

Esmerelda looks up into his face. She smiles. "I warned you. You can daydream about Janet all you want, but when we're together, we share our illusions. I'm teaching you that: remember?"

"But . . ." He stopped. Esmerelda is right, but he feels wronged.

"You must love her very much," she said.

"I do. I don't think I can explain how much."

"It's different for me," Esmerelda said. "I've nothing like that back there. It's all here."

Doyle knew part of the story. She had been the wife of a councilman in Rome. Her careful ear and wily flatteries helped keep the festering boil of radical politics from breaking open. In her importance, she was much like the others Doyle had met. The German, Max Gunther, had been heavily involved in security as a paint man between NATO and the Warsaw Pact countries; he was a thoroughbred cynic who believed no good could come of politics except that no side be allowed to win.

And there were others, hundreds of thousands of others: A Samizdat publisher from the Ukraine; a South African fusion scientist, a lobbyist for the European space program, and a corporate farmer from Kansas.

Esmerelda was certain what had happened: "We've died and gone to Heaven."

She told Doyle in detail what her life had been like. There were sweaty liaisons with obese, warty men—to secure someone's appointment. There were hours of inane conversations, often focused on her breasts—just so she could plant a crucial idea in an otherwise idealess brain. And there was her husband, a man so stupid he thought he was the power in the family.

"You can have that world," she said.

They sat in the Overton Park shell and watched the rain. "This isn't bad," Doyle said to himself. "I could learn to live with this."

"C'mon," Esmerelda said. "Time for something new."

Time passed. If there was time.

The absence of time bothered Doyle more than anything else. Here, all time must be subjective: Did that mean, despite the months that seemed to have passed, that he had yet to be noticed missing back on Earth? Was Janet yet sleeping beside him?

And if not . . . what had happened to her in the time that had passed?

He felt guilty. "But what can I do?" he wondered. "Nothing. Keep my eyes open for a way out is all."

He looked for loopholes in this cosmic contract.

"Can't you see? We're it: the Saviors," he argued with Max. "Earth will collapse without us."

"Crap," Gunther said. "Earth is probably

gone, and we're on some sort of lifeboat. We're the rats who escaped—and, from what I've seen, we're the ones who caused most of Earth's problems in the first place."

That led nowhere, Doyle decided.

He worked at his illusions.

He learned to take shapes. From his memories, he created lush woods vital with squirrel and rabbit, and creeks, and wildflowers. He and Esmerelda became deer and grazed together.

The Italian was unlike any woman he had ever known. He knew he could never love her as he loved Janet, though: Esmerelda was too real, too wise . . . too traveled. Besides, he could never be unfaithful to Janet. It was not in him. It was old-fashioned, he knew—but he was old-fashioned. He had come in from back-country West Tennessee to Memphis. He'd been raised by a lay Baptist minister and farmer—a non-smoking, non-drinking giant of a man. Certain values were deeper in him than his genes, he felt. Fidelity was one of those.

And he loved Janet. On bad nights, he admitted to himself he feared giving her any reason to leave. She had almost left once before, but she had come back. He did not think he could face that again.

His morality—his "stuffiness," Es called it—did interfere with his relationship with the red-haired woman. But they learned about each other. They were friends, he told himself.

Doyle's powers grew. After a while, he could bring Max into the illusions with him and Esmerelda.

And his powers grew.

And the dreamworlds he created began to change.

Little things at first: A rose would smell of soured milk. A rainstorm would rise up during a picnic. A convertible he created had four flat tires. He struggled against himself, but he knew what the problem was:

Paradise was not perfect.

Esmerelda needed his help. She wanted to visit her home island of Corfu. The island was off the coast of Greece.

"To make it real, I need help," she said.

"I'm having trouble," Doyle said. "You know that."

"I trust you," she said.

"That's a mistake. I don't even trust me."

"C'mon."

She remembered the hills and olive orchards for him. He began to see the dark greens, feel the breezes, smell the oil. They chose for their visit a cloudless day in mid-June; they appeared on a knoll near an abandoned water mill. The grass was lush. They supplied themselves with a wicker basket containing food and wine.

"Lovely," he said.

"It's better with you," she said.

Then came the ants. The ants were the size of hamsters. "You didn't have to remember these," he said.

"I didn't. You must have done it."

One of the ants seized a half-pound of cheese and began to carry it off. "Whoa, there," said Doyle. He jerked the cheese loose. "You think it would be safe to stomp 'em?"

"It's you," Esmerelda said. "It's your lack of discipline—but I'll teach you to erase. It's fun."

She worked on the ants until they were the size of dime-store turtles. "You try it."

"You sure I can?"

"Sure."

The technique was difficult, but Doyle's powers helped. Soon the ants were the size of fleas. Then they disappeared completely. He checked around, but could find no more.

They settled in to eat and drink in the warm sun.

"And thou," she said lazily. She stretched out, her hair gleaming brightly against the emerald grass.

But Doyle could not quite get comfortable. His mind kept wandering. He slipped in and out of the picture. He would forget that his job was to reinforce Es's vision. The first thing he knew, he'd created a Jersey cow from his family farm. It wandered over a nearby rise.

"What is that thing?" she asked.

"A milk cow."

"I mean, what is it doing here?"

"I forgot myself," he said sheepishly. "I was leaning back and remembering a good day when I was young, then pop! Here came a cow."

"Well, get rid of it. This is my illusion and there are no cows in it."

He nodded. There seemed to be so much to master that he had yet to even start learning. Part of the problem was his power, of course: His strong images meant, at any time, one of his stray thoughts became visible to others. He was better now, but hardly perfect.

Max still guffawed over Doyle's debut. His imaginary love-making had indeed been what brought Max and Esmerelda to his side. Doyle still suspected both Max and Esmerelda wanted him to replay that dream—and they wanted to be invited in.

"It's still there," said Esmerelda, rising up onto an elbow and looking at him.

"I know. What kind of animals do they have on Corfu?"

"Pigs."

"I don't want a pig," he said.

"All right: A goat, then."

"A goat." He began to reshape the cow. It was not an easy business—but it was easier than trying to erase something that size. He thought so at first. He found he really didn't have a very clear picture of a goat in his mind.

"Yuk," she said. "That's a goat?"

"No. A banioxle—from Greek mythology."

"Good Lord. Can't we just have a goat?"

"If you want—I just figured, it being a Greek island and all, you'd . . ." The words trailed off. He wasn't comfortable with his invention, but he knew he'd never get a goat right. Not now, anyway. His creation had eight legs.

"It's ugly, but I suppose it's harmless," she said. "Leave it in."

"Right," he said. He studied his creature carefully for future reference—in case she ever remembered it and wanted another one, or in case she wanted to show Max.

Finally, his interruptions stopped. Esmerelda—backed up by Doyle's power—was doing a good job visualizing her world. Doyle realized he did not know what kind of grass it was beneath them. The air had a golden, toasted quality he had never known. And the smells: wood and leaves, cheese, together with a kind of homey mustiness.

Esmerelda was far better at her craft than Doyle was, but she lacked his power. Without his help, she couldn't sustain a complete world. Constantly, she ad-libbed. The musty smell, he realized, didn't come from anything nearby: It was simply a good smell she had added for spice.

"Nice job, Es. I could stay here forever."

"If we stay too long, we'll be trampled by herds of cows," she said, grinning.

"So long as I don't create any Baptists, I think we're okay," he said.

They rested in the sun. Doyle felt ease. A breeze came up and played in her hair. He remembered few times in his life when he had felt this unhurried and unbothered. Really, there was no point in missing Janet—not now, not while there was nothing he could do for her. Having worlds at his fingertips wasn't bad. He'd stopped feeling the compulsive emptiness he usually felt when Janet wasn't around. They rested in silence.

"Come closer?" she said.

He hesitated, but then moved closer. Their sides touched as lightly as leaves. He could feel her beside him. She was warmer than the afternoon sun. Her arm moved slightly and her hand came to rest on the top of his thigh.

"Es . . ." he said, gently. She didn't answer. She didn't move her hand. He felt he wanted to be closer to her, but he didn't want to move. He was afraid to move. If anything happened, he didn't want to face the guilt.

She shifted again. Her body molded to his.

They were still. He put his arm under her head. Her head rested in the V of his shoulder and arm.

"Kiss me," she said.

"Don't," he said. "Please don't."

"Just a kiss."

And that would be all it was, he told himself. They weren't in real bodies. This was an illusion.

Their bodies were ornaments. They were figments of their collective imagination. How can you be unfaithful in a Fun House? he wondered. He remembered the old injunction from the Bible, the one that warned how a man could commit adultery in his heart. He wondered if it was possible the old scribe had been through this same situation?

Then he thought of her lips. His quibbling stopped.

He leaned toward her and their lips met. It was a friendly, gentle kiss. Warm, without passion. And that was it.

Once again they leaned together.

Time was on hold. He was happy.

Forever, it seemed, they were frozen in the moment.

And then he heard the funny sound. He rolled up on one arm and looked around. "My God, Es. You've done it now."

She sat up. "What?"

He pointed.

There was a minotaur at the top of the hill. The noise was its two hooves scraping. The hooves were on human legs. As the two watched, the minotaur bellowed. The sound was like thunder. It was a terrible sound.

"I didn't do it. I haven't thought of minotaurs in years. Why should I?"

"I thought the, ah, banioxle might've reminded you, and you got to thinking, your mind wandered, and—"

"Not me. It must be yours."

"No. Even when I make mistakes, I have a feeling that I've done it. This is different. That's not mine."

As they watched, the minotaur began to move. It moved toward them. Its bull's head spewed steam from its nostrils and its great egg-sized eyes gleamed with ferocity. The minotaur had the body and trunk of a man—but the body was that of a Sumo wrestler.

The way it moved didn't seem friendly.

"Well, we'd better get rid of it," Doyle said.

"Don't think I'm not trying. It won't erase. You try." There was the beginning of panic in her voice.

Doyle cast his thoughts toward the minotaur, straining to imagine nothing in its place. He was still rusty at the technique, but there was something else wrong. There was some sort of wall blocking his thoughts. It was as if someone else was aware of what he would try and had moved to block him.

"Max," he said. "Would Max play a joke like this?"

"Max would have tanks or Wagner. Not this."

Unless he was jealous, Doyle thought. And then . . .

The minotaur shook its head and bellowed again. Its great arms raised and shook against the sky. It began to move faster. It began to run. Its footfalls were like pile-drivers.

The banioxle wandered in front of the beast. The mighty bull-thing roared. The banioxle froze in fright. It had yet to move when the minotaur picked it up and ripped it in two.

Blood splashed freely from its hands.

"Let's not play, Es. Fold it up. Kill the illusion. All of it. Now!"

But the world didn't begin to fade. It didn't tremble or waver. The minotaur remained real.

The minotaur rubbed its wet hands dry on its sides. The bull-man was about thirty meters away. The damn thing was nearly four meters high. It was moving toward them.

"There's something interfering with my control, Charley. Something's reinforcing the illusion against my will. I'm not strong enough."

Scratching the whole illusion would normally be easier than erasing a single part of it—but this was Esmerelda's dream. Doyle didn't know how much he could help.

His mind pressed out and around. He felt another will there. It was a powerful will, almost as strong as his—but it was also a trained will, unlike his. Weird.

Doyle began to wonder, Can you die in an illusion? What happened if you couldn't get out and that thing got hold of you? He saw the ruined shape of the banioxle and shivered. Paradise wasn't perfect, for sure: not if things like this happened.

"Run, Es."

"What're we going to do?"

"Run, dammit. Run."

He started running himself, but slowly enough to let Esmerelda gain ground on him. When she passed him and was at full speed, he angled away—making himself a decoy. The pile-driver sound was louder now, much louder. He turned and yelled. The minotaur turned toward him.

"Now what?" Doyle wondered.

The minotaur stopped. When it moved again, it moved slowly and warily. It didn't seem to trust Doyle.

Green letters flashed in the sky:

"How does it feel to have the tables turned?"

"What?" But Doyle didn't have time to wonder. The minotaur was picking up speed. It was close enough now so Doyle could see how high it towered over him; he could see the froth on the jaws of the beast.

"Now," he thought. The world was protected against them; this thing was directly protected. Only one other thing might work.

Doyle summoned his powers and spat them forth—but not at the minotaur. He aimed slightly ahead. A gaping hole opened just in front of the charging beast. It had no time to react. Into the dark gaping mouth it fell.

Quickly, Doyle pressed out. He had succeeded. Whatever—whoever—was guarding the illusion had been distracted.

"Fold it, Es! Fold it now!"

And the edges of the world wavered, the sky darkened, and Doyle fell out of the imaginary island of Corfu.

"This is some swell Paradise, folks," Doyle said. His image flickered in the company of Max and Esmerelda. Another half-dozen friends and acquaintances had gathered. Most were dressed formally to show their concern. It was an odd gathering. Over the months, most people here had become addicted to their pleasant fantasy worlds. It had been entertaining and harmless—until now.

"You probably jiggered the thing up with your overactive imagination, Charley," the British mathematician said.

"Yeah. Making banioxles—something I've never even heard of, and wouldn't want to meet," another added.

"You shouldn't think of those things," Max said. "Not with your power. You could really mess things up."

Doyle regarded the group sourly. "And it's some really big-hearted angels in this Paradise, I ought to add. Haven't you heard a word either of us said? Es and I both felt something outside us."

"If I may speak frankly?" It was Benson Tiller, the neuro-anatomist-psychiatrist-guru from The Johns Hopkins University. He had a Freudian beard and eyes that looked like someone had squeezed them as far back in their sockets as they would go. Doyle respected the man, but liked him not at all.

"Sure," he said. "Why should you miss the barbecue?"

"I don't mean to speak with malice—"

"Of course not."

"—but you'll agree to having problems none of the rest of us have suffered?"

"Right," Doyle said. "Hamster ants and pink suns. So what? They're not dangerous, and I knew they were mine."

"Let's say—just for argument—that your right brain/left brain coordination isn't what it could be. You're a very bright man. You are also very specialized. It's not unusual for such types to having warring identities. Do you agree?"

"Go on," Doyle said. He was growing suspicious.

"It's not unusual for the two minds to have different goals, either. And I think we're seeing a concrete manifestation of that."

"I'm not sure I follow you."

"It's simple," Tiller said. "One side of you wants to stay here in Paradise. The other side wants out—and it is resorting to some very powerful images to drive you out."

"I think that's bunk. What about the green letters?"

"A perfect left-brain judgment. It's in words, the left-brain territory. It is the side that wants you to stay here."

"So it creates a minotaur to run me out? Professor, you're not making sense."

"The minotaur was right brain. You heard the words about the time you thought of the hole, right? What better way for the left brain to react? Sort of, 'That'll show you.' It works."

"No, it doesn't work. The words were directed at me." Doyle punched a finger into his chest. "This me. They weren't directed at the bull. Furthermore, if I'm all divided and fighting it out in the air, how come the battle is visible to others?"

Tiller made a tsk-tsk noise. "Your body is a projection, remember. Your 'mind,' your literal mind, is hidden away. We don't know where or how. There's no reason both the bull and body can't be right brain. And the words, 'How does it feel to have the tables turned?' are a perfect description of how the left brain would react to the right's actions."

"I have this terrible feeling you've convinced yourself of something, Benson. And it doesn't matter that I'm absolutely certain it's something else *outside me* that's the problem, does it? Can you explain why I feel that?"

"Sure: left-brain rationalization. And I do have a conclusion. You are developing schizophrenia."

"Shucks. I thought you were serious."

"I am."

Doyle screwed up his face. He made a spitting motion. "Well—for the sake of argument—what do you think ought to be done if what you say is true?"

"I think you ought to be treated. You probably should be confined, for your own safety—and the safety of others."

"And how do you propose to do that?"

"There are enough of us here to hold you, I think. We've talked it over and most of us agree. It's safe. And I could work with you. I could treat you. It would take a while, but we've got time."

Green letters:

"No you don't. The man's got things to do."

Doyle smirked. "What about that?"

"There's no need to be threatened, Charley."

"Me? Threatened? Have you gone blind, too? Don't you see those letters?"

"It is back," Esmerelda said. "Whatever it is."

"No," said Tiller. "Esmerelda, don't let yourself be trapped by his illusions. He's still projecting. Your friend is a very sick man and he's getting sicker."

Letters again. They flashed bold and bright:

"Ho, ho, Charley. I told you you'd end up like this. Would you listen? Oh, no. And then you turn on me, your old friend. Serves you absolutely right."

"Christ, Benson. Don't you see it?"

Tiller nodded. "Sure. So what? It's just him." He pointed to Doyle. His expression was the same as if he'd discovered the evidence of a puppy's accident. Doyle would be the ruined carpet.

More letters, more words:

"Haven't you got a clue, goody two shoes? I'm just trying to get your attention. I need you, man. I— "

"Meriwether," Doyle said. The light dawned suddenly. "It's him, Es. That nigger."

Benson said, "He's losing control. Now. Everybody."

"Max—don't help 'em, I'm warning you." Doyle backed slowly into the surrounding darkness. He could feel the phalanx of wills closing on him. It was like the Iron Maiden, he thought wryly. "Back off," he said.

Green letters flashed again. Doyle was too busy to read them.

"Es, take care."

And then he thought of dying. He popped from sight like a candle going out.


In the black and the nothingness, Doyle held himself still. He floated quietly. His mind was as blank as he could let it be. He used the old Zen trick, thinking only of the spaces between the freight cars of his thoughts. In this way, he hoped to hide. He could not afford to "be" —that would almost be a spotlight leading others to him. He must wait until they tired of their search. Then he must begin his own search.

For now, he was safe.

He was safe from the doctor. He was safe from Meriwether.

Soon, he would have to search. He knew what he would have to search for. Her name was Charlotte Bistro. Her image was burned into his mind.

When enough time had passed, Doyle began to sift through the Nothingness, looking for that image. Sometime, somewhere, Meriwether would think of the white girl. Doyle was sure of it.

If he did, Doyle would follow.

Charlotte was something else now, he thought bitterly.

Charlotte was bait.

"How's it going, Es?"

She looked up and saw Max. He walked across the grass toward her. She was back on Corfu.

"I didn't invite you," she said.

"Since when must best friends be invited?" He stopped, looking at her. "Never mind. I know. Since best friends are replaced by lovers."

"That's a joke," she said. "If you only knew."

Max crossed his legs and sat beside her. There was a small breeze. Cotton-ball clouds were stuck here and there in the sky. Now, one of the cotton balls passed in front of the sun. In its shadow the two of them were cool.

"Is he crazy, Max?"

"You'd know better than me."

"He's not crazy."

"I wouldn't bet he is," Max said. "But he's unhappy. He's unhappy in a place where happiness is always a thought away."

"Is it?" She sat up and shivered. "Are you happy?"

"I don't have to look over my shoulder anymore. I don't sleep with a gun under my pillow," he said. "I don't wake up and hear thunder and think, 'It's started. I've failed.' If it's not happiness, it'll do."

She looked at him closely. His eyes were gunmetal blue. They mirrored like sunglasses. "I hurt you," she said.

"I think I was happy, before he came. I was happy with you. I know I was."

Her eyes scanned the horizon. She frowned.

"What is it?"

"Nothing. No minotaurs, no banioxles, nothing."

"He'll be back. Tiller's still watching."

"It seems like weeks."

"It hasn't been."

The long time passed. They sat. *He'll be*

*there until I move,* she thought. *If it takes forever.*

"Do you want to make love?" she asked.

"Do you?"

"I asked first." She flashed him a smile. "It's not like we never had."

"I want you," he said. "It's not love."

"It'll do," she said.

In the long empty stretches of the search, odd thoughts nibbled at Doyle's consciousness. He didn't mind. If they were still looking for him, they would be looking for Janet's image. He was doing the same thing, looking for Charlotte's. He felt like a trout cruising a stream, looking for a pattern that meant food.

And he thought of Esmerelda. He missed her more than he liked to think.

He felt he had been frozen in nothing for months when he felt himself tense. There was a golden glint of something that had touched his mind. It was golden hair.

"Careful," he told himself. "Steady."

He opened his mind to the image and saw the little girl. She was in a park. It seemed to be Overton Park. She was not alone. Doyle held himself tight, struggling to keep his mind silent. He must watch for his moment.

Meriwether watched the girl from a bench.
He was stretched out like a cat. His dark skin
set off shining eyes. His lips were full, almost
pouting.

"Well, hello there," he said. "Whose little
girl are you?" He licked his lips; his right
hand was in his jacket pocket.

Doyle kept himself invisible. *What does he
have?* he wondered. *A gun, a knife?*

The delicately fingered hand came out of
the pocket. It opened. In the palm was something red and white.

Peppermint.

Doyle felt his stomach twist.

"Do you like candy, little one?" Meriwether
held out his hand. "Aren't the red-and-white
swirls lovely? You can have some if you
want."

The girl was obviously tempted. "My
mother says, 'no.'"

"Your mother's smart," Meriwether said.
He unwrapped the peppermint and put it in
his mouth.

Doyle kept himself steady. "None of this is
real," he told himself. "Whatever happens is
only an illusion. Wait and get the proof. There
must be no question. Keep still. Make sure.

"Then get him. Goddammit, get him."

He watched.

Meriwether produced another bit of candy.
It waited in his open palm.

"Jesus, she looks like Janet when she was a
little girl," Doyle thought.

And then he knew he'd made a mistake.

Meriwether was sitting upright on the bench. His eyes searched the park quickly. "Charley? Charley Doyle?"

And Meriwether laughed. "Doyle! I know you're there. C'mon out. You have no idea how long I've been waiting. This was the only thing I could think of to lure you ... Well, c'mon, man. Show."

Doyle thought, but only in words. He wanted no clue to his location out yet. "Not yet, Meriwether. There's some questions you have to answer."

"Get off it, Charley. I've been messing with you, and you know it. Just like blowing your car: You knew I wasn't out for you. If I was, you wouldn't be here now."

Doyle was uncertain. This seemed like the man he'd liked and admired for years. *But it's not*, he told himself. *He's up to something. He's changed. You'd know exactly how much he's changed if you hadn't made that fool slip.*

"All right, Charley. I've been friendly. I've made my nicest offer." Meriwether spoke, then stood slowly at the bench. "You're a real pain, sometimes. I taught you half of what you know—and you treat me like this. So we'll keep playing the game. You're going to appear. You're going to talk to me. I'm going to make sure of that."

Doyle floated, watching only. He didn't know what Meriwether planned. He told himself there was no reason to be afraid. *He can't*

*hurt me here. Until I know where he gets his
strength, I'm not moving.*

He ignored the nagging question, "What if
I'm wrong?"

"I'm sorry to have to do this, Charley. I'd be
happy to wait you out—if there was time. But
you also said a bad word. You called me n-i-g-
g-e-r. I know you're white trash, but you know
better. And I'm going to make you apologize."

At the edge of the park, a woman appeared.
She was dressed in a light, loose robe. Doyle
was curious, but could not tell yet what was
going on. Then he recognized her by her walk.
He knew who she was long before he could
make out the details of her face. It was Janet.

She came nearer, but the details of her face
didn't sharpen much. That was reassuring,
Doyle thought: Meriwether obviously hadn't
studied her as much as he'd like Doyle to believe.

Shadows appeared behind a couple of nearby trees and at several shrubs. The shadows
grew solid. They were men. They reminded
Doyle of Meriwether's old crew, although he
knew that was not possible. But a new crew?
Very probable.

Doyle wanted to laugh. That explained
Meriwether's power, of course. But also he
thought it was funny that here, in this place,
Meriwether was again gathering power.

Meriwether was no fool.

"You've got a few minutes," Meriwether
said. He reached into the air and produced a

lighted French cigarette. "Nice, huh? I'm getting good at this." He put the cigarette in his mouth and puffed. "I'd rather you come out than have to play this game through. You're lousy at games. You always lose."

Doyle almost assented. He was curious. He liked this Meriwether more than most of the people in Paradise. *You're slipping*, he thought. *He'll con you yet. Hold off.*

He had already been trapped once by Meriwether, he remembered. It had been on Esmerelda's island. To bring himself to flesh would put him back under Meriwether's power—and he had no idea yet what Meriwether wanted. To give in could be deadly.

Doyle needed help. He could think of only one way to get it. It would mean taking a risk. Things might happen to Janet for which he could never forgive himself. *But it's not her. It's only an illusion. Remember that . . . and wait.*

He didn't know whether it would be worth it; he didn't know if he had the resolve to stand by and watch. Already he could feel his calmness evaporating. Images flickered in his mind and he had trouble keeping them invisible.

"Those men are recruits," Meriwether said. "One's KGB, and there's a guy from the Argentinian security service, and a guy from the Attica pen. Nice guys. What they're doing in Paradise beats me. Think about it."

The woman who was Janet was close to

Meriwether now. He turned to her and nodded. "You're Janet Doyle, aren't you?"

"Yes. And you're?"

"Answar Meriwether, a friend of your husband's. He may have mentioned me?"

"Weren't you a policeman?"

"Once. I've crossed over." Meriwether signaled with one hand. The shadows began moving in.

"I'm sure, if he's mentioned me lately, it wasn't very nice. He thinks I'm some kind of murdering pervert, which is a slander. But fairness isn't one of Charley's long suits," Meriwether said. He grinned.

Janet's eyes widened as she remembered. She took an uncertain step backward—into the waiting hands of Meriwether's men. "I have business with your husband," he said. "But he seems to think it's better I use you for my business. I'm sorry." Then, as an aside, he said, "There's still time, Charley."

"Charley? Are you here? What's going on?"

Doyle tensed. Meriwether had gotten the voice down perfectly. Fear was sharp in her voice.

"I'm scared, Charley. Can't you help me?"

Meriwether made a clucking noise with his mouth. "I guess he can't," he said. He held out his hand like a surgeon. One of the men slapped a switchblade into his palm. He held the knife blade up in front of Janet. He shrugged. He made the knife flash. It cut effortlessly through the knot of the shoulder. The robe fell away.

Doyle saw a needle-thin red line where the knife had kissed his wife's skin. Anytime, his control could break. He couldn't watch—but he couldn't turn away.

*She's not real, she's not real, she's not real.*

He still needed time. *Where are they? Aren't they still searching for me?*

Janet's white, nearly nude body stood in the clearing. "So lovely," Meriwether said. "It's a shame. I'm sorry."

The knife moved down her smooth stomach and then into the elastic band of her panties. Meriwether tightened the elastic with the knife point. Sun glinted on the blade. The moment held achingly for Doyle. The spongy smell of oak trees filled the air. Wind rustled through the trees with the sound of sheets.

The blade cut. The panties fell away.

The two white columns of her legs appeared. They rose from sandaled feet to their dark joining place. Janet half-turned her body away, as if trying to hide. The move frightened Doyle more than anything. He felt her terror in him.

She whimpered.

He acted in desperation. He made the sound of sirens fill the air. Their sound grew loud in the park.

Meriwether laughed. "That's stupid, Doyle." He took the knife and made a quick scratch across her stomach. Blood oozed from the white. It was not a deep cut. It was a warning.

"I could mess her up good before they got
here, Doyle. And I doubt your police could do
very much."

Doyle felt sick. He understood what Meriwether meant. *I'll get you, I swear it. You'll
pay.* The police would only be Doyle's addition
to the scene. It would still be Doyle's will
against the combined wills of Meriwether's
team. Doyle remembered the awesome power
of the minotaur and accepted defeat.

He killed off the sirens. He erased their
sound.

*Where are they?*

Only one thing could be wrong. This Janet
wasn't vivid enough to attract Tiller's search
party. Doyle was depending on Janet's image
to attract Tiller, who would be looking for
Janet's image in order to find Doyle.

He would have to make Janet more real.

*I can't. God help me, I must.*

It was the only thing that would work. He
would have to put his image of Janet into
Meriwether's scene.

*Is it worth it?* he wondered. *What do his
crimes matter here? Can I risk her to catch
him?*

He didn't ask: *What if it doesn't work, and I
lose her?* To think that would blow his control. All he had suffered—that *she* was suf-
fering—would be wasted.

He had made his decision.

Meriwether laughed at the siren's absence.
"So the old street cop can't take a little slash
and cut?" The laugh was from hell, an execu-

tioner's laugh. Meriwether's face hardly moved as he made the laughing sound.

Doyle forced himself to carry out his plan. He worked on the image of Janet. She had a series of moles that began slightly below the cleft of her breasts. There were four moles; they moved in a half moon beneath her left breast. They appeared. *Janet, forgive me. I love you*, he thought. The skin was not so taut between the points of her pelvis; he softened it and let the skin cup. *It's because I love you, Janet. Because I want this scum out of your world*. He kept thinking he must cry. He couldn't cry. To cry would bring his body into focus. He worked.

Janet had always carried her right shoulder slightly higher than the left, because of a slight spinal defect. He made her left shoulder droop. Detail after detail, he added. He added until his Janet stood before Meriwether.

Doyle shook at the edge of his control.

"What's this?" said Meriwether. He had not moved during the minor transformations. "We're getting to him. He's drawing himself in." He turned, addressed the trees. "I don't want this, Charley. I don't want to do this. Come on out."

He waited for a count of five. "Have it your way. Fyodor, take her left ankle." A man moved around from behind Meriwether. "Mario, the right. Good. Now put her down gently. Careful: We don't want this to hurt more than it has to."

The four men did as they were told. Two held Janet's arms and two held her ankles. Janet was stretched on the grass like a Greek cross.

Meriwether began to unbuckle his belt.

The sound tinkled in the clearing like a bell.

Janet began to twist. Her noises became louder as she began to understand. She called to Doyle; he listened to her voice, and he was ashamed. *This is going too far*, he thought. *But it hasn't worked. It's got to work.*

Meriwether knelt, his naked legs between Janet's.

Green letters flashed in the air:

"All right, Charley. You're disguised, but we knew we'd find you with her. Just relax."

*Thank God*, Doyle thought. He stayed hidden.

"What the hell?" Meriwether said. "You can't fool me, Charley. I know you too well."

Tiller appeared. "He's crazier now. This is sick." Max flashed into view. Then came others. "We're all around, Charley. We're your friends. No sudden moves, and everything will— "

"Break out, men. Scramble it!"

Fyodor and Mario vanished. Two others faded out and then reappeared. "They've got us walled or something," one called out. Meriwether's face began to shine with sweat.

*Perfect*, Doyle thought. *It worked perfectly.* He did not move even yet. If Tiller's net broke, he would have to pursue Meriwether yet again. But he didn't think he would ever be chasing Meriwether again. If all went well, Meriwether had played his last game. He began to work a new image in his mind.

"We've goofed," Max said. "That's Janet—but that's not Charley." Esmerelda appeared. She was inspecting Janet, who had now begun to fade. *When I clear my mind, she'll be gone,* Doyle thought. *She doesn't matter to anyone else.*

"I protest," said Meriwether. "The ground rules—as I understand them—are no one is to involve themselves in another's illusion. Not without an invitation, anyhow."

"He did the minotaur," Esmerelda said. "I'm sure of it."

"Look at the facts," Tiller said. "Charley's slipped off the deep end. He's disguised, but he's also crazy. Ask yourself: Could anyone else have imagined Janet so precisely?" He turned to point at the woman's body, but Janet had ceased to exist.

Esmerelda shook her head. "No," she said.

"Look at what he was doing here. You know how he felt about his wife. He'd have to be crazy to do this."

"This isn't him, I tell you."

"It's not. My name is Answar Meriwether, and I am nothing like Charley Doyle. Nothing."

Max was studying Meriwether. He turned to Tiller. "It isn't him. The aura is all wrong."

For once, Tiller appeared uncertain. "You're sure?"

There were nods all around.

"Should we let him go?"

"Maybe," Max said. "But I'll bet he can answer some questions."

Doyle moved. This was one argument that he wasn't going to let be lost. He pulled into the scene, emerging from a nearby thicket in the uniform of the Memphis Police Department. He walked confidently up to the group —just like any cop on a beat.

He pulled his gun and held it on Meriwether.

"Charley," Esmerelda said.

"Doyle? What the hell— "

The hammer on the pistol cocked.

"Careful. You're going to—"

"Charley, listen to me," Meriwether said. "I had to get you out and that's the only way I knew. I wouldn't have gone further. Charley, I'm your old squad-car buddy. Charley—"

Doyle pulled the trigger.

Meriwether's body exploded in the chest. Blood splashed wildly as the dum-dum bullet rolled through. There was no expression on Meriwether's face anymore.

Meriwether was dead.

Doyle holstered his pistol. "I don't know what happens next," he said.

The tone of the group reminded Doyle of being before the Grand Jury. He had known something like this must happen, but he'd had hopes that Tiller's grand theories would derail any investigation. It was Tiller's idea that Doyle had cured himself through some sort of radical reality-therapy. "You're not a danger anymore," he had assured Doyle. Doyle assured Tiller he had never been a danger—except maybe to psychiatrists with over-active imaginations.

Max was the one who destroyed Tiller's grand theory. He'd vanished even before Doyle pulled the trigger on Meriwether. "I thought I recognized the guy, and I did. It was Fyodor Holub, a Polish KGB agent. He's a snake with a heart of stone, but an ace. A winner . . . I'm surprised," he said, "if Meriwether's the villain you made him out to be, that Fyodor joined with him."

After that, some thought Doyle should be tried for murder.

"No corpus delicti," he said. "Besides, I only killed an illusion. A projection."

"You don't believe that," Esmerelda whispered. "You meant it."

Doyle found he could not lie to her. He ignored her. "How could I kill something that's not there? We've all agreed our 'brains'—if that's what they are—are in no way connected with the bodies we imagine. I would have to kill the brain to murder, and I didn't."

Uneasily, his argument was accepted. Doyle

spent some tense times after that. People were suspicious of him. Too, he was afraid he hadn't done in Meriwether. At any time, the man might reappear. He should reappear, in fact.

*But maybe I blew him all the way out of Paradise? What then?* He had a chilling moment when he thought it was possible he had returned Meriwether to Earth. *Back where he could get at the real Janet? No, I couldn't have.*

He should have thought of that before, he realized.

"Why did you do it?" she asked. They hovered together, just the two of them, surrounded by the thick blackness of absolutely nothing.

Doyle was silent. He had no answer. Now, from this perspective, the years he had put in chasing Meriwether made little sense. Worse, how could he explain to her the terrible hollowness he felt now that the chase was finished?

"There was no honor in it," she said. "I expected honor from you. To just walk up and pull the trigger: Where's your all-mighty justice in that?"

"I don't know, Es. I didn't really know what I was doing. I had some notion of making him feel the terror Janet had felt—and I just kept going. It seemed right at the time. Now—I just don't know," he said. He looked at her with pleading. He needed assurance from her, not this. He couldn't take this. "I feel as if I killed a part of myself. When he went down, when I saw the blood, I saw he was just another man. And yet the power he had in Memphis. He could have done so much good, Es. It's not like he was evil. It's like he was a twisted good. See: He had the ability, and he wasted it. That's the crime. And then came the real crimes. It was like he was horrified at what he got away with. Do you see?"

"No, I don't see."

"Maybe I don't, either," he said. "Maybe I'm just trying to sort it in my mind. He'd become something special to me, as if—by bringing him down—I could bring down the whole rotten system. As if by killing him, I could kill out all the rottenness. It seemed—there at the last, when I was almost crazy, or thought I would go crazy—that he and I were the only balance points in the city. That we were it, the yin and yang, the positive and the negative. But now . . ."

"The city's gone," she said.

"It's hard to believe that."

"Believe it. For me."

"No," he said.

She swallowed hard. "You're hard-headed, you know that? Well, maybe this'll help. You know Max, he's been in hog-heaven since this

entire problem erupted. He's checking under
beds, everywhere. And he's talked at length to
this Fyodor."

"So?"

"Fyodor said he joined Meriwether because of you. Meriwether had convinced him,
Mario, the rest, that you were the villain. That
you—left by yourself—would kill Paradise."

"I'll be damned."

"Maybe you should be," she said. "You've
made one hell of a start already."

Doyle looked at her for a long time. His face
didn't hold pleading anymore. In the darkness, he nodded in agreement. The nod was
barely perceptible.

Meriwether was dizzy among the stars.
Everything was behind him now. Ahead was
unknown. Before, he had always been responding to the world around him, but no
more: Now he was in control of himself. The
stars pinwheeled around him.

For his part, he could have spent eternity in
Paradise messing with Doyle's head. That had
been fun.

The fun ended when Doyle appeared in the
clearing, wearing the uniform and carrying

the gun. And then the gun had come up. Meriwether had seen the crazy gleam in Doyle's eyes—the gleam he'd always seemed to inspire there. Doyle's eyes had burned like a lighthouse.

"Hey man, listen to me," he'd said. But Doyle wasn't listening. Desperation came. He'd felt the stink of fear in his body. And then the gun had come up. It had all moved so slowly. Meriwether had been aware of birds singing in the trees, that lovely woman of Doyle's, the sunshine. The grass had seemed more permanent than Astroturf. Everything was as he'd wanted.

And then the gun had come up. And then the boom, the muzzle flash.

And death had come into his chest like an angry swarm of bees, stingers out, buzzing for the honey of his blood.

And blackness had come.

And sorrow. He'd awakened in amazement and sorrow—amazement that he had awakened at all; sorrow at what he knew he had lost. He'd looked out through another's eyes, the eyes he'd left on Earth, and he'd seen pictures of barns where the girls' portraits had been. He had tried to protest, but he couldn't speak.

Someone else now owned his body. He could feel how different the someone was. It was him and it was not him. Meriwether had come back to Earth, but still had not returned. He felt the changes that had been made. He felt sick.

To Meriwether, there had always been an underlying pattern to the world. He'd had a sense that the chaos had purpose: that today's mayhem led to tomorrow's millenium.

*By King's spirit, was I wrong!*

The old Meriwether had always kept a lid on the petty violence of his neighborhoods. He had no patience for those who knifed old people, or for those who broke into the houses of the poor and took their goods and peace of mind. No. You ripped off the Man, not your neighbors. He'd taken apart two or three punks, and the message had gotten through:

There's no Miranda ruling from Meriwether, man.

No due process. No Court of Appeals.

Only judgment.

And he'd thought Doyle understood that. Crazy Doyle. But this other thing, about the death of the little girls. Meriwether hadn't known about it, until it was too late to stop the series. He couldn't bring the little girls back. Deep down, he accepted the murders as his fault: He should have known better about Tiny. But he hadn't. All he could do was punish Tiny.

He did it. He did it better than the Man could do.

Tiny peed like a girl now.

But would Doyle give him a chance to explain? Hell no.

And now some punk had taken over Meriwether's organization. *When you got no home,*

*nigger, anyplace else is home.*
   He'd found a clue.
   He was headed to the stars.

   Orion is yesterday drinking of a star. The power he feels is enormous. He knows his thoughts perfectly: reads their subtleties into the angstroms. *Color, ah color: the particular color of an aging G-type star just before its surface explodes; the color of a dust storm blown by star winds through space, and the lush green of this last planet he works before.*
   It is said, and Orion does not doubt it, that he was born a cold-blooded lizard type on some jungle planet two cycles before. Possibly. It is long ago, and he has forgotten. Rather, he is erased of it. Those thoughts are not-good, meaning not-essential. Why should the butterfly care about his cocoon or need memories of being a caterpillar?
   Orion can imagine no sound reason.
   He shimmers as he thinks. He still wears a light ornament. It is a thin connection to the physical world. Orion fears, as he ages, that he is becoming sentimental. Or sick.
   Immortality through reason; power through reason: Those things were at his core as

a Nothing Maker. Reason, pure and brilliant and perfect, cannot co-exist with a demanding physical reality. Besides, Thought is more real than the physical. Someone, cycles before, had discovered the link between the quantum world and the infinity beyond. That torturous path, Orion had followed. He could now be Nothing—yet, since that last Egg, he had held on to his skeleton of light.

*Why?*

The minds belonging to the Nothing Makers were salvaged from physical worlds threatened by destruction, or had always been so before. Now an Egg had been created simply to salvage one end of the galaxy: The rules of their use of power had subtly changed.

*But for the good, for the good*, Orion thinks. Blue and mawkish orange and rainbows of black.

*Or has it?*

Interharg is disturbed; others are disturbed. Orion, ashamed of his own light skeleton, is outraged and horrified at the number of young Nothing Makers who now affect them.

*The poison is deeper than we know.*

*Forget it*, he tells himself. What is important is the next size of infinity. The concept is curious, intriguing—and it is a treasure picked up from the poison planet. The hulls there had invented classifications for sizes of infinity. Orion had picked it up from an engineer's mind he had mapped. The engineer knew the work of the once-hull Georg Cantor. Cantor had designated the different infinities by Aleph numbers. Aleph Null was the smallest infinity; Aleph One was the next largest-sized infinity, and Aleph Two had been the largest Cantor had been able to describe.

Orion, once he thinks of it, knows there must be a three, and immediately sees there must be a four and a five. *Is there a six?* he wonders.

He ought to be able to figure out a six.

He has not yet, however. It might take a while. The life of a star, perhaps. Beyond the end of this universe and into the next cycle, maybe. But Orion has time.

He has all-time if he wants.

His thoughts are interrupted by Eskelion, whose beaming hypercharged presence is always annoying. After a hundred thousand years, you'd think the creature would calm down some. Some beings, Orion supposed, are just not suited for a thinking life.

Eskelion, he is sure, is one of those. Perhaps it is Eskelion's background as a plant? Perhaps.

Mauve circles burn umber, speckled with steel gray, as Eskelion stumbles his way through the high dialect of the Nothing Makers. "One coming. Pale light unblended, and speedily, and opposite."

"Star drink to you," Orion responds, dipping his aura the requisite shades of blue. *Who can it be?* he wonders. A dozen Eggs are scattered through this galaxy. Somewhere, a

Paradise is hatching. New beings are matured to the edge of Nothing Making. It is an interruption, but not an unpleasant one.

"Feel cross-spectra, feel light dark," Eskelion continues. "Interharg, Calfi, Ortle: feel much brown."

"Assure. Side-skipping I go."

Orion sets out in welcome.

More than anything else, the fact that there was no way of keeping time in Paradise annoyed Doyle. He wanted desperately to know how long he'd been away from Janet. It seemed like years, but it might only have been months. Or moments. There was no way to know. He did the only thing he could: He worked to master his power.

If he became powerful enough, he might break out.

Always, he faced failure. Always.

Some demon inside him seemed intent on destroying his art. Oversized ants were the least of it; banioxles, at this stage, would be a pleasure.

For guinea pigs, Doyle used Max and Esmerelda.

They suffered his failures.

One more time, he begged them. Just one more. "I've mastered it now," he said. "This one's simple. It's perfect."

"No way," said Max. "You're too risky."

"One last time," Doyle pleaded. "I won't ask you again."

"You've said that before," Max said.

"Trust me," Doyle said.

"What is it this time?"

"Doves," Doyle said. "What could possibly be wrong with doves?"

One last time, they went along.

He began to remember what he had done. He remembered the sharp pain and sudden blindness as he swooped down across the golden field. He remembered and relished the exquisite fear he'd felt as the dove. His illusion had been perfect as the angular face of the red-haired dog had appeared above him and opened its mouth.

Then had come the teeth, the beautiful teeth.

And then came the wonderful saving blackness.

And then . . . this frightful, fearful nothingness.

And Doyle was ashamed at what he had done.

Dim light began to surround him as he brought himself back under control. His "body" coalesced as his thoughts focused once again. He waited.

A glimmer appeared.

Max and Esmerelda materialized.

"I'm sorry," Doyle said. "I had to have it *real*—I couldn't take any more sweetness and light."

Esmerelda seemed to have been crying. Max's face was cloudy with anger.

"Sorry?" the German said. He thundered. "Sorry? You scare us half to death, and you're sorry? You tell us you've got it perfect, and we trust you, and it's back. 'Sorry,' you say. 'Doves,' you said. 'What could possibly be dangerous about doves?'! Doves! Doves in the middle of hunting season! You should pick loons."

"I tried, Max. I really tried. It's just— "

"Yeah, you tried. Like the time you took us on the ocean trip, and it turned out to be the Titanic? And you were trying when you took us on the sight-seeing trip through Jerusalem —and the bus was attacked by grenade-throwing terrorists? Trying?"

Max vanished. He left behind a whiff of brimstone. Deliberately, Doyle was sure. He looked at Esmerelda. He colored his features with sadness, so she would understand how he felt. "Paradise," he said softly. "Isn't that what we call it?"

"Yes," she said. "And for me it is—or was—Paradise. I was able to let my dreams flower, to wear the body of my youth, to never again have to seduce some party hack for the 'greater good' —it's closer to Paradise than I ever expected to get. For most of us, it's like that. We spent our lives beating our heads against the walls of duty and honor—like you, just like you—and we don't have to hurt anymore. We've earned the right to have things our way. I can't see what's so distasteful about it, either."

"Nothing," Doyle said.

"Nothing? You don't mean that. When you're lying, you lose control. Your body fades in and out."

"Okay, so it's not nothing," Doyle said. He steadied himself. "It's a very big something. I'm scared of what's happening at home. I'm scared for the black women who're being pulled into a squad car right now and being raped, and whom no one will ever believe. I'm scared because NATO's getting the edge on the Warsaw Pact countries—or them on us— and Max isn't there anymore to juggle power so all sides come up even. I'm scared because in Rome there's blood in the streets, because Esmerelda doesn't hurt anymore."

"It's not like that. It couldn't be."

"No? Look around us. How many hundreds of thousands of us are there? And who are they? Movers and shakers, the doers and thinkers. There's not a token among them."

"You would like that, wouldn't you? Proof of your importance?"

Doyle stared hard at Esmerelda. "If you think that . . ." he said. He couldn't go on. They shared the silence, both knowing what must happen. They weren't really arguing.

"But the cyberneticist—what's his name?"

"The Englishman? Steve?"

"Uh-huh. He doesn't think there's any reason our bodies would had to have been destroyed."

"Yeah. I talked to him, too."

"Maybe it's like he said: We're an experiment. I think that's kind of nice."

Doyle scowled. "An experiment? If there was only a handful of us, maybe. Even if the selection wasn't so damn impressive, I'd say maybe. But to get us all? There must be more than a million of us. At least."

"So?"

"So, if it's an experiment, a handful would have done. Not this many. This many scares me."

Esmerelda didn't say anything at first. She was toying with her body, making it glow from the inside. While Doyle was undoubtedly the master now at projecting illusion, Esmerelda had him beaten when it came to controlling self. He was entranced.

When she spoke again, her voice seemed dreamy and far away. "I don't mind your wanting to save the world," she said. "Really, I don't. And I wouldn't mind if you admitted

that was only a part of it. But the way you ignore the other issue, that makes me know I'm
fighting to lose."

"You mean Janet," he said.

"Yes. Janet."

"The way I see it, if someone had wanted me
to stay here, they wouldn't have sent her here
with me. They didn't. They want me to go
back."

"You know damn well why she isn't here."

"No. No, I don't. Tell me."

"Because she wouldn't fit. She's no more
your equal—or mine—than a cabbage. I'm
here, though—and I'm your equal. Or your
better, if you could even grasp that. What I'm
not is a doll you can worship and keep on a
shelf. You can't dress me up and pretend I'm
Joan of Arc or whatever the hell it is you think
Janet is. I may not have flesh, but I have mind.
I'm more real than Janet could ever be—and
you'd never know the difference. We could
make this Paradise."

Doyle watched as Esmerelda's clothes melt-
ed. Her body changed. Her breasts became
smaller and her hair went from red to blonde.
"No," he said. "No." But he watched anyway.
Whenever he'd dreamed of Janet, it had always been just a dream. She had been most
real when she was before Meriwether: That
was because, interacting with someone else's
will, she had no longer been his puppet. But
Esmerelda as Janet . . . that would be even
better.

Involuntarily, Doyle reached out. He caught a scent; his nostrils widened. The smell was wonderful, transporting: the scent of apricot. Esmerelda's thinking of that detail was more than simple consideration; it was an act of love. And Doyle knew it. And he also knew, if he accepted, he would have betrayed Janet.

That he could not do.

Worse, Esmerelda's trying to please him would be an even greater travesty than his own images of his wife. It would be another fakery, another sham. More of that he didn't need.

"No, Es. I can't let you do it."

She beckoned, luxurious in her nakedness.

"Dammit, no."

And suddenly she was clothed. She wrapped herself in funeral garb: a shroud. And then she began to laugh. Doyle saw that it was real laughter and not a cover-up. "Okay, I tried. I did my best," she said. "Only a fool would go farther—or care more. I am no fool."

"I never thought you were."

"That may be what I did wrong, then," she said. She shook her head. Her hair was red again. It moved like flame. "I guess you'd better get back to your little girl."

"But how?"

"I don't know any better than you, but I've got an idea. You're making the same cop-out as the rest of us when you imagine Janet. You imagine her perfect. If you could really see her, warts and all— "

"She hasn't got any warts."

"She has something. Moles. You know. And until you see those clearly, you're stuck here. Paradise is ruined for both of us. I want you to get out, so I can have some peace."

She disappeared.

She left behind a scent of rose.

She left Doyle behind. He was trembling. He knew she was right. He knew what he must do.

Doyle pressed out with his mind, exploring the cage of nothingness. He felt the wall through which his thoughts could not push. But he must push. He pushed until the effort blacked him out. He came to with the smell of yeast and a feeling of stickiness, and he was lonely. He fought his way out of the blackness. He pushed again.

Time, even the imaginary keeping of time, ended for Doyle.

He imagined being a time-traveler, and a space-traveler, and a traveler-between-dimensions. None of it was right. None of it worked. None of it was real.

"Janet is real," he thought. "Making love to Janet is real."

He remembered nights, afternoons, the first time they had stayed together. The awkwardness. He remembered the first time she had wakened him, her lips moving gently along his back. Times of laughter, times when anger moved their bodies like whips, and a time when she was close to him, afterwards, and his cheek touched her hair, and his cheek felt a cold wetness there that was his: These he remembered.

And each time, afterwards, he blacked out. With each cycle, his need for her deepened. It was never enough. The wall stood. As it had been with her, never enough. The need would not end. He learned to hate Janet. He learned love again.

He remembered her leaving him. He remembered the twistedness of his stomach, and how he'd thrown up. He was sick to his soul at sharing her body: When she'd come back, he'd felt her body was like a disease. And she'd said, "We can't be lovers anymore—just friends." He determined he would have her again, then drop her. It was what he wanted.

Gently, gently he had worked: listened, nodded, fingers like thieves.

And she had opened her body to him again.

And he had not had strength to turn away.

Still, though the anger burned in him, it was not enough.

The blackness, the stickiness, the yeastiness returned. He hung suspended in the nothingness and wept for his need.

And it was not enough.

Then came a time when Doyle's vision was clearer than it had been before. She was so real to him that his hurt and the want that combined into love filled him. Tears ran down his cheeks and he laughed. When he could have killed her gleefully, and killed himself, and chose neither.

This time it must work.

He smelled the apricot from her shampoo. Her gold hair glistened in the moonlight. The two of them rested together on clean cotton sheets, like pants and shirt discarded together.

She was naked. The T-shirt she usually wore was missing. Her odd modesty required that her breasts be covered—but she always left her slim legs and the place of their joining uncovered.

*I think/remember that she is ashamed of her breasts. The heat outside is terrible, and I'm happy. I am fatally in love. Love*, he thinks. *Not lust*.

Passion moved through them; their bodies became slick with sweat. She was almost a shining thing in the darkness. Doyle drifted in the illusion, happy, happy.

And then she spoke. It was so quiet at first he did not understand. She was pregnant, she said. And joy exploded over him.

"I want to marry you," he said.

"You're sure?"

"More sure than anything."

And they moved together again, and she
agreed, and then . . . and then . . . Blackness
threatened Doyle. He could feel the yeastiness
gathering around him. *No, not this time.* He
fought. He was dizzy. He was afraid. And
then . . .

It was another night. It was a night much
like the first, when he proposed. But it was
different, what she said. She said she had miscarried.

She said to him she had miscarried.

To him she told: I miscarried.

And he believed her absolutely, and they
married anyway. It was good. It was good. It
was good.

Only he knew she had not miscarried. She
had had an abortion.

And the blackness was suddenly everywhere, swelling over him, calling to him. This
blackness was different; it was kind. So kind,
so soothing, so comforting. Here are your
dreams, Doyle. Have your dreams.

Have Max as your friend and Esmerelda as
your lover.

Have anything you want, Doyle. Anything.

And Doyle flared. Intensity was on him like
lightning, and he laughed at the blackness. He
remembered the pains that had come before.
He ridiculed them. He turned toward the reality.

*She killed my son, and I love her, and I don't
care. Father: hear me, she has killed my son.*

*And I love her. Father, Father . . . forgive me
for the son you never had.*

Doyle passed through the wall.

It was like waking up at work time, only to
remember it was Sunday and there was time
to drowse away the morning. *I'm back*, he
thought. *I'm back in my body.*

It was true: He was home.

He knew it was true because it wasn't quite
what he had imagined. The world had changed. Pain, there was pain. A backache nagged at
him. But . . . there was also the smell of apricot; he felt the massage of thick carpet beneath him and warmth from a fire. Wine, he
tasted wine.

*Liebfraumilch*, he thought. *Funny: I hate
Liebfraumilch.*

As he locked more firmly into reality, he began to see just how faulty his illusions had
been. He opened his eyes and a flood of unfamiliar details poured in, but only one thing
counted:

Janet was beside him.

She had gained some weight, he noticed.
She was napping beside him on the carpet.
Neither of them wore clothes. Her stomach

was still flat, however, and now it was tan, dusted with yellow hairs. Her delicate breasts were banded in white from the protection of a negligible bikini top; the nipples were bright red and slightly swollen.

More detail poured in as he put together the strangeness of carpet, fireplace and sweet wine: *Where the hell am I? This isn't where we live.* This was a sleek townhouse and it reeked of prosperity. The walls were paneled. There was a wall-sized TV.

Whatever doubts he'd had about really being back in the real world vanished. Never would he have imagined this. Even in a nightmare such details would have escaped him.

And then final details began filtering in. For the first time, Doyle felt alarm.

Doyle began to feel the sleepy, sated rhythms of other thoughts. The thoughts were threateningly close by. They seemed all around him, throughout him, as if they were in the body with him. The thoughts beat gently with this single emotion: *This is home, this is comfort, this is what I've always wanted.*

At first he could think of no explanation for the thoughts. As his eyes swept his body again, he began to understand: This body was not the one he'd imagined for use in Paradise, but it was not the one he'd left behind, either. The body was well-tanned, for one thing. Doyle spotted an unfamiliar scar—but he also saw a gash he'd gotten as a boy, when he'd tripped and fallen into a barn fan.

It could only be one thing: The body had gone on without him. It had been at least months, likely years, since he'd been here. And the thoughts he felt? They must be ones that had developed since he'd been gone.

With a growing feeling of panic, Doyle began to explore those other thoughts. Doyle was suddenly aware that he did not quite "fit" anymore; there was a lack of harmony between him and the body. It took great concentration for him just to open his eyes. He felt like the top of a Tupperware container that had been fitted onto a too-small container: Most of him fit perfectly, but part of him would not snap into place.

*But it's me, it's her*, he thought.

He reached out and made contact with new memories. He had quit the U. S. Attorney's office and gone into private practice. He spent his free time sailing. He remembered dancing, dancing, dancing, with music pounding his ears to marshmallows—and he remembered his joy at it. There were new memories of being with Janet—and memories of being with someone else.

*My God, Christ—how could I?*

The woman had been sleek and black-haired, but she had been no Esmerelda. Nowhere near. And Doyle and this woman had been out for kicks—nothing else. No love. He couldn't believe it, not with his Baptist upbringing. But that wasn't the worst part. No. It was the simple act of unfaithfulness that

staggered him, confused him. How could he
have been faithful enough to fight his way out
of the nothingness, across the black barriers,
through the wall, through the pain of the
abortion, to come back—and find he had been
unfaithful here?

It wasn't possible; it couldn't be. *Betray her,
maybe,* he thought. *But to betray me like that?
No way.*

He began to shake. The body began to
shake. Janet moved beside him, stirring. Her
eyes opened and the simple sight of her looking at him made him feel calm.

"Something wrong, sweetheart?" Her voice
was sweet. It touched his ear as ripe apple
touches the tongue.

Doyle tried to answer. He felt clumsy. He
couldn't quite make his mouth work; he began
to feel he was fighting with someone or something for control of his vocal cords. "I'm, I,
ack," he said.

"It's all right," she said. "I'm here."

Doyle, the man who had been to Paradise
and returned, Doyle 1, suddenly realized what
he was fighting: the Doyle who had remained
behind, Doyle 2. The two of them, each in control of one part of the brain only, were fighting for control of the tongue, the lips and the
lungs. Doyle 1 had the stronger will; it was,
finally, his words the body spoke.

"I want a cigarette," he said. *A cigarette will
calm me down,* he thought. *A real cigarette!
That's worth the trip back right there.*

"What?" she said.

"A cigarette," he said. "I want one."

Her eyes narrowed. Doyle 1 had forgotten that look, the bitch beautiful; the demanding princess. She said, "I don't believe it. You haven't smoked for over a year, and you're going to throw it away? Just like that? After quitting as a Christmas present to me?"

As the words registered, Doyle 1, shaken at her words, let his control slip. *What else could happen?* he thought.

Doyle 2 seized the chance. "I don't know what's got into me. I haven't got the slightest urge for a cigarette. It's—"

*You lying unfaithful sold-out bastard: You'd crawl through fire for a cigarette right now. Where the hell have you hidden your guts?*

Doyle 2 began to stutter. The face of the body went white. Words came in through his ears, but Doyle 2 was too upset to answer. "Charley, what's wrong?" the words said. "Talk to me, please. Please talk to me."

The body mumbled nonsense as the two Doyles fought.

*Who are you? WHAT ARE YOU?* Doyle 2 wondered.

*I'm you, more or less. I'm the man you used to be.*

*What are you talking about? What's going on?*

"Talk to me, honey. Do you need a doctor?"

Doyle 2 tried to respond—and Doyle 1 decided to let him. At least for now. *He doesn't know anything has happened; he doesn't understand.* Doyle 1 needed to know some things before he tried anything else. A mistake now could be fatal—for both of them. *Whoever did this had to leave a clue. The answer has to be in here someplace. Somewhere inside the brain, something has got to show. It has to, or else . . .* But he couldn't imagine an "or else." *This was done for a reason, and I aim to find out what the reason was.*

He let himself flow along the electrochemical pathways of the brain, as he tried to develop an understanding of the chemical messages scuttling from axon to dendrite. He was overwhelmed by the activity that surrounded him. There seemed to be billions of flashing lights, as if he'd found himself inside a galaxy-sized pinball machine. Finding his way around was like trying to find your way around the world, using a Technicolor roadmap that had been reduced to the size of a dime. *That part fits, and that part,* he thought. *Here there's something new.* He aligned himself with the neural circuits and pressed himself against them. A wad of golfing memories erupted. Suddenly, he knew the grip needed to correct his slice. *Damn, double damn: Has this geek no shame? Next I'll find he's been peeping in windows at night.*

Deeper and deeper he probed, ferreting out the memories that made Doyle 2 different from Doyle 1.

*But where did the changes begin? This is*

*like me, but there's no passion. No anger. He's gone mellow. Something had to do that, and that something has to be here. But where?*

And these are ONLY his memories: Where did I come from? *Where are my memories?* He found things he thought he remembered, but they were always slightly different than what he recalled. Sometimes there were major differences: This Doyle thought of growing up on a farm with fondness.

The answers must be deeper still.

He clawed and sorted through three years of memories. He began to see how this Doyle had changed to meet Janet's demands—and those demands, he saw, had caused Doyle 2's unfaithfulness. *Hell, he missed the point: Janet's always been headstrong. Sparring with her was half the fun.* But he did not like some of the things Janet had made this Doyle do. Quit smoking; switch from whiskey to soda-pop wine. Doyle felt a grudging sorrow at this Doyle's life. *Like he has no center, no point. No point and no passion. No joy,* he thought.

He came at last to a place where the flickering trails of light began to thin. It seemed the neurons had been weeded here. There were gaps. Where brain cells should be, there was a scar smoothness. Doyle pressed against a scarred place and felt a barrier of black.

*No, not again. I can't do it again.*

But it was too late. He felt himself becoming folded into the blackness. Now, he had to struggle. He thought he had no more energy; the idea of struggling any more was enough to defeat him. He could not take this.

Doyle was tired. He only wanted sleep.

He groaned and gathered up all the energy he had left. He pushed once more. He pressed hard into the darkness. The vision exploded around him.

Lights danced.

Doyle's mind flooded with the sudden knowledge of life between the stars. He grasped at once the notion of bodiless minds roaming the emptiness between stars. A rainbow danced toward him. The rainbow introduced itself as Orion. The rainbow wished him well. He said it in lights, but Doyle understood.

"I have done this to you, and you have struggled with honor. You are here because you cannot accept the lack-of-struggle."

A thousand pricks of light flashed into Doyle's mind; he felt himself run through with light, crucified in light.

"Here, here, you will find us here."

One pinprick leaped out from the rest. It expanded, grew fuzzy, became a galaxy.

"In the space between this double-star and this red giant, you will find us," Orion said. "You are free. The mold we made from your mind is destroyed. You have learned to hold your thoughts together without body. You are us are we."

The vision faded.

Doyle 1 lingered. He now knew alien smells, copper and chlorine; he had tasted the insides of stars; he had seen dances in space.

But he didn't want it.

*I am free*, he thought. *I choose. You had no right.*

But there was no one to answer. Orion's image was gone.

Doyle had fought his way out of nothingness for Janet; he would not abandon her now, not for a promise. Not for another pipedream. Not for a drink of the stars.

"This is mine," he announced. "This is my brain and my body, and I claim them."

The vision had left him dazed. He felt torn, beaten. Groggily he backed away from the dead-ended part of the brain. There was nothing there but scar now. He had absorbed the message left behind.

Doyle began to rise through the circuits of Doyle's brain.

Lights flashed more brightly and more frequently.

He prepared to fight.

Doyle 1 again began to hear Janet's words. They were indistinct, as if he heard them under water. Still he rose. Upward, upward.

"Better now?" she was saying. "Good."

He saw again through his body's eyes. He did not try for control yet; he did not want to alert the other Doyle. When it came time to kill off Doyle 2, it would be done quickly. He would depend on surprise. Surprise was the best way.

Her face smiled into his. She nestled

against his body, and Doyle 1 thrilled at the actual, real, physical closeness of his wife. Closer now came her words.

"I love you," she was saying. "God, it seems like . . . Did I . . ." She turned and looked into his face. Her sharp features were smoothed and seemed cut from diamond. Her lips were wet. She licked her lips nervously.

*They're going to make love*, Doyle realized suddenly. *And when he's tied up with that, I'll strike. And then it will be over, and she and I will be making love. At last. This whole nightmare will end. I'll be home.*

She kissed his body gently, then pulled away. "You've grown so much," she said. "You're so much more loving. Did I ever tell you that two—maybe three—years ago I was ready for a divorce? I was, I really was. You thought of nothing but your work, nothing but your crusades. Never of me. And then you changed." She smiled. "It seems like another life now, I'm so happy."

The body answered without Doyle. "I can understand. I don't know why you put up with me so long."

They kissed, the body and wife. They were tight against each other.

And Doyle was screaming inside himself.

He wanted to tear out the neurons that had allowed him to hear her words. He dived inside the brain again, conjuring his own thoughts and forcing them into the brain's circuits. He flooded Doyle 2's mind with images from a cesspool: chunks of waste floated in a yellow-green muck. Doyle 1 jammed the ion pumps for the sodium and potassium channels along the axons. He felt the body going into seizure.

"Die," he said. "Die."

But nothing could erase her words. It was too late for that. The words played through him like knives heated white-hot: the words burned, but they also cauterized. Doyle began to fit the pieces together. He saw that, as much as he had loved Janet and wanted her to share his world, she had loved him—and wanted him to share hers.

And she had won, over his body.

And she had lost him. And she didn't even know.

Doyle was washed through with a powerful, healing desire for light and distance. Carefully, gently, he reversed his attack on the body. He soothed the body; he put in images of sunlight and soft rain.

When it was done, when the damage was repaired, he began to break contact with the body. He began to feel and hear and smell in colors. He began to glow. *I had Paradise, and that wasn't good enough. I had reality, and I couldn't face that. I guess some people are never satisfied*, he thought.

He rippled in sad gentle laughter.

Contact after contact, he broke free.

"What's the matter?" he heard Janet say. "You just about scared me to death. Are you all right?"

Doyle heard her voice as violet.

"Jesus, I don't know," the body said. "I just had . . . the weirdest feeling." Still the body trembled, but it was calming now. The body reached for his wife. Its other hand reached up and wiped at its eye.

"You're crying," Janet said accusingly.

"I guess I am." He sounded surprised.

Doyle heard the words in yellow speckled with green. It was the last thing he heard. He burst free of his body.

When it happened, he knew he had made the right decision. He could "see" the world as a magnificent ball of interlocking energies. It was a celestial Christmas tree. Doyle was free of it, however. He was leaving it.

Up he went through the jet stream and higher, until he cleared the last wisps of atmosphere. He hummed blue, seeking. At last he matched the pattern of stars overhead with the map Orion had buried in his brain.

Following Orion's instructions, Doyle began to give up the idea of mass. It was the hardest thing: the last barrier. He did it. He was now free to move at any speed. He began to accelerate. Faster and faster he moved, toward M31. Past lightspeed, because that only held back mass.

The last contact he broke was even thinking of Earth. One sensation lingered after the rest.

It was the smell of apricot.

Orion is anxious as the first of the newborn approaches. Each mature intelligence brings gifts, he knows from experience. To predict what they can teach is useless, and he does not try. Still, he is excited. Each thing learned will be partly to his credit. He is the master craftsman of Paradise.

He waits.

Soon he notices something light-like hurtling his way. Orion's senses are spread over a million square kilometers—and he is puzzled. The incoming direction indicates that the arrival is from the last Egg created.

"Absurd," he thinks. "Impossible."

He rechecks the direction and he has not erred. The being comes from the poison planet.

Quickly, Orion considers. This is dangerous, he thinks. He is cloaked in gray.

He decides to shape himself into a human-like form. He will make the body silver, translucent and blank-faced. Such a body should create a little awe and terror in this first arrival, Orion thinks.

That will give him time to see if anything has gone wrong.

When the Earth-being nears, Orion flares his new body. He is pleased to see the newcomer halt quickly and awkwardly.

"Brother in peace, I commend you your journey."

Meriwether blinked and made a quick de-

cision. He shaped a body identical to
Orion's—only black. "You jiving me, man?"

Orion is momentarily confused. He studies
the shiny humanoid before him. He senses
no awe or terror. *Jive?* he wonders. *What
color is jive?*

"Hear me," Orion said. He said it carefully,
still trying to get an analysis done of this
creature. "Brave you are, and honored we are.
But danger/strangeness still there is."

"No lie, ace, and it's getting badder all the
time. That crazy honky's steaming right behind me, I'm telling you. I'm going to have to
skin that mother to get him off my ass. You
saying you'll help?"

The confusion level was high, Orion
thought. This being showed none of the or-
dinary arrival symptoms. He seemed pleased
with his primitive vernacular, too. Odd. It was
not unknown for this to happen, but it was
rare. It was a disorder usually associated
with sexed beings: *Aha*, he thought.

Meanwhile, Meriwether decided to shuck
the street talk. It had served his purpose and
bought him time. This dude was off guard
now; Meriwether could drop the act.

"I saw your picture in my mind back there,"
he said. "It's some job you people have done,
I'll admit. And I'm honored to be in on the
scam—if that's what it is."

Orion translated "scam" and tried to explain. He started with the problem of the
poison, then the problem of maturing minds.

He described the necessity of the raid and how it was accomplished. He explained the process of evolution whereby Meriwether had "hatched" from Paradise—but he was interrupted.

"Hold it right there, Jack. I didn't leave voluntarily. I was blown out of there."

"Blown?"

"Blown *away.*"

A flashing of lights, a question: Which way?

"Killed," Meriwether said.

The revelation stunned Orion. *How can this be?* "This other man tried to end your thought processes permanently?" he asked. It was hard to believe.

"Well, he shot me point blank—it usually works out to that, yeah."

COUNCIL, COUNCIL. I, ORION, CALL COUNCIL.

"And he'll try again when he gets here, I imagine. Doyle has a lot of determination for a white boy."

"Here? He would try to unmake you here?"

"If I'm here, he would."

"Not in this place. He couldn't. Such a thing is not-good," he said. Even as he protested, however, Orion began to believe. In the first place, only such a peculiar series of events could explain the speed with which Meriwether had arrived. The evidence he needed to believe was before him, in the person of this unawed and cocksure being who dared mimic his design.

If this one existed, there were probably more.

COUNCIL!

COUNCIL IS ASSEMBLED, ORION.

"Let's start all over again," Orion said to Meriwether. He explained how Meriwether had evolved to join the Nothing Makers; how he was now beyond sight and sound.

"Sex?" Meriwether said. "I've lost sex?"

Translation: Yes.

"Horse hockey. I'd just soon go on back to Paradise, if you don't mind. Just show me the door."

Orion's mind spun rapidly, making the necessary connections. Where was the honor this being should feel? Paradise, Orion said, was something like a nursery. You don't want to go back to a nursery, he said. All that goes on in nurseries is games. Games, he said, are for children.

"But games are also fun," Meriwether said. "What's the point of living without fun? Just like Doyle and me: We've been jacking around now for years. It adds spark to being."

"To make 'dead' is fun?"

"Well, no. Not if you get stuck there—but I'm not, am I? I'm still breathing."

Orion was baffled. He tuned in to Council, and he could feel/smell/touch their bafflement.

Orion had a feeling, as the conversation went on, that fitting these people into the Nothing Maker society would make finding

Aleph Six a breeze.
    Secretly, he hoped so.

    Eskelion was too young to belong to Coun-
cil, but he listened as its members delib-
erated. He heard this Meriwether speak and
was fascinated.
    When he had heard enough, he made himself
absent. He Thought. A single Thought consum-
ed him, overwhelmed him: The sense of Earthmen he had gotten from Orion and Meriwether. These newborn might well be a way
out, he thought. They were not the kind to
easily relinquish their homes—but they must
be warned. They must be told of Orion's enormous power, of Council, of their incredible
lures. Once your body was ash—as Eskelion,
painfully, knew—there was no going back.
Once home was abandoned, it never worked
to even try.
    In his throat and his bowels, Eskelion felt
his terrible loss. He was not so blatant in his
physical being as was this Meriwether, for he
only covered his thoughts in physical terms;
he did not actually have a "body" as did the
Earthman. But he still thought and longed for
his physical self. The lovely gray-green of his

planet's surface, the trunk-deep waters, the stumpwater smell: all were gone. The loss ached at him day and night, and it was this that made him hyperkinetic. It was not youth, but the burning of unfulfilled desires. Orion and the others could call it "youth," but they did not know. They had forgotten.

Eskelion decided he must go. He must meet this Earthman Doyle.

He bounced.

Doyle's excitement had been building for the last dozen or so light years. He felt he was a transparent being bulleting his way through space. The unwinking pinpoints and star clusters around him seemed a symbol: He had emerged from the narrow world of his birth, and now was a son of the universe. He recalled the Stanley Kubrick classic, "2001: A Space Odyssey." He imagined that he had become the baby hovering at the end. Kubrick had originally planned to end the movie with bombs going off on Earth's horizon, Doyle recalled. The ending had been changed, though, because Kubrick feared it would be too much like the ending of "Dr. Strangelove." Very well:

Doyle would be that different ending.

*What lies ahead*? he wondered.

A person named Orion. A being of light.

Peace settled onto Doyle as he hurtled. Soon there should be answers. He could find the reason for the cycle of madness and despair he had lived through; perhaps the weight of his cynicism would lift. These people, to whom bodies were as irrelevant as the laws of physics, must surely have answers.

Surely.

Surely.

And the peace he felt deepened.

He began to feel that he was nearing Orion's homeplace. A new tingling filled him. He recognized in the tingling a more sophisticated system than that he and his friends had used in Paradise to locate each other—but the principle was the same.

He thought it was the same.

About this time, Doyle also began to feel watched. That was likely, he thought. Surely sentries would be posted to watch for new arrivals. The feeling persisted.

Doyle began to slow. He began to feel an uneasiness, the way you feel when someone sits too closely, someone you do not know and do not want to know.

He slowed more.

He stopped.

The feeling was strong now. He'd hoped it was a hangover from his childhood. He could remember walking early in the morning—3 or

4 a.m.—to get the cows. You'd get the feeling
of being followed. You stopped, the feeling
went away. If you went on, the feeling returned. Later, much later, he realized he must
have been hearing the echoes of his footsteps
off the long walls of the barn.

Stopping hadn't worked here, however.

He *was* being watched. Inspected even, he
thought.

"Hello?"

Nearby, a light began to swell from a pinpoint. It was as if a faraway star was going
nova. Doyle hung in space, surrounded by
black and flecks of light, feeling the rhythms
of space rush through him. He realized how
stupid it was to think of empty space: Space
was full.

"Hello." Doyle felt the thought this time.

Something shaped like a football and glowing pink was growing from the pinpoint of
light. When the shape was finished, it was the
size of a bus.

Doyle himself had no shape.

"Hello?" the thing said. "Are you an Earthman?"

The quality of the thought felt somehow
childish. Doyle remembered children, when
he was a street cop, looking up to him and ask-
ing, "Are you a policeman?" This felt the
same.

He wondered just how many *other* people
were zipping along this freeway in the sky.

"Yes. I'm from Earth."

"That's so marvelous."

Doyle wanted to ask what was so marvelous about it, but he held back. "Are you Orion?"

The football shifted from pink to bright green. Laughter, Doyle supposed—or shame. He did feel humor in the next wave of thought that reached him:

"No, not me. I am Eskelion, and I have been wanting to meet an Earthman. I've been wanting to since the first one arrived."

*The first one? Who else could have made the transformation? Esmerelda? Doubtful.* It could be anyone, he supposed. "I'll be happy to satisfy your curiosity, if you'll tell me how I can find Orion."

"Orion's in Council—but they've been expecting you, this light-time or next. You'll see."

"Ask your questions, then. Shoot," Doyle said.

"Shoot? Then you do kill? Are you Doyle?"

A terrible feeling came over the Earthman. Shoot-kill-Doyle: How could that combination mean anything here, unless . . . But it couldn't be. It just couldn't. That would be a travesty of justice.

"Why do you say that?"

"Because of the dark Earthman."

"Does he have a name?"

"Doesn't everyone?" the football asked.

"I mean, what is his name?"

"Meriwether."

Doyle could see it clearly now. He imagined

the Rulers of the Universe posting rewards
for him. Spectral bounty hunters were even
now sifting space for his aura.

What do you do instead of beating your
head against the wall when you're in a near-
vacuum and have no head? Where do you go,
when you've been everywhere and been re-
jected everywhere? These questions were becoming important to Doyle. But mainly this
one:

*Why me?*

Doyle considered. He could answer none of
the questions.

And he had tried to kill Meriwether.

That probably didn't set well with Universe
Ruling-types.

But an eye for an eye, a tooth for a tooth?
Surely, they wouldn't be so primitive? Besides, he had neither eyes nor teeth. Surely—if they read thoughts—they could see
through Meriwether's lies. Surely.

*Meriwether, oh Meriwether: You sly SOB.*

"He says I'm a killer, does he?"

"Oh yes," Eskelion projected. "Dedicated
beyond all to the ending of his thoughts forever. It's romantic is what it is. I admire the
passion, Sir. It is a passion we have not had
here in many star-times. Star-lives, I daresay.
Feel star-killers; feel ooze blood, feel beauty!"

Feel vastly confused and entangled, Doyle
thought to himself. "It may not be all that you
think."

"The thought is in you. I feel the thought.

The thought is equal to the action, here."

"Swell, just swell."

The football enlarged.

"No, you don't understand," Doyle said. "Right and wrong *must* exist apart from thought." It does! he thought. "It is true: Right exists apart from thought, and Meriwether is right or wrong regardless of what I think. And I, I am right—or wrong—regardless of what you may think. It is immaterial."

Doyle felt himself glowing. He thought, "So I am the Earthman/killer? I bring passion to the places between the stars?" He imagined a place like Paradise, only more removed from reality. Memories tens of thousands of years old would be the only link. "Is it possible, from my own ignorance, I may now know something? Possible. I know there's something outside thought, anyhow."

His thoughts were pushed aside by Eskelion's. "Sir, breathlessly listen," the creature said. "This my story is for your own hearing. To other's ears told has-not-been. This is waited time-over-time for you."

Between the stars, between strangers, in words and not-quite-words, Eskelion's story came.

Do you know what spring is to the soul of a planet? When the orange sun rides to the lip of the forest, and then rises higher, higher? It is the when of cross-seeding. It is hope. Spring is always to remember a good thing, except for me. Spring is other for me. (He said.)

I had grown to the height of many stalks. (Doyle had a sudden vision of plants something like corn, but their husks were filled with rubied fruit. They would taste like ginger ale.) Many seasons had I grown. Tall and sturdy were my many bodies. Good tongues fell from my branches to soil. And then came the mighty is-not-spring-but-is. Leaves rolled up as if touched by fire. The cross-seeding did not come, despite the high sun. Flowers closed their petals without once feeling the downy touch of pollen fall. Seed borning was not.

Something ill from Father Sun touched me: Something was twisted in his warmth. He who was life was now poison, and that light that had made us food was now killing our many selves. I—so small, so young, even at my height—felt shuddering in the runners that connected me and us. Life was being washed from them, trashed, being sucked. Words not are for this. This is among the should-not-be.

We made the words to know. A name must be—a name you, as Earthman, must know. Is death. Not death as had been known, as I had seen and had been inside myself all time. Old death is always there, always a part, not like this new death: not all-things-ending.

And all things were ending.

Not old deaths, this.

(There is a groping between minds, as Doyle and Eskelion attempt to share understanding—as Doyle attempts to comprehend the anguish he feels from this alien soul.)

It is so. Each of your bits of skin, those cells, each of them has the old death and its end is not a hurtful thing. That is the death of which we knew.

Now came the big death. Grandfather forests browned and their bare fingers—empty, scarred, scaled—clawed and then stopped clawing at the sky that had turned enemy.

The big death took many, many. All who were left were weakening, and would know the big death. All would die, from the twisted light of Father Sun. Except the Nothing Makers came. Our cries and many deaths had reached them, and they came. They came and saw the all-many of us dying. They came as gently as pollen fall to a land without flowers. No flowers there were, among the many.

In the one only were there flowers. None had blooms except I. Except me and not-us. Except us that is me.

And a new home was given me and us.

Here.

It is a home of no big deaths—and no little deaths.

It is a home without flowers.

This home is no mulch to take root in. No

breeze stirs my limbs where no breeze or
limbs can be. Where there is no pollen fall and
no season of resting. Where all that matters is
not.

Where even big death, the only hope, is not.
Until you came.

(It grows silent and quiet. Doyle feels an
amazing tenderness. He, too, had been "res-
cued"—kidnapped was more like it—and he
had lost the physical world: He had lost Janet.
He recalled lines from a poem he once quoted
for her. They were lines from John Crowe
Ransom's "The Equilibrists." He repeated the
lines for Eskelion:)

\* \* \*

"For spin your period out, and draw your
  breath,
  A kinder saeculum begins with Death.
  Would you ascend to Heaven and bodiless
  dwell?
  Or take your bodies honorless to Hell?

  In heaven you have heard no marriage is,
  No white flesh tinder to your lecheries,
  Your male and female tissue sweetly
  shaped
  Sublimed away, and furious blood es-
  caped."

\* \* \*

Eskelion heard the words and hummed. His hue brightened; his color was scarlet. Doyle heard Eskelion's thinking: It is true and wise. You-we in Heaven not happy are to be.

Doyle agreed: You-we are not.

Eskelion: But your furious blood is not left you.

Doyle: It has not.

But another thing Eskelion believed, and this too he told Doyle. Father Sun had not become sick on his own. Somehow, Eskelion said, the Nothing Makers arranged it. By purpose or by accident, he did not know. They could do it, however:

"They have done it to your sun, Earthman."

"What do you mean?"

Eskelion explained how the sunspots now swarmed on Earth's star. The Nothing Makers—led by Orion—had put them there. "It was a necessary-good thing," Eskelion said. "They believe it so—but now I see that they have a poison in their hand, maybe even a poison worse than that you have made."

Doyle listened in disbelief. If he understood correctly, Orion and his friends had jiggered with both Eskelion's and Earth's sun. On Earth, perhaps the effect would be negligible. To Eskelion's world, however, the new cosmic rays had brought death. "Could it be killing Earth?" he wondered. And then he thought, "No—even the cowlike spirit in my body would have noticed that. I would have picked up some clue."

Still, these Rulers of the Universe seemed
not all that competent at their jobs.

"What do you propose?" he asked Eskelion.

"Friendship."

"Done," Doyle said.

Meriwether had finally been plugged into
Council. At first, he was overcome with
awe—but his feeling soon changed. This felt
exactly like the times when, hat in hand, he'd
approached government agencies back home.
Back then, race and money had been all that
counted—and you could tell which one counted most, because it was the one that wasn't
mentioned. White mouths moved, but nothing
came out. It was only at the agencies that
Meriwether could work up an unself-conscious
hatred of whites.

For the opposite reason, he had always
liked Doyle. Doyle was straight—as far as he
could be, anyhow. For Doyle, only two things
mattered: right and wrong.

Everybody had their power words, Meriwether thought. Like here. Here the taboo-
word was "force." No one had yet mentioned
the possibility of stomping Doyle flat. It was
the only thing Meriwether felt had a ninety-

per-cent chance of working. Lectures, the
Nothing Makers proposed. Blockades were
suggested. Hiding, even. And the talk went on,
while Doyle neared.

Meriwether could always feel the Man
closing on him. He felt it now. The Man was
Doyle.

Time was running out.

"May I speak, honored Council?" he said.
He was quickly learning the chromatic in-
flections of the Nothing Makers. They—unlike him—appeared mainly as wisps of color.
They seemed to be meeting in a kind of ad-hoc
amphitheater. It was as if someone had taken
the tree from out under its set of Christmas
lights and then turned the lights over: Council
was an inverted cone of blinking colors. What
Meriwether could not manage—but what was
going on all around him—was simultaneous
conversations. Orion would be color-linked in
a dozen conversations at once.

"Any and all may speak."

There was a patronizing tone to that. Meriwether bridled. It was like the last white
mayor of Memphis telling him, "We listen to
blacks in this city." Sure, fella.

*Swell*, he thought. *Once a nigger, a nigger
the universe over*.

He spoke—or rather thought—as loudly as
he could. He thought hard at the Council and
blended his thoughts with colors skimmed
from his emotions. He tried to picture Doyle
fairly, to show the goodness and blindness of

the man both.

"This man is coming here," he blinked and thought. "If he comes here, you will not stop him. You will not sway him by good thoughts, by good actions or by hiding. I have hidden—and he has found me. This man has power. He broke me out of Paradise; he alone broke free by strength of his will. Have others done this? Are others *like* this?"

Meriwether had guessed the answers. Brown shudders from the Christmas tree affirmed it.

"If you wish to change him, you must stop him. To stop him you must hurt him—cause him pain—beat him senseless. Know me and decide." He remembered his scenes with Doyle, embellished them, and turned them loose before Council.

It was an argument he planned to lose: He sensed that the Nothing Makers would veto any dangerous attack on Doyle (even if such a thing was possible, which he doubted). But he wanted to nudge them into action. He wanted them to compromise—on a plan he had already worked out.

Orion snorted in a flurry of blood-tinted orange and blue-greens. His thoughts were cutting. "Child, child," he said. Boy, boy, Meriwether heard. "We have put force behind us. It is not needed. This man cannot hurt us."

"You plan to let him amble in and wreck the place?"

"No. But the matter must be handled . . . wisely."

"A two-by-four up side the head would be wise."

Council turned away. Lights and flickerings increased among those gathered. Meriwether listened for his opening.

Interharg, a seeming equal of Orion's, seemed annoyed at Meriwether's presence. *Good*, Meriwether thought. *If I can annoy them enough, they will not want anybody else around who might annoy them worse. And Doyle would.*

"We have strength," Interharg said. "Reason is," an explosion of shifting colors, "the same as imagining this one here could be swayed by reason." There came a multi-chromal snort; Meriwether sensed chuckles and guffaws.

"Strength without force must be," Orion flashed.

"The appearance of force, a thing that would seem harmful, but is not: Such is needed."

And Meriwether chimed in: "Like a trial." He flashed them a scene of the old-time City Court. Doyle, he let them know, had been among the crowd associated with the system: Naturally, he would have an oversized respect for its function. Put Doyle on trial for his crimes and let him sweat the verdict: That should do, he argued.

"Trial" became a new color in the Christmas tree. Questions came and more chatter

—but the arguments began to shift. They were no longer "what" but how.

Meriwether was pleased:

This was something he'd wanted all his last ten years.




The straightforward pledge of friendship pleased Doyle deeply. It was a remembrance and reminder of good times he thought he'd never see again. It was good, after his trials, to have someone he trusted.

He trusted Eskelion. He felt his soul thoroughly and could find no reason to doubt that trust.

"I think perhaps they have gotten involved more deeply than they know," his new friend said.

"How so?" The two of them were moving, Eskelion leading the way.

"This Meriwether I like. You also. And yet you are enemies. Here, an enemy is the not-good. There is no gray. It is a composite of the what-is-known that is hard and fast and permanent. They have picked as good this Meriwether. You are not-good. Side by side, I think they confounded will be."

"What they haven't experienced is lies.

That's where Meriwether shines."

"He lied when he said you had killed him?"

"He's not dead, is he?" But Doyle wasn't happy with his answering Eskelion with a question. He should try to explain. Eventually, he knew he would have to explain. He might as well get in some practice.

"There was a child on Earth, a child that Meriwether killed for his own pleasure. It was my job—my responsibility—to avenge that death. To provide justice."

"Justice is kill-him-too? This is allowed?"

"Ah, no," Doyle said. "It's a little more complicated than that. Normally, there would be a trial to decide his guilt. At the trial, the punishment would be decided. But now Meriwether has escaped justice. It's up to me now, if justice is to be done. Maybe it has been done already. I don't know."

Eskelion, it seemed, had no knowledge of crime. There had been none on his world and there was none here. Plant people, apparently, didn't rape and shoot and steal. Or murder golden-haired young girls.

"What passions do you miss?" Doyle asked.

"Sunrise," Eskelion said. "Rain."

"But those aren't passions, really. A passion is a fire, a dream, a want."

"I dream of sunrise," Eskelion said. "I want to feel the cool mists clearing and the upper leaves beginning to warm as the work of the day starts. I want the all-through tingling of the spring, and the deep lovely sadness of leaf-fall."

"But—wait a minute."

Doyle "shook" his head. He thought, for a moment, he heard sirens. He heard the hi-low siren, and then the wail. The "sound" became louder.

"What's that?"

"I know not. It is a new kind of thinking."

The siren sound grew louder. It was odd, hearing sirens with no ears and no air.

"Look," Eskelion said.

Doyle saw. There were eight blue bolts coming toward them through the blackness. It looked like something out of a comic book, he thought. The bolts were a shimmering bright blue. The bolts were square columns. They looked like square striking snakes. Once Doyle had seen a Navy flying team doing a *fleur de lis*: The jets had come up, belly to belly, and then peeled out in different directions to make the bloom of the flower. That was what the bolts did as they approached.

And then the bolts began closing on them.

Doyle realized, "It's a cage."

Blue: The color of police.

Cosmic police.

"Eskelion," he said. "Don't say a word 'til we get a lawyer."

The bright blue colors closed tight. Doyle found it harder and harder to think. He could hear garbled thoughts from Eskelion, but they were growing weak. His own thoughts became dim. He stopped thinking.

His mind had frozen fast.

Fog filled Doyle's mind. He was vaguely
aware of people. People surrounded him.
They were not giant pink footballs. They were
not blinking lights. Just people.

His thoughts moved out of the molasses
state. He seemed to be in the old City Court,
upstairs in the downtown police station. But
the old courts had closed years ago. He
smelled the cheap perfume and unwashed
bodies and boozy breath. It was real. Any
minute now, his case would be called. He
would stand up and walk forward and argue
an 11-month, 29-days for some shoplifter. And
he would hate it.

Wood benches and linoleum floors: He
hated it. Here, the city sieved the poor.
Familiar faces surrounded him, people who
were here time after time and fine after fine.
No one big. Nothing important. Just tiny
people who fell through the cracks in the
system. He hated it.

His eyes focused more sharply. He looked
around. He saw the ageless and interchange-
able faces. But something was wrong. He
rubbed his eyes and looked again. The eyes,
there was something in the eyes. He looked
more closely and saw. The eyes flickered. Inside the eyes of the people flickered stars. The
eyes changed color. They weren't eyes at all.

"I'm daydreaming," he thought. He looked
again. "No."

He'd testified here to many a drunk as a rookie cop. He'd pushed for convictions he didn't believe in, because it was needed for the next step. Finally, he'd said goodbye—and left to pursue Meriwether. He wasn't sure, now, the dues he had paid had been worth it.

"Woolgathering, sport?"

Doyle had been expecting the voice. "Meriwether," he said. He didn't turn. "You slime. I wondered when you'd show."

"Some warmth you show for your old squad-car buddy. I thought you'd like this. It reminds me of home. Good job, don't you think?"

"Shove it. Go away."

"I can't."

Doyle turned now, interested. "Are you arrested, too? They get you for perjury?"

"Hardly—although it may work out that way. They want me to be your lawyer."

"My what?"

"Lawyer. L-a-w-y-e-r. You were one once, remember?"

"You're judge and jury, too, I suppose?"

Meriwether grinned broadly. He looked to Doyle as if he were embarrassed he hadn't thought of that. "No, not quite. A man named Interharg will be the judge. You haven't met him. He's a real killer. The planet he evolved from, they ate their weakest children. Swell guy."

Doyle felt sweat gathering in his palms. He wanted to rebel, but thought it wouldn't be wise. He'd better play along—for now. He needed to know what the aliens had planned.

"Orion will prosecute," Meriwether said. "He's the man you met inside your head. The man who engineered us. He and Interharg are the top men, here—if they have top men. They are among the most active, anyway."

Doyle looked from his bench toward a man with razor-cut hair and cleanly chiseled features. Blue eyes wore the blue suit. "Is that him?"

"Yeah. Like the body? I tailored it myself. Thought it would impress you."

"They did all this just for me?"

"Of course. You're a big deal. I convinced them of that."

"I'll bet you did," Doyle said. "Is it out of line for me to know what I'm charged with?"

"Some goodies, Charley: attempting to end permanently the thought processes of an intelligent being—"

"You, I suppose. They'll never prove the intelligent part."

Meriwether chuckled. "Maybe not, but there's more. There's obstruction of racial progress, vandalism of cosmic property, reckless disregard of the good, bad form and general obnoxiousness. Enough, I think, to brand you a habitual criminal—if we were on Earth."

"If we were on Earth, I'd be rolling in the aisles over those charges. You didn't have anything to do with them, did you?"

"Of course. I always did think general obnoxiousness should be a crime."

"But not murder?"

"Now we get to the nut of it, Charley boy.
The purpose. Not theirs: mine. I want you to
comprehend once—just once—that you can be
wrong." Meriwether paused. "And besides
that, it's going to be fun."

"Fun? You've gone beserk. You're—"

"You're yelling."

"I haven't begun to yell. Let them hear."

"There's an interview room just outside.
We've got time, I think. We need to talk."

Doyle started to say, "No." It was what he
wanted to say; it would have been easy to say.
He was stuck here, now, and Meriwether was
critical to his becoming unstuck. The least he
could do was hear him out. Meriwether signaled the bailiff, and that brought a guard.

As he walked, Doyle thought, *I just wish I
still had a gun. This time I'd be sure. This time
I'd be right.*

The guard stayed outside. The two of them
took seats across from each other. Between
them was a scarred, rickety table of oak.
Initials had been carved over initials into it.
The room smelled of tobacco smoke and
sweat.

Doyle felt astonished when Meriwether
grinned.

"This makes one hell of a lot of sense,
Charley. You and me. Why'd they pick us? Me,
I understand. You—I would have understood

once. Not now."

Doyle closed his mouth. *Absurd. He sounds hacked that they chose me! Of all the megalomanical ideas.* He forcibly calmed himself, waiting for Meriwether's grin to fade. He waited. Meriwether's teeth disappeared behind his lips. He waited some more, and then said, "I'm curious why you think they chose you."

The grin started to come back, but stopped. "At least I haven't sold out. At least I'm no gummy shill."

"A child-molesting murderer is better?"

"No. But that doesn't change your selling out and your leaving the streets," Meriwether said. He shook his head slowly. "Until I heard you say it, I didn't believe. You've hinted around, and hemmed around, but never said it. It's crap. I thought you would've had it straightened out by now. You, the hotshot prosecutor! Trying to lay a crime off on me that's years old, and a crime I didn't commit."

"You're lying."

"Listen to me. Listen once. If you'd ever gotten off your high-horse before now, you'd have seen it—and we wouldn't be here. Remember that. Now: I did not kill your little girl. I was not involved with her in any way. It was one of my men—Tiny, you know Tiny?— he did it. Shouldn't have happened, and I take responsibility. For all of them. But Tiny was punished. I punished him."

"I don't believe you."

"Gentry knew. And he knew how I fixed Tiny."

"You're lying."

"Why should I lie? He would have told you, if you'd ever asked. He didn't know why you wanted me so bad. He thought it was some code-of-honor about me leaving the force and turning to crime. That made sense, anyway."

"You can't bluff me, Meriwether. I worked the street. I know. I heard."

"You know and you heard? If you know so much, how come you never came up with one witness in my skin business, or on my gas-running and gun-running? You couldn't get those, and they'd squeal about murder and rape? Didn't you ever ask yourself that question?"

Silence. Doyle rolled it over in his mind. But he had overheard conversations; he remembered tips that had come in by telephone. And Tiny.

Tiny had talked.

"My God. Tiny was the big one, and he said you did it. The rest I sort of put together."

"I'd like to fix it so he couldn't talk, knowing that—just like I fixed it so he'd never rape."

Meriwether watched Doyle closely. "So there. It finally sinks in? You admit you were wrong?"

Doyle's face reddened. "No. If not for that, then what you tried to do to Janet."

"I did nothing to Janet. Nothing. She was an

illusion, the only thing I could think of to bring you face-to-face with me. It didn't work out—but she wasn't hurt. Not even the illusion was hurt."

"And the pictures? The pictures of the little girls?"

Meriwether swallowed. He rubbed at his temples with his fingertips. He looked around the room before looking back at Doyle. "Listen, you know how I grew up?"

"Some. We used to talk."

"There wasn't a virgin in my house after age twelve, and I had six sisters. Uncles, drunk friends of my old man: Seeing all that messed my head about women. Women older than that are ... dirty. Something. And the little girls are innocent. It's their innocence, the un-sexiness of them, that turns me on. And it's not sex, not at all. It's something I love that I've never had. And it's harmless. Least, it never harmed anyone but me. I swear that's the truth. I swear it."

"I'd like to believe you, Meriwether. I really would. I've seen you lie and con your way through so much already—I can't believe this isn't another fast one. It's very convenient, there being no way I can check."

"Charley, you were my friend once. Believe me for that."

Doyle stared at his old friend. His lips were dry. He was feeling things tear inside himself. Even to admit he was wrong would be horrible.

Just then, Eskelion materialized. He fitted not very well into the cramped room.

"You should believe him, my friend," the alien said. "I have read his thoughts and they are true. They are facts and meaning together. He is not my friend, however. You are my friend, and for that I tell you. I— "

Meriwether rose, trembling. "You've been reading my thoughts? You scum-eating stink-ing— "

"Cool it," Doyle said. "You know they can."

Tears appeared in Meriwether's eyes. "It's not right. I swear it's not. I told you, Charley. I never wanted anyone else to know. Never."

Doyle reached across and touched the man. "Thanks. I accept that. I think that's real."

He said it before he knew it. Inside him, the storm still whirled. He remembered the years and they were wasted. Quitting the force, the sentences in law school and the city courts: all for nothing. He remembered the gritty feeling of the pavement beneath his uniformed knees, as he'd sworn above the girl Charlotte's body he would see her revenged. And he'd carried that promise with him like a burning coal, and it had burned him all those years, and it was for nothing.

Until a few moments before, his hate for Meriwether had been the only solid thing left him. The hate had been as solid as his love for Janet. Could he let that go?

He couldn't. He couldn't.

"Look at me, man. Look at me the way you used to."

Doyle looked. "I look at you and I see blood. I look at you and I see the green you've gotten be selling your brother's horse. I look at you and I see one crime left: a man who had brains and guts, and who sold himself out."

"No, Charley. It's still not right. Think: Why did the Nothing Makers choose us? Us. Both of us. You have some brains, and you care, and you were trying to cleanse a rotten system. I—I have some brains. I care. And I was fighting the system that already was killing my brothers. Can't you see?"

And Doyle thought: *Yes. Yes and no. I see—but I can't have been so wrong. There is no way I could have been that twisted all this time. And I've lost it all.*

"Eskelion, friend," he said. "If you can read me, you know what's happening. What giving this up means. A man is the sum of what he thinks, and what he believes, and what he does. And I've lost all those . . ."

"You are wrong to think your beliefs have changed. You have not abandoned the beliefs, but merely outgrown the symbols you used for them. You hate that for which it seemed Answar Meriwether stood, not the man himself. You will grow to see, I assure you."

"I don't believe it."

"Trust me," Eskelion said.

"I trust you."

"Good. Mr. Meriwether?"

"I've always trusted the pompous, self-

righteous and otherwise obnoxious SOB—but
I've known he meant well. If he's stopped
shooting at me, I'm happy."

Doyle turned to examine Meriwether once
more. He looked as if he expected the man to
disappear and become something new—but it
didn't happen. "So. Partners. Until there's
proof otherwise."

"There won't be proof."

"Let's go back then. I want to see how you
defend me on the charge of 'obnoxious.'"

The trial began and seemed as if it would
never stop.

"The defendant has ignored all grounds of
sense," Orion was saying at this particular
point in eternity. "This is the real charge, the
case we intend to make. Granted the opportunity for growth—of learning to develop his
powers of mind for honor, duty and wisdom—he spent most of his energy scheming
to return to his shallow world."

Doyle listened without interest to the
charges. His life seemed to have gone out of
him; he didn't care. He wondered if this was
the way all prisoners felt—as if nothing that
went on at their trial was of concern to them.

He'd seen boredom on the faces of defendants before, but he'd never understood it. Now, understanding came naturally.

*What do they charge me with?* he thought. *Homesickness. I was homesick. This is the crime of which they convene an interstellar court? What next? Charges of horniness, of angst? I'm guilty, all right. Guilty of not taking them seriously.*

Shocked, Doyle realized that this, too, was something people in court must often feel.

"He has ignored the possibilities for inner exploration that Paradise provides. Instead, he wallowed in visions of flesh. He could not break himself of his obsession with physicality—a perversion that warped and critically wounded the Paradise he had been given . . ."

"By God," Doyle said. "They *are* charging me with horniness."

"You were," Meriwether said.

"What's this about wounding Paradise? I didn't do that."

Meriwether whispered his answer. "They don't know. They're checking. I told them Earth courts were always half cocked, so they didn't wait for the answer."

"You what? You're my attorney, remember."

"Sorry. I guess I got carried away."

"Well, object, dammit. Tell 'em they can't do that."

"I don't think it'll do any good," Meriwether

said. "But I'll try, for auld lang syne." He stood. "Objection. These charges are irrelevant, not germane and out in left field."

"Objection overruled," Interharg's voice boomed.

"I told you," Meriwether said as he sat. "I may have primed 'em too well. Just like back home: Everything's stacked for the prosecution."

"Screw that. Did you, with your street savvy, get them to disclose their evidence?"

"No. What's that?"

"If you were a real lawyer, I'd have you disbarred."

Orion droned on. "What we are seeing is distilled discontent, the inability of this creature to accept or understand the Good. He is unable to use his surroundings for his own growth and happiness . . ."

"I don't believe this," Doyle said. "This is insane. I've got to get out of here."

"We will," Meriwether said. He sounded confident. "I've got a real show-stopper of a summary planned."

"Jesus. Don't you understand? This isn't real. This is an illusion—and our friends may be dying while this farce goes down. We've got to get back, see if we can help. We broke out. Maybe we can show others how."

"Quiet in the courtroom," Interharg said.

"You be quiet."

"If the defendant makes another outburst, he will be declared in contempt."

"I am in contempt. I'm full of contempt. I— "

Lightning struck Doyle's head. There was a blinding flash and then something seemed to explode between his eyes. When his vision cleared—smoke still curled from his eyebrows—he saw Interharg glaring from his bench. The judge's face was alabaster and craggy with corruption. This, Doyle knew, was Meriwether's vision of a judge. *Good God. He's stacked the decks against me and he didn't even mean to. He's seriously trying to defend me. Meantime, he's poisoned the aliens with his warped idea of justice. I'm going to fry.*

"You stupid son of a bitch," he said. "If you had brains, that plus the bone would break your neck."

"What's eating you?"

"You've framed me. You didn't—"

"No. You've got it wrong. I'm on your side —but this is the only way out. I've . . ."

And the voice of Orion droned on about the crimes of Doyle.

Eskelion emerged from Thinking. He had been feasting on rich images supplied by

Doyle, images of healthy trees and blue skies and clear rains. It was in a place called Tennessee. It was a place he could put down roots.

He could again be the soul of the forest.

After his Thinking, he felt for the first time in many centuries that there was some goodness that the Nothing Makers had not accounted for. He felt there was goodness missing here—goodness missing, where goodness should be all.

"What I need," he told himself, "is more feeling and less Thinking. Thinking gives me headaches."

Illusions weren't satisfactory after all. He had known this, but thought it was a sickness in him. The Earthman had reassured him—had made him give weight to his own feelings for the first time.

As he returned to his chosen shape, Eskelion felt a moment's concern for the Earthman. *But it's all right. Orion said it's all right. He's just being tested, is all.* He trusted Orion; he knew he meant well. *But meaning well isn't enough. Doyle doesn't make me small-feeling. He doesn't make me stupid-feeling.*

"Orion doesn't have a choice," Eskelion said. "I understand why he is that way. He was born a lizard."

"Not a lizard, little one. The image is not right."

"Orion? Blinded lights be I," Eskelion said. He dimmed profusely.

"Do not apologize. Share feelings with me," Orion projected.

Eskelion felt a series of brooding images. Orion was concerned that Eskelion had become contaminated by the Earthman, and that the contagion would spread. "But there is more, there you are right," Orion said. He showed images of the hurt he had felt—the hurt he now missed.

What Orion could not bring himself to say was that he himself was infected. That the point of focus, the place of Council, was poisoned. The fragile, pure and abstract Rules of Reason could only hold in the absence of physical knowledge. It was, after all, an almost ghostly existence. Certainly, that was how Doyle and Meriwether would see it.

And perhaps they were right.

*Dying colors if they are. Dying . . . and reborning.*

But he did not tell Eskelion. Eskelion, stupid Eskelion, seemed instinctively to know some things Orion was still trying to work out for himself.

For Eskelion's benefit, he painted a light picture of the horrors the humans themselves had experienced.

"This is the not good you feel," he said.

"Sir. I thought you were in 'trial,' sir."

Orion projected. The trial was in recess, a tradition that must be honored. It seemed to be going well. Doyle and Meriwether, he was given to understand, were using the recess for

traditional purposes: They were berating
each other. "They would kill each other, I am
sure, were it not for our power . . . and they
have power. They are interesting animals.
They are not even so wise as you, a plant's
soul," Orion said.

"But he understands my passion, in ways
that here are not honored," Eskelion said.

"I understand," Orion said, in shades of
sympathetic mauve. "I must Think of what
you feel. Of what we both feel."

And he was gone.

For a moment, Eskelion was flattered that
Orion had seemed to understand. It was star-
tling, however, and in its way was frightening.
Orion was the rock of the Nothing Makers; he
was a keystone of Council. He had been
among those without doubt. That he doubted,
Eskelion feared, meant the Earthmen might
indeed be dangerous.

"There is nothing to fear," Eskelion
thought. "We are sworn-and-true friends."

He considered. He faded himself out.
Urgently he began to search for Doyle's aura.

Before the sham of the trial could continue,
Orion realized he must make a decision. Despite the words of Meriwether, the trial was

not having its intended effect. Doyle was un-
cowed; he was unafraid; he was still a danger.

*Danger*. Orion savored the spectrum of his
emotions, enjoying the rare combination of
lights that word permitted. *Danger*. How long
had it been since he'd felt that thrill? Certainly, it had been since before he joyfully
escaped his body and became Orion. *Danger*.
It had nothing to do with cool, precise reason-
ing. No. Reason had first carried Orion to
Earth, where Good was arranged to counter-
act a Bad. But that had not worked. That idea
was shot. Now all Good was contained in one
word: *Danger*.

*Neither Doyle nor Meriwether are playing
the game*, Orion thought. *They don't make
sense. They do not recognize the Good against
the Not Good. But what else is there? I must
know*.

Orion had looked deeply into Meriwether.
He had sifted his thoughts and copied
thoughts from the man, thoughts Meriwether
must have never expected anyone to know. *He
seems so brash, yet inside he is broken glass*.
Orion resurrected a crucial scene from Meriwether's mind. He would experience it now.
He would go through it completely. He would
suffer what he must suffer, in order to understand.

The image came alive for him.

Sight. (A young girl, schoolbooks under
arm, her plaid dress like a flag above white
knees.) Sound. (She is singing to herself. She

sings off key and the words are nonsense, but the music seems perfect.) Touch. (A spring wind licks at his arm; the same sun that beats warmly on his face beats gently down for her.) Taste. (Peppermint on the tongue: How cooly it rolls! Perhaps she would like a taste?)

Desire. (I will never have such a child, Meriwether thought and now Orion thinks. I could never be the parent to such innocence. Being around me would spoil the innocence. I will be childless. I will forever be a father without a child.)

Action. (Meriwether calls his friend and orders another portrait for his office. He describes the girl. "I want her looking pure and chaste," he tells his friend. "I want to be able to see in her face two things I've never known.")

Orion wondered: How can he do this to himself? How can they hurt so strongly? How can they bear to remember?

*And why*, he thought, *do I find myself being pulled into their feelings like some ill-fated comet falling into a sun of disappointment and desire?*

He could not comprehend Meriwether. He did even less well understanding this new one. In ways, it seemed Doyle must be more twisted than the other.

Orion recalled a scene he had stolen from Doyle's mind. It was a misty, faded scene—one of the few he'd been able to copy while Doyle was trapped in the blue bolts of Council's collective will. He experienced this scene fully, too.

Sight. (A barrel-full of downy yellow chicks. The barrel is in the back of a pickup truck roaring down a highway. The day is cold and gray.) Sound. (A hundred thousand peepings come from the barrel, driven like ten-penny nails into the ear.) Touch. (The chicks are light as nothing in the palm, and warm as biscuits.) Smell. (The brood smell, with wet feathers and sawdust added.) Emotion. (Pity. The chicks are all males and so are useless. They are divided by sex and the males go in this barrel. The barrel goes in the truck. The truck goes to the dog-food plant.) Words. "Pretty pretty birds. Nothing I can do. Someday, little chicks. Someday.") Tears.

Orion is torn with the feelings of the boy. It seems to him the tears are important. The thought angers him. *Foolish!* he thinks. *Pity is wasted on the non-sentient. Only the sentient trapped in pain deserve pity, and pity should be spared them—if salvation can be found. The sentient are given the Egg, and then they are free. Then they are beyond pity.*

*Paradise nourishes them and their dreams. When they mature—if they mature—they may move among the stars and drink of them. That is our gift. It is better than pity.*

"We have given them that," he thinks.

He thought: We have taken nothing from them.

*Nothing but the tears and the sadness.*

Orion steadied himself. He focused himself on a single frequency inside the visible light spectrum. He was bright blue, a perfect blue. A perfect being. He began to feel calmer as his reason returned. "I have been unworthy of myself," he chastised. "I am not a young fool like Eskelion.

"I am not.

"But" —he couldn't help himself— "I may very well be an old fool."

When Doyle and Meriwether returned to the courtroom, there was a disturbing energy in the air. The people, including judge and jury, seemed dead. Their eyes were blank. Only Orion's eyes seemed alive. He studied Doyle with an intensity that made the Earthman dizzy with discomfort.

Eskelion had entered with them. He had taken the body of an elderly, balding black man.

Doyle leaned toward him. "What do you feel? Can you tell what's going on?"

"Orion has summoned Council. He wishes to forfeit his position as prosecutor."

"I know that," Doyle said. "But why the change?"

"Meaning what?"

"His wish will be granted. He is Orion."

Eskelion shrugged. Doyle thought the gesture seemed natural, which surprised him. "He has veiled his reasons," Eskelion said. "He only says he must Think."

It was eerie, Doyle thought. He felt chill as the flickering reappeared in the eyes. The bodies were still frozen. The flickerings grew more intense, with an occasional set of eyes spewing sparks as if from a welder's torch.

Without warning, the body Orion had inhabited slumped and fell forward on the slick wood table. It made a grisly thump. There was the sound of smashed flesh.

And then the body raised up. Flattened features rearranged themselves and the appearance of the face was normal again.

"Antis has taken over," Eskelion reported. "This is not pleasing to Interharg. Antis was one of those who petitioned against the shutting down of your sun. The—"

"Quiet," Meriwether said.

They turned and watched as the prosecutor stood. "If it please the court, we would consider a lessening of the charges in exchange for a guilty plea."

Under his breath, Meriwether said, "Bingo."

"This is highly irregular," the judge said.

"These are highly irregular circumstances, your honor," Antis said. "If we could perhaps meet with defendant's counsel in your chambers?"

Interharg surveyed the courtroom with a sour face. "Very well," he said. "Court recessed for ten minutes."

Meriwether looked at Doyle. "You want me to ask for you to come along?"

"I doubt they'll agree. This is your court, remember. Just get back and talk to me before you agree to anything."

"Right," Meriwether said.

Doyle watched the trio leaving the courtroom. He'd been having a growing feeling that he was trapped, and now he felt the bars were about to snap into place. *Meriwether: I may have trusted him too much. But did I have a choice?* He still felt the odd passiveness he'd felt since the "trial" began. These conferences and recesses: They were all things he'd once considered an essential part of the legal process. Now he doubted. It seemed like sleight of hand. He began to feel a grudging empathy with Meriwether—not much, but some.

The first thing he saw on Meriwether's return was a big chiseled smile. He wasn't reassured.

"Well, brother—I think we've done it," Meriwether said.

"Done what?"

"Found our way out of this box, what else?"

"And?"

"You plead guilty to a 'willful violation of Thought,' and it's over. And then we go back to Paradise."

Doyle considered. Paradise was better than this—but he still needed Earth. But if he could see Esmerelda again, maybe that would do. Maybe that would be all right.

"I don't know," he said.

"What's to know? You cop a plea, and they build us a Paradise."

"Build? What's wrong with the old one?"

"They're not sure it still exists. If it does, we'd contaminate it."

"You can't be serious. You are absolutely out of your mind. First, we have to know what's happened to Paradise. Second, we have to know what's happening to Earth. We have to know: Only then can we make a decision. But I can tell you this: I'll choose Hell over a Paradise with you."

"What's this crap? I'm helping you."

"From my point of view, it doesn't look like help. And—frankly—I'm still trying to figure out why you'd want to help someone who tried to kill you."

"I blew up your car: same difference."

"You knew I wouldn't be in it."

"Right," Meriwether said. "And you knew you couldn't kill me."

"To hell I didn't. I wanted to see you dead."

"C'mon, Charley. I'm your old squad-car buddy. You don't expect me—"

"I don't expect anything from you," Doyle said. He added icily, "Partner."

Meriwether studied him. "I still don't believe it. Anyhow, I told the judge it was up to you."

"Thanks."

"I, too, vote Earth," Eskelion said.

"You?" asked Meriwether.

"Him," Doyle said. "And if he can see it, maybe there's hope you'll see it. Maybe there's hope the judge will."

"I need a forest," Eskelion said. "I am only whole as the soul of a forest."

Meriwether looked from alien to Earthman and then back. He looked as if he were trying to figure which of the two was more strange. "That cooks it," he said slowly. "I quit. I'm stuck here with the last of the McCoys and his feud, and a football who wants to be a Boy Scout. I'm getting out. I'm—"

There came a hammering from the bench.

"All rise," and the judge entered.

Under his breath, Doyle whispered to Meriwether. "A new Paradise would just be a pretty prison. Think about that."

"If the defendant will approach the bench."

Doyle stood. He swayed slightly. One shaky step at a time, he made his way to the bench. His mind whirled, but nothing appeared in his mind that would help. He looked into the face of Interharg, high above him, and he saw dark galaxies whirling in those eyes.

"Are you ready to make your plea?" The voice rasped.

"Not guilty, your honor."

Interharg stared violently down and Doyle felt anger in the stare. Bright specks and flakes in the eyes seemed to grow dangerously bright.

"Fool," the judge said. "You are a scab on the face of sentient being. You mock duty and honor and wisdom. I am filled with loathing at you and your farcical idea that justice could come from this abscess of a system."

He paused. "It is not allowed, but there are few punishments even in the bloody and malicious history of your race that I would not now deem suitable for you."

"Your honor," Doyle said. He began shaking. He felt the merciless and almost dispassionate way Interharg expressed himself. This was not anger the judge expressed: It was simply and truly his verdict. And that was frightening.

"Your honor," Doyle said, beginning again. "These things you say of me are not crimes. The charges brought against me are not crimes. But I—I have been kidnapped, a crime —and threatened, a crime—and held against my will, a crime. I have been separated from my wife, my work and my world. I ask that you consider that."

"I have. Do you wish to change your plea?"

"I cannot make a plea without knowing the possible punishment," Doyle said.

Interharg snorted. "What has punishment to do with your guilt or innocence? You are guilty, or you are not. I lose patience with your unreason."

Doyle thought: *How simple, how straight, how true. And maybe I am guilty, and maybe I should be punished. But what does it mean?*

He thought of a Paradise containing only him
and Meriwether—and he thought he understood Hell. *Eternity like that? Nothing we
have conceived could be so cruel . . . and yet
they could put me on a cross and make it last
forever. They could burn me at the stake and it
would last forever.*

"I am guilty of breaking no law. I am guilty
only of being a human being."

"That is guilty enough," Interharg said.

The bleeding in Paradise continued. The
images they were able to conjure became
weaker and weaker. There were friends that
Max and Esmerelda could no longer find.
Their auras had gone elsewhere, or they had
ceased to be.

No longer could either of them sustain an illusion by themselves. Even together, their
illusions lacked all the color and vividness of
previous time.

They now shared a small gray-walled room.
In it were two easy chairs. Baroque music
filled the space. Now and then, a frightening
eddy of blackness whirled through a wall. It
was becoming harder and harder to make the
wall hold.

"He was your lover," Max chided. It had become a recurrent obsession of his. He spoke in the tones of the eternally unrequited lover. He was Esmerelda's friend, and that pleased him—but that that was all he would ever be was a living hurt.

"He was not my lover," she said.

"Not because you didn't try."

She shrugged slightly. There were lines on her face—lines she had deliberately added, lines that began to offset the soft beauty of her face. "I could have had him," she said angrily. "I could have any man."

"Man? Yes," Max said. "He was no man. He was a child, too young to understand love. What a man he was, your lover: the man who killed Paradise. He was crazy."

"Crazy?" Esmerelda said. Her voice was fierce. "Crazy? Because he would not let himself become addicted to pipedreams? If courage is crazy, yes—but only if that."

"Courage is not to fear love," he said.

"Courage is not to fear pain."

Max bounded from his chair and began to pace. "You cannot tell me about courage, woman. You have not slept in the mud, beneath bushes, knowing that to give in to the aching heaviness of your eyes meant death. You—"

"I don't want to hear it, Max."

"Of course not. You want only to hear his praises."

"No," she said firmly. She fixed her eyes on

him and felt great love and great pity. "I want to get out. I want to know what Charley did—he knew the way. I want to know what he would do."

"Simple," Max said. "He would tear something down. He would break something—or kill someone."

"And he would get out."

"Maybe. We have no proof that he did, only his sign: a world dying around us."

"We should try to follow," she said.

"We?" Max laughed bitterly. "*We* should try to find him? I don't want to find him. I'm glad he's gone."

"Are you glad we're dying?"

Max looked at her. He did not answer for a while. The two kept company with their own thoughts. They were both sad and alone, and they shared that. When Max finally answered, Esmerelda had almost forgotten what she'd asked.

"Yes," he said. "I think I'm glad."

Eskelion had released his human shape, but he still floated pink and nearby. Doyle and Meriwether sat in a cramped concrete-block room. He wondered at how strongly they were attached to physical shapes, to their physical selves. Interharg, raging, had ordered another recess. For these two, it meant only blackness.

The alien felt their awful disharmony with each other as well as their futile groping toward an answer. He pitied them their futility: They could not think clearly enough to accept that they had no choice in the coming answer. Even Council was baffled by the problem: What could mortals do?

Eskelion admitted to himself that theirs was a different life-form than his had been. They did not know the fierce quietness of the forest after dusk, before the night-things began their hymns. That, he would return to.

What they seemed to want was a return to pain. Their pain was everything—even their joys were wrapped like thick-skinned nuts in shells of hurt.

It seemed to him they thought progress could only be made through pain: *If hurt means progress, they surely will go far*, he thought.

"Friends," he said. "Be still."

"Your blimp is back."

"Esk," Doyle said. His shoulders were bent; he was stooped. The bickering with Meriwether had left him looking dark and drawn. His lips moved once, twice, before he actually spoke. "Do you have any idea what they're going to do?"

"They can 'do' nothing. They can only let you do to yourself what you are already doing. It is like—"

"Riddles," said Meriwether. "That's all I get. Honky politics make more sense than this. He's telling you you're going to be punished by the Golden Rule."

" 'Them that has the gold makes the rules'?" Doyle asked. "If only this were conventional power, then I would know something. But they keep shifting rules."

"Friends," Eskelion said. "Maybe I can help."

"He's your Friend. I'm your Not Enemy, remember?" Meriwether said. "Even blimps are racists."

"Get off it," Doyle said. "You and your—"

"Me? You've got right to talk. You and your refusal to plead not guilty to some folderol, when—"

"It's the implications. I've got to know what it means."

"It doesn't *mean* anything. It's a charade, a game," Meriwether said. His forehead was creased in anger. His hands opened and closed like claws.

"I wish it was, but I don't know."

"Do you honestly expect to know? Christ."

"Can you expect me to now want to know?"

"Know what?" Meriwether shouted. "Know slime-sucking what? We know they're bigger than we are, and they've offered us an out, and you won't take it. I know that. What in the name of Martin Luther King do you want to know?"

"I don't know," Doyle said.

"He doesn't know," Meriwether said. He spat the words. He turned toward Eskelion. "He doesn't know and you don't know. I'm just a nigger from South Memphis, but I think I know—at least I know more than this fireball DA here—at least as much as this cosmic Easter egg. But nobody listens."

But someone was. Interharg floated silently, invisibly, and he took it all in.

Orion reached position outside the Egg and he penetrated the shell. The shift from the hard emptiness of space to the nourishing interior was pleasant. It was, he knew, a return to the womb. All his kind began in one of these.

But not one like this. He could feel the snarled patterns of overlapped minds around him. Some mind-patterns had lost their focus and would eventually seep into nothingness. Other minds had fused and two personalities now groped together, learning to be one. And Doyle had done this.

Orion hummed orange as he examined the break that marked Doyle's exit. He had never before seen anything like this. He felt a fluttering of fear and danger. *This isn't supposed to happen. Where did he get the power to do this?*

It had something to do with lust, with passion: Orion knew that, but it did not help him understand.

In a way, it no longer mattered.

Orion focused himself as best he could. He let his aura out like a net. His mind touched on thousands of identities and let them pass. He moved faster, faster. Many of the souls were broken: many would never heal. The stench of miscarried emotion was overwhelming.

Finally, his net began to close. These were the two: This was the Max; this was the Esmerelda. Orion gently began to insinuate himself into their pitifully weak illusion. Their world was small, simple, bare.

The music interested him. It moved by mathematical progression—quite complex, quite intelligent. He sieved for a name and found it: Bach.

He must remember that name.

He could not reveal himself yet. He needed to know more of these two before he acted: Already he had learned how misleading Doyle's imaginings could be. He spread himself thin and listened for their feelings. He let their energies play though him. He detected a pattern that seemed vaguely familiar. *How can that be?* he wondered. Then he realized. *Doyle. Doyle has a pattern like this buried in him.*

The feeling was the same as Orion had felt from Doyle, and now he felt it again: It was a give-and-take, a battle, a struggle, between opposing kinds of energy. It was the Doyle-energy/Janet-energy, only it was here, too. It was the male and female energies.

"We could make love," the woman was saying. "I would like to make love."

"No you don't," the man said. "You want to make love to Doyle, but you can't do it alone. Using me, you could imagine him. You would."

"I wouldn't. You would know," Esmerelda said.

Max went on, ignoring her. "Making love is one thing your Doyle wouldn't do. Remember? Not even to get himself out of this fix—which is something I doubt our love-making would do."

"I would like to make love," she said.

Orion analyzed the tone. He was intrigued. Her voice and tone carried almost as much nuance as his colors. He was stunned by the things she seemed to say, all without words. It was a knack Doyle needed but had never developed.

Among other things, Orion heard these: Yes, she would like to make love. Yes, she would like to make love to Max. Yes, she would also—perhaps more—like to make love to Doyle. But those things were irrelevant, she was saying:

She just wanted to make love.

And Orion felt this from her:

Making love was healing. Making love was balm.

Orion considered. This was unlike the "making love" messages he had from Doyle. For Doyle, love was proof. It proved who he was; each time proved he could be loved.

And, now, Orion understood Doyle.

His mind shut cleanly. He now Knew.

All proof of love had been eradicated from Doyle. Only anger and bitterness provided him directions now. They were the source of his uncontrollable strength.

And it could be channeled. One way.

Orion decided it was time to make himself known.

First, he gently swept the minds of Max and Esmerelda. He needed a strong, credible image they would accept; probably any such image would do, so long as both accepted it —and so long as the image was neither Doyle nor Meriwether. Orion probed, searched and gambled.

He had only one shot to hit the target.

He chose his form and materialized in the gray room.

"My God—I mean, Max!"

"Sweet Jesus," Max said. "I mean, Holy Father?"

Orion turned gently, letting his robes flow airily about. Apparently, he had chosen well. He at least had their undivided attention.

"Is it really . . .?"

"It can't be . . . can it?"

"I don't see why not, Es. Maybe we were more right than we knew."

"Children," Orion said. It seemed in character. "Children."

"Do you see them?" Esmerelda said.

"What?"

"The nail holes. They're bleeding."

"It can't be, Es. It can't be. He doesn't exist."

Orion felt more awe than was warranted; he also felt fear from these two. It was time to downgrade the illusion. "I am not Him," he said. "But I am of Him."

The woman was making the sign of the cross; to Orion, it did not feel like something she would normally do. It was an overreaction. He had chosen an historical figure, a figure both this man and this woman associated with absolute truthfulness—and yet, with the Man before them, both expressed doubts. *May I never understand the human kind*, Orion thought, *for if I do, I am surely doomed*. He spoke to them:

He gave them his name, Orion. He held up his hands and said, "These hands have created this Paradise." He told them he had hoped they would learn quality and thought, and that he had failed. He said, because he had failed, this Paradise was doomed—as might be other worlds.

"There is a friend of yours, a man named Doyle," he said. "He is without purpose, but powerful and dangerous. Until he learns control—indeed, until control matters to him—he is a fire that threatens to burn all."

The man named Max muttered. "Hell," he said. "Doyle has created Hell of Paradise."

Orion stopped. For the first time, he saw the transcendental meaning of those words. To Doyle, they were mere symbols, to be used sarcastically or not at all. It wasn't the same with these two. To these two, Paradise might be real.

The humor of the idea startled Orion, and yet he did not see their belief as far-fetched.

"He has not created Hell," Orion said. "He has not yet entered the Paradise of which you think. He needs too much. I think," he said to Esmerelda, "I think he needs you."

Interharg had heard what he needed to know. He signaled, and his allies began to move. This farce of a trial must be ended. It must be ended now, before Orion returned. *It is this or chaos*, Interharg thought. *I choose rightful order.*

Meriwether was still explaining his ideas to Doyle and Eskelion. For a few moments, the alien had been pulsing suddenly with odd colors. "Friends, I think— "

"See, dammit? Nobody listens."

"Esk, I think you ought to wait," Doyle said.

"I feel danger," Eskelion said. "I feel I must . . . I must." Eskelion ballooned pink and large, and then the spheroid began to halve.

"Now what the deuce?" Meriwether said. "It's not enough he looks like a sideshow, he has to introduce a new, improved version."

"Listen," Doyle said. "Can you feel it?"

"Feel what?"

"Just feel."

Meriwether tried, and he felt it. It was hard to miss. Tightness he felt, as if the air around them were being compressed. He felt the slight terror, like when you're below water and the stuffiness in your lungs says it's time to surface, and you suddenly don't know where the surface is.

"What is it?" he asked.

Doyle shook his head. "I don't know—but I recognize the force behind it: Interharg. The judge. He's— "

A bolt like that which had clobbered Doyle in the courtroom came racing through one of the walls. The walls shattered, and they were surrounded by blackness. The interview room was gone. The bolt circled widely around them. It angled in. It hit Eskelion. The alien was cleaved in two.

"Friends," they caught from him, and that was it.

Twin specks of lightning appeared in the darkness.

"Move," Doyle said. "Run."

"How?"

"How we got here. The same way. This is it: They've made their decision, and now— "

Meriwether screamed as a bolt glanced off him.

Doyle grabbed at Meriwether's flesh. Already, the flesh was beginning to fade. "Answar, dammit, you can't let go. You can't. You have to hold together."

Doyle side-skipped, pulling dead weight. He remembered the giving up of mass, but Meriwether dragged. He tried it anyway. His speed increased.

"But where do we go? Paradise? What's *left* of Paradise?" he asked himself. Surely they would follow them there. Where else? There was only one other place he knew, and that one place was Earth.

*So it's home again, like it or not.* He could feel the pulsing of Meriwether's thoughts. *Thank God for that.* And he remembered seeing half of Eskelion burn—but he had no tears to weep. *I did it*, he thought. *Me.*

*Dear God, please: Let me just this once do something right.*

Max wept. He floated in a gray room, and the music had stopped, and Esmerelda was gone. He could not bear to follow her back to Doyle. He couldn't.

He would not.

Esmerelda was gone, and Max wept.

Max wept in a dwindling place called "Paradise."

Esmerelda and Orion made good traveling companions. They were fast, but there was still time for her to learn—and for him. For the first time since the Earthman had appeared to begin destroying an orderly Universe, Orion felt some hope. This woman was a special being, he thought. She had an understanding that the men lacked. With her, he felt there was a chance that the two men could be made to see reason.

And he told this to Esmerelda.

She laughed. "Male chauvinist pig," she said.

He probed her mind at her request. He understood her meaning and laughed. From something he learned, he said, "Shameless hussy" —expecting her to laugh.

"Please don't," she said. "Please. It's

different than you understand. I think it's different than you can understand. That phrase belongs to Max . . . Max . . . was a good man, and he doesn't deserve what has happened. He doesn't deserve to be left alone."

*Here at last,* Orion thought, *is a human capable of feeling empathy toward the situation of others. Empathy: the thing that has been lacking: the thing that can bring Meriwether and Doyle into harmony with That Which Is.*

"I like you," he said. "I like the other humans, but they baffle and annoy me—and I feel to admit like would be to give them a weapon. You I like, and I can understand."

"Never tell a woman that," she said. "She will never love you if you do, and she will never trust you if you don't. But I can tell you about men: I understand."

Their sharing expanded as they neared the focus point of the Nothing Makers. Orion had nearly forgotten the troubles he had abandoned. They seemed easy to solve now, and he was not worried. He felt a great ease.

The ease crumbled as they materialized. Fear returned. A fire was sweeping through the point of focus.

"Hell does exist. You lied," she said as she took in the towering flames in which they appeared.

"No. Do not worry. I am safe, and my safety protects you. COUNCIL! I, ORION, DEMAND COUNCIL!"

There was a fluttering in the flames and she drew close to him. Suddenly, they seemed to be standing in a marbled clearing—but they were knee-deep in ash.

Lights flickered and flashed around them. The fire was now a circle around them.

"This is the fire of purging," Orion said. "By whom?"

"Interharg," came the answer.

"Against whom?"

"Against the two Earthmen and the one he calls 'renegade.' "

"Against me? I defy it. I defy the Council's ruling."

"Not against you, much-honored Orion. Against the soft one, the muddled thinker: Eskelion."

"This is a ruling of the Not Wise," Orion said. "I judge it so. It reeks even of the Not Good."

Dark shudderings and ominous, eerie light played around the two, the being of light and the woman with red hair. She felt panic around her and consternation, and more.

"You cannot make such judgment."

"I do. Honor binds me," Orion said. "I challenge Interharg; I demand his appearance."

"That cannot be. He is gone. He and Eskin and Rolff and others of the Hard Thinkers. They pursue the Earthmen who escaped the purge."

"The Earthmen survived?"

"Against all odds, yes. It is this that made need of pursuit."

The thoughts twisted and whirled rapidly, until Esmerelda found she could no longer follow them. Occasionally, she felt Orion's thoughts sweeping past her—but before she could read them, they would join in the eddying flow of the other thoughts. Orion burned scarlet, flamed orange, then disappeared and reappeared.

"I make demand," he said. "I demand revenge upon Interharg."

"One being against another? It cannot be done."

"To allow a purge without approval of full Council: This cannot be done," Orion said. "And yet it was."

Meanwhile, Orion noticed Esmerelda's confusion and began to feed his understandings to her. He explained to her of the Fire of Revenge, of purging. Interharg had taken it upon himself to complete the purge.

He would track Doyle and Meriwether and slay them. If he succeeded, he would shut down the Earth's sun. That would be the final Fire of Revenge, according to the judgment. That would be an end to the twisted thinking of the green planet.

Esmerelda read something else from Orion: His honor, his power, and perhaps his life were also on the line. He was fighting an avalanche of wills, an avalanche that now moved of its own power. Interharg had the initiative;

inertia alone could carry him to his goal.

"Hear me: I am Orion. I put as bond my power over suns. I demand that Interharg's power over suns also be removed. Let us do battle in honor. Let the survivor's judgment stand."

Flurries of light followed. Furies of light. Esmerelda felt her senses burning in the commotion; her "skin" tingled; her body ached with the violence of the arguments.

"Bond, then, is accepted. Your demand is granted. Upon honor must rest the judgment. On your head be it, Orion."

"On my head. I bend to honor."

And then there was silence.

The flames circling Orion and Esmerelda began to move closer. Tongues of fire licked high in the unearthly blackness. The flames were high and hot, and Esmerelda felt herself dying in the flames.

"We go," Orion said.

A deer watched from the shadows of the wood. Sunset was almost finished, and darkness descended. The doe had been nibbling at the green shoots of corn in the nearby field. Now she was nervous. Something strange was in the woods. Something there was both un-known and different.

With a sudden start, she vaulted into deep cover. She ran, an awkward fawn at her side.

"See that?" Doyle asked.

"What was it? A cow?"

"A cow? Nixon and Carter, no: a deer."

Meriwether peered at the brush where the two deer had vanished. "A deer? I thought they were extinct."

"Hardly," Doyle said. He could see the faint spectra of Meriwether, the different energies, fading in and out. Around them stretched Doyle's home county in West Tennessee. It was spring. There was a silent coolness to the air. Doyle felt good at the sight, but also per-plexed. He'd left home at fifteen, thinking never to return. Yet here he was. Here, he knew, he would fight his final battle.

He chuckled drily. "We're ghosts of our former selves, Answar."

"Funny man. You're a funny man."

"I think it's time to make the crossover. We must shape real bodies for ourselves."

"It could bind us permanently," Meri-wether said. "I don't like it. Maybe we should just float for a while, just wait and see."

"Maybe—but look at it this way: We are still in Interharg's realm without bodies. If we make the hurdle back across, then he'll have to follow. He'd be on our turf."

"Your turf," Meriwether said. "I don't know if that's what I want."

He looked around, taking in the open spaces. He'd never imagined that this kind of emptiness existed, yet here it was. It was a little bit frightening, he thought. He could see a black line weaving through the distance, finally disappearing in a cut through a hill. Doyle had said this was once his father's land, and that here they would be safe. Meriwether didn't know that he agreed.

"That's the old road. I used to walk a mile to the Bennett grocery, where I caught the bus," Doyle said. Meriwether didn't reply; Doyle could feel the man's indecision, and he felt sorry for him. Meriwether had no home. "Interharg will be here soon," Doyle said.

"You got that right. Maybe we should skip back to Paradise."

"No. He's bound to check there first. And I've got a hunch Orion may be there. I don't trust him any more than Interharg."

"You never could tell your friends from your enemies, Doyle. I'm telling you Orion's okay."

"Can we take the chance?"

The darkness was deep now. Locusts purred ratchet-like in the trees. A smell of silage came rich and pungent from somewhere in the distance.

"I've got to go over," Doyle said. "This is my place. This is where I'll be strongest."

"You're still crazy. You know that?"

"More and more I know that. What I don't know is why it's a bad thing. Out there, among the stars, they think they're sane. Ultimately sane—and you've seen how crazy that is."

Meriwether said, "I never even drank of a star."

"What?"

"Something Orion promised me: I could drink of a star. I would get drunk on the beauty of a star. He said I could do it, but I never got the chance."

"Now's your chance. Go."

"No. I'm going with you."

"You don't have to. I'll be all right—besides, it might be safer for us to split up."

"No. You're the only thing I've got, Charley. You're as close as I've got to someone to care for. Where you go, I go."

"I don't understand," Doyle said.

"*You* don't understand? You think I do?"

They flickered for a moment in the silence. They were will-o'-the-wisps, shadows, not much more than nothing. Doyle extended his transparent hand. "Friends," he said.

"Friends," Meriwether said. "Now let's do it."

The sweep of Paradise had wasted precious time, Interharg thought. He had sensed it

would be worthless—but it had been a chance
he had to take. Doyle must not be missed.
He ordered the team toward Earth, and they
moved.

Interharg loved command. He loved orders,
and he loved having his orders obeyed. It was
an opportunity not often allowed among the
Nothing Makers, where all were supposedly
equal. Theory fell to practice, however, on
missions like this. Interharg and his five
chosen flashed through space, angling along
the slight energy-line that seemed to be Doyle
and Meriwether's trail.

They were better than bloodhounds, he
thought.

Faster, too, and more deadly.

"Here we go," Interharg said. "This is the
sewer they call their home."

The green planet turned comically beneath
them. Earth was like a thousand other planets
Interharg had seen: too much water, too much
air. It took a bad place to produce bad minds,
and this place proved it. If Doyle and Meriwether had come from a good place, a place
where struggling to live required all one's
energy, they would know more of reality than
they did.

And this job would not be necessary.

But it was.

Interharg was absolutely opposed to the
taking of a mind's right to think. Absolutely.
That was the final Not Good, the darkest and
most shameful action. But—and it was a cata-

strophic development—these two had wreck-
ed Focus. They had already poisoned the wise
Orion. Others would fall. It could not be
allowed.

Interharg must abdicate honor, live in
shame.

The Good must be preserved.

"The trail is being covered by the poisons
emitted from the planet," Rolff said.

"It was sure to happen. It is no problem,"
Interharg said. "I know their minds. I know
the few places they will feel comfortable in
going. Downward, now. It is time to go down."

"What if they have returned to the material
world?"

"They haven't the power. They lack the
skill."

"The twisted one has used his power well."

Interharg had not wanted to think of the
possibility. It had been star-lives since he had
assumed shape. The risk was small, but it was
a horrible risk. Only in the flesh did a Being of
Thought risk death. He feared more than
knew that he might be forced into making the
decision. It was too bad Orion wasn't along;
Orion was good at that sort of thing. He never
flinched at becoming physical.

*And he will be along. I wonder what Orion
will do then?*

"We will decide when it is time," Interharg
said.

Clumsily, they began to filter into the city
from which Doyle and Meriwether had been

plucked. Clumsily, they sifted intelligences for a match with the minds of the two. None fitted.

"This is sewer work."

Interharg flickered in agreement. "Barely minds at all. Barely beings at all."

The work continued.



There was a pain in Meriwether's foot. He hadn't wanted a pain in his foot, but there it was. He sure hadn't put the pain there deliberately. It was the single flaw to his body, and he had fixed his other flaw:

Now he was white.

Doyle had advised against the change, but Meriwether insisted. Meriwether had come through white.

Doyle appeared in the world as black.

Meriwether didn't know what to say, so he didn't say anything. He did think: *Smart ass. This time he'll cook in his own juices for sure.*

"Over there—years ago, too many years—I stuck a horse in the mud. It was something. It was an old brown mare named Dolly, and I'd ridden her out here to bring in the cows for milking. It was a godawful gray, rainy afternoon. Seems like it had been raining for weeks. And I was riding the horse along, when the horse comes to a complete stop. Stops flat, right there in the middle of the field, with nothing anywhere to stop her. I reined her left, went maybe fifteen meters, then tried to go forward again. A couple of steps and the same thing happened: She stopped. Went the other way, tried it again. Same thing. It was getting late and I was getting hot. Mad. I popped the old horse with the reins and she leaped forward, and splat! There I was, sitting with my feet on the ground and the horse underneath me. Seems they'd put a natural gas line through there and the dirt hadn't packed yet. You wouldn't believe how I apologized to that horse."

Meriwether listened in slight amazement to Doyle's soliloquy. In all their years in the squad car together, Doyle had never mentioned this story. He'd scarcely mentioned growing up on a farm. Now was different. Now it seemed the land they crossed had grown storybooks instead of cotton.

"How'd you get the horse out?"

"That's funny: I don't remember. Seems like we got a pickup and some sort of harness. Maybe the front legs weren't all the way in; it was just the back legs. I don't know. When that horse died, she just wandered out in a pond and drowned herself."

Even Doyle's accent had changed. He sounded like a 'neck, which was doubly weird because of his black skin. Meriwether hoped the combination wouldn't cause problems.

They were moving off the land, down a dirt road, toward the blacktop. Doyle said there was still some family land about three klicks away—land with a cabin, a pond, a place for them to wait until they could plan what to do next.

"Until Interharg catches us, you mean."

"Or Orion," Doyle had said.

"I'm hoping for Orion. Your track record isn't too good at judging folks."

They walked in silence. Something seemed to have blocked Doyle's monologues.

"I somehow can't think of you as a farmer, man."

"I wasn't much of one—but my father, you should have known him. He was a bred-in-the-bones farmer."

Meriwether chuckled. "The man in the big house, right? I should have guessed."

Doyle laughed. "You'll see."

Leroy Brown, who had spent the last fifteen years of his life eking out enough money from truck farming to pay off the mortgage, sat on the front porch of his three-roomed house and enjoyed the cool evening. Days were getting longer, but Brown somehow felt they would never be long enough again. Time had gnarled the dark hands in front of him, the hands that now twisted white paper around the sweet-smelling tobacco.

"Well, Mama, looks like the corn's going to do all right," he said. His voice was deep, but cracked. His words hung in the spring night like fireflies.

She, too, was on the porch. She sat in her wicker chair, her back to the world, her eyes focused inside the living room on the glow of the black-and-white TV.

"Tomatoes, too," he said.

Brown listened for a long while to the familiar sounds of the country. He listened and was alone with his thoughts. By and by, he heard other sounds. Talking and footsteps, but they were soft.

"Hear that?" he said.

She didn't answer. Inside the house, someone was doing something to someone, and she was watching. Brown never watched. TV was only white folks doing dumb things to each other. No one on TV ever worked. Brown resented that. No one ever had to go out and earn an honest living on TV.

He listened to the footsteps and tried to decide whose they were. Most likely, the Tiller boys were sneaking their way over to old man Phillips' pond. Old man Phillips, he'd been a case. He'd stocked the pond and then wouldn't let nobody fish: Just like an old

white man. Weren't nothing in the pond anymore but stunted cat.

Brown listened harder. It wasn't the Tiller
boys. Too quiet. Maybe it was shiners. He
didn't like shiners, always trying to slip a still
in on your place. That way the sheriff would
get you and not them.

But it didn't sound like shiners, either: too
loud. Shiners slipped around like snakes. You
heard 'em hiss.

Too loud. It might be the sheriff, though,
out for shiners.

His old eyes peered into the darkening
night. There was no moon. The night was
thick and deep. He thought, "Sheriff would've
told me, sheriff would."

"Mama," he said. "Hand me out my gun."

She grunted. In a moment, her chair creak-
ed and he knew she was doing his bidding.
Still his eyes watched, his ears listened, and
his mind worked. It'd been a while since anybody came for chickens, but you could never
tell.

Mama came to him and handed him the gun.
She gave him the two shells he kept above the
book shelf. He loaded the gun carefully: right

barrel was buckshot; left barrel was rock salt.

"Got something coming across the back. You call the sheriff, Mama, you hear anything."

A grunt.

Leroy Brown lifted his aching bones and stood on the hard-packed earth. The gun had a good weight on his arm. He remembered, long before, when the shotgun had been the only thing that kept him safe on his land. White trash around here was mean: You didn't kid with them, no fooling. If you carried a gun, though, you might come out okay.

In the darkness, Brown was all but invisible. His overalls and cotton shirt blended with his dark skin, and he was silent. He walked silently, his ears hearing the footsteps and infrequent words. He tracked the noises like radar. He knew this land. There wasn't a wrong step he could make.

He saw the two faces before they saw him. He stood and waited as they came closer. Closer, closer. Brown shifted the Remington slightly, ready to pull it up. He listened.

"That's Leroy Brown's place over there. You'll meet Mr. Brown. I don't know if he's still alive."

"Spare me country niggers."

"Not this one. Not Mr. Brown. There's not many blacks around here that went by mister, and they all earned it. He earned it. Nobody messed with him."

Brown recognized the voice, but he couldn't

quite place it. It sounded like one of the Doyles, but that didn't make sense. They'd owned the big place down the road and sold out years ago. The young Doyle had left home and then the old Doyle just came apart. It was too bad. The old man had been tough, hard and the Lord's man. The young Doyle had been all right, but the boy had been strange: always about half-scared of his shadow.

"How much farther?"

"Not much. Just down the road, and we'll see what's left of my grandfather's place."

So it was Doyle's voice: the young Doyle. That, too, was strange. Young Doyle and his grandfather, old man Phillips, had never really gotten along.

He started to call out.

"I hope you know what you're doing," the unknown voice said.

"I don't. You know that by now. After all these years, to be here. To come here to be safe—and maybe to die. It bothers me."

The two men walked within feet of where Brown stood. They didn't see him. Brown felt an odd kind of excitement: *There's something wrong, and they're running.* He'd known that feeling, known it well.

It had been years, but he would never forget. He sometimes thought it was the last thing he'd remember before death. It was after Alicia was dead, dead because of what happened on the schoolbus, that Brown had done what he had to do. He'd ride that bus, he

vowed. The children would get to school safe-
ly. No one else would take the job; after years
of drawing and re-drawing school districts, it
was done. The yellow buses had come to take
the black children to the white schools. And
something had happened: Some said it was a
drunk, but Brown knew better. Somebody had
deliberately run that first bus off the road.
Nobody had been hurt much, except little
Alicia. She had apparently hit her head, but
there wasn't a scratch on her to see. She
looked sleeping, but she was dead.

And Brown had taken the job of driving the
bus, and this same shotgun had gone with
him. Nobody tried again—maybe they was
sorry, white trash generally didn't mean
harm, they was just dumb. But they'd drive
by in the night, honking and hollering. The
sheriff would come, but nothing ever happened. And Leroy Brown would lie in the night,
next to Mama, sweating even on those cool
nights in October, listening, feeling fear.

It was the fear of a man who's run as far as
he's going to run, but who will run no farther.
Who has chosen to make his stand, no matter
the consequences. That was the fear Brown
recognized in these two's voices.

They were past him now. Maybe it wouldn't
be good to speak. He'd check on them in the
morning.

Brown turned and picked his way through
the hedgerow back to the path behind the
garden. He felt a chill at the back of his neck

and looked up.

There were those damn lights: the 'FOs, Mama called them. Been a long time since they were around, he thought. Three, four, maybe five years. Not since that big rush of 'em, when you could go out in the night and watch 'em until dawn. It was the summer the troubles had started, and that made Brown wary. Cities had gone crazy, he'd heard. Even Jackson, you hadn't heard too much good from in those days. People had stopped going into town, too. There had been no need. There was nothing there anymore.

Things had recovered since, not entirely, but mostly.

The return of the lights wasn't good.

Brown studied the lights and, just for a moment, wondered if there was a possible connection between young Doyle and that other man. Could that be what they were running from?

"No," he said aloud. "That's too much even for a white boy."

Gun gingerly cradled on his arm, slightly tense now, Brown began the final walk to his house.

Interharg and his team searched, moved on, searched and moved on. All the while they felt the poisons from the minds that must be screened for the identities of Doyle and Meriwether.

"Much more of this: I cannot take."

"You must endure. Honor demands it. To turn back now is to forfeit our duty."

But Interharg, too, had his doubts. If Doyle and Meriwether had remained bodiless, they should have been found by now. If they had taken bodies—either created them or stolen them—the situation would be dangerous. He had hopes they had created bodies: That would drain them of their power. It would make them weak. Then, he felt, he would still have a chance for purging.

He considered the idea of taking a body for his own. To once again feel and see and touch and smell: The idea appalled him. It frightened him.

"Interharg?"

"Do not. I am Thinking."

Silence. "But I have found them."

"Yes?" Interharg tried to mute his feelings.

"They have crossed over."

*So it is the nightmare. Skulls of dead stars and vomit of fusion*: "Gather," he said. The message rolled out to all of the team. The report from Rolff continued:

"Here: Feel three life patterns. The one close to them is not involved. He seems to be only in the watching mode. The other two:

Feel them: They are the ones we seek."

Interharg studied the patterns. "They have crossed over, but they are weak."

"They have made their own bodies, and yet they still walk. How do you call them weak?"

"What of it? We are still strong."

No one answered. None of the team disagreed. They did not agree, either.

Great pain greeted the wakening baby. It had been a spore it knew not how long. There was no other with it, and it felt a terrible loneliness. The loneliness was as big as the blackness all around, and as many-pricking as all the bright stars that shined on its misery.

Hurt. Lonely. Hurt. Lonely.

Its memory slowly began to form, and strong in the memory were two friends. Two friends.

There was a pale friend and a dark friend, and they had promised the baby a present. If he could find them, they would give him the present.

And maybe it wouldn't hurt so bad, and maybe it wouldn't be so lonely.

It was getting dark now in this room that
had been gray for so long. Once, Max remembered, there had been music here. He
tried to remember how the music had sounded, but it wasn't his music. It had been her
music. When she had left, all the music had
gone.

Max tried to remember her. She had a
name. It had been a smooth, sweet name. He
tried to remember the name. Carolyn, he
thought. But that was not it.

"Kathleena," he said. The word glowed a
faint green in the air, and then faded. But that
was not it.

Max thought it was important to remember
the name. All else he remembered were night-
mares—and they had been twisted, interming-
led and spattered with blood. There were
nights he remembered when he had moved
through fields with explosions going on all
around him, with a thousand screams push-
ing through the air. Falling into a deep muddy
hole, smelling the deep stink of its muck, he
remembered: he remembered a stick had lodg-
ed in his side and he had tried to pull it out.
But the stick, when it came loose, had had
fingers. On the fingers was the marriage band
of a friend. And in his dreams, the killing
never stopped: The killing fell like rain, and
he walked soaking through it, swearing, "I
will live beyond this, even this."

In the darkness, Max said, "I will live beyond this, even this."

He wondered. "What has happened to me that is so bad?"

It had something to do with the name.

Rose Ann? Xavier? Hanalora?

Max stirred. He was frustrated, bored.

"I am waiting on death," he remembered. It didn't seem like a terribly good idea. "Should I die because of a name I can't even remember?"

And he thought of other names:

Heinrich. Jackson. Lieb.

They were names that had died beside him, and beside whom he had sworn that he would live—that this war would not happen again.

In the darkness, Max flickered brightly.

"What are those bastards up to?" he growled. "Who now is massing the tanks, who now has the balance of terror?"

Brightly he glowed. He felt alert. "I have abandoned my post," he thought. He began to take shape. "I must get back. I have a sworn duty." His shape grew firm, strong.

With the shape, his memories became clearer. He remembered that he was in Paradise. "Paradise," he spat.

And there must be a way out. Too many had left for there not to be. He could leave if they had. Yes. And he must. He had a job to do.

And then he remembered her name.

"God damn you, Esmerelda," he said. He was smiling.

"There," Orion said. "Do you feel him?"

Esmerelda tried. She had still not adjusted to this bodiless, weightless realm. Her vision and senses did not work properly. She suffered from synesthesia. Earth—if it was Earth, as Orion said it was—"looked" to her like a giant brass band would sound. It "smelled" of angles.

"I feel geometry, which is stupid," she said. "How can I explain this? I touch and it feels triangular, with a little box and a circle to it. Does that make sense?"

"I can understand," Orion said. "It is common. 'Squeeze' at the box, and tell me what you 'see.' "

Esmerelda tried. "I 'see' something that smells like the squawk of chickens."

"Squeeze harder."

She tried. She could "feel" perspiration on her forehead. The drops of sweat were obtuse angles.

And then she "saw" chickens. They looked like chickens.

"I see chickens."

"Reach out and try to touch them. Can you feel them?"

She stretched and she stretched and she stretched. Finally, there was smoothness against her fingers. "Feathers! I feel feathers!"

"Good. Concentrate on those images and let everything else go. Ignore everything but the feathers. Try to smell them."

Smell them? What were feathers supposed to smell like, she wondered. She could remember the rubbery smell of plucked chickens at the market. Surely, that wasn't it? And then she smelt a smell she could not name. It was chickenish.

"I've got it," she said.

"Now look for Doyle," Orion said.

Esmerelda tried. Something was funny about looking for Doyle by way of chickens. "I feel him," she said. "I can't see him, but he feels close."

"Good. It may be the best you can do. He has returned to the physical. There is a wall between us. He runs, I think," Orion said. "He cannot run far enough to escape Interharg, however. He and Meriwether are outnumbered. They have shaped themselves bodies: They are weaker than they know." He held himself stable, trying to think. "Interharg will not waste energy on creating a body. He needs enough energy left to return. He will enter a body and control it."

"Steal a body?"

"Yes."

"What will happen to the person in the body?"

"If Interharg were not in a struggle, he should live. But not in circumstances like this. The person will stop thinking. He will die. It is wrong, but Interharg has poisoned himself in his quest to stop Doyle's poison."

Esmerelda felt thickly nauseous. Had they come all this way, had miracles been done, only so that Doyle must lose? Then she, too, must lose.

"I must join him," she said.

"You cannot. You lack his power."

"I do," Esmerelda said. "But you have power."

Orion was silent.

"You have the strength. You can put me across."

"No," Orion said. "It would drain me. I would not be strong enough to confront Interharg when he returns."

"If he returns, he will have killed Doyle," Esmerelda said.

"It is so. But if he returns and defeats me, then your sun will also die. And Doyle has already lost. It is too late for any other result."

"No," Esmerelda said. "No. You can intervene. I may not be able to help, but you could."

"And I would lose my world. I would lose the stars," Orion said. "I would be condemned to flesh. I would be condemned, then, to death." He sounded tired and resigned.

Esmerelda raged inside herself. This was unfair; this was not fair, damn it. But she could see only one outcome, the cruelest: "I do not need to cross," she said.

"But you would be here," Orion answered. "You would be alone here forever. And if I go and am to return, I must take a body—not create one. I would have to kill."

She understood. To save Doyle, she and
another must die. It could be a stranger or it
could be Orion—but someone else must die.
Could she ask Orion to give up immortality?
No. Could she ask him to kill? No. No, she
couldn't. "No, I can't," she said to herself. But
she knew she would ask. Otherwise, nothing
mattered. She had been stripped from her
world, stolen from Paradise, and now she had
only this odd bodiless realm as her own. She
would be no one in a Nothing place. She had
nothing else, except Doyle's survival. Without
that, there was truly nothing.

"Take the body," she said. She said it
quietly.

"Kill?"

"Yes. Kill," she said.

"And you? What of you? He will be saved,
but he will not be saved for you," Orion said.

"I know. It doesn't matter."

"You will be lonely. You will be lonely forever. You will live in this blackness, and you
will have no one, and it will be that way forever."

Forever, she thought. Loneliness forever. In
a way, hadn't she already begun that long suf-
fering? She had stood it; she could stand
it . . . forever. At least this way, the loneliness
would have some purpose. In a century, the
purpose might not seem so much. She would
be bitter in her loneliness, she knew. She
would be angry at the choice she had made.

But not now.

Now, she could only make one decision. She must save Doyle.

"I understand. I accept."

"Can you tell me why?"

And she tried to tell Orion. She told him of other loves, and of her life before Doyle, and of what it was like to live for things totally outside yourself. For years, the thing she had lived for was the survival of Italy. Now, Italy was gone—but there was Doyle. Doyle must survive.

"We are all so small as individuals," she said. "We make ourselves big only through commitment."

Orion listened until she was through. "No," he said. "I cannot kill for this Doyle."

"For Doyle—*and* for me," she said.

"You will be worse than dead—and that will be two deaths on my conscience, two deaths—where there need be only one."

Esmerelda waited for him to explain. What was this? she wondered. What had she missed?

"I have lived too long," Orion said. "Now, for the first time, for the first time in star lives, I feel alive again. This is better. We will cross over, the two of us."

"Then you must be the one to die?"

"Yes," Orion said. "But I will have some time before that happens—more than you, probably. Enough."

Interharg chose the mind and leeched himself to it. Quickly he seized control of the
command axons, the controlling dendrites—
the connections he would need to make this
body his. The struggle was enormously more
difficult than he had expected:

Interharg swore at Orion as he struggled.
"Didn't he choose the strongest minds? Then
how is this one so strong?" The only answer
he could figure scared him, that all the minds
in this Earth were strong. But how was that
possible?

The body/mind that Interharg had chosen
fought on, and Interharg felt he must soon
win. Soon this body would be his. And he
cursed his team: They had refused his orders
to cross over. They would not kill, they said.

Interharg was alone.

Now it was he against the two Earthmen.
With luck, if he won, he would still be able to
cross back. He began to plumb the memories
of this struggling mind for something that
would help in the battle to come.

Max could feel Paradise churning and erupting even as he twisted free. Others, myriad

others, were struggling loose.

"We have survived," he thought in wonder. He remembered a maxim from one of his friends: "That which does not kill me makes me strong."

"We are strong," Max said.

"Smoke?" Doyle asked. He and Meriwether sat in the sun, their two cane poles lifted above the dark waters of the pond. The white-washed cabin was behind them; the key to the cabin had been hidden exactly where Doyle remembered. Doyle felt the particular plea-sure one feels from having gotten a good night's sleep. He could smell cattle and grass. They smelled good.

"I don't know why you'd build a new body just to begin poisoning it," Meriwether said. "If it weren't for this bizarre episode, I'd never have been able to quit. I'm not going to start smoking again."

Doyle shrugged. You couldn't explain smoking. But of all the things he'd missed while bodiless, two stood out: sleeping and smoking.

He had both again. He was happy.

"This is some place you've got here," Meriwether said.

"Nice and simple. Janet and I used to come up here on weekends." He wondered to himself how long that had been. Three years had passed since he last "visited" her—how much more time had passed since he'd been to the Nothing Makers? He started to tell Meriwether they needed a calendar.

"Someone's coming," Meriwether said. "He's got a gun."

Doyle glanced up and saw the stocky man coming down the hill toward them. It was Leroy Brown. Doyle felt a sudden pleasure at seeing the old man again.

"That's Mr. Brown—I told you about him. We passed his place last night. He's just coming over to see who's here. He's always kept an eye on the place for us."

"He walks funny," Meriwether said.

Doyle had already noticed the man's odd gait. He suspected it was age or arthritis, or both. Brown would be getting on in years now. He walked as if he were not quite used to having his balance, as if he were unsure of his legs.

"Good morning," Doyle called. "Get a pole and come on down."

"Better not," Brown said. "Got too much business to attend to." He was still up the hill and he shouted—but the words had a garbled quality.

A stroke, Doyle thought.

"There's something wrong here," Meriwether said.

"Not a thing," Doyle said. "You're more
paranoid than me. I've known this man all my
life."

They watched the old man approach. The
man was playing with the gun. Something
about the way he held the gun made Meriwether nervous. He glanced at Doyle. Doyle
was beaming empty-mindedly. *Jesus Christ:
Of course*. "Idiot: You're black. You better
start wrestling with some excuse," Meriwether said.

Doyle blinked, looked shaken.

"Charley. I didn't think I'd ever see you
again," Mr. Brown said.

"I'm surprised you recognize me. I have a
skin condition. It brings out the melanin and
makes me dark."

The shotgun shifted slightly. Meriwether
tensed.

"A skin problem? It's a mind problem,"
Brown said.

"What?"

The shotgun came up. It pointed squarely at
Doyle. Meriwether saw Brown's fingers tight-
ening on the triggers.

"I had no idea it would be this easy," Brown
said. "I regret what must come, but Council
has ruled."

"Interharg?" Doyle said.

"Vengeance is mine. For duty, honor and
wisdom."

Meriwether jumped even as Brown's finger began to move. Even as he moved, he saw the barrel begin to swing. That idiot Doyle had yet to begin to move. He had one chance: He had to knock the gun away.

The shotgun blast caught him squarely in the chest. His voice choked out of him and red touched his lips. This time it was no dream, he thought. This was it. He was falling backwards. "Run, Charley. Goddammit, run . . ." Then the air stopped moving in his throat and his throat filled with liquid.

Doyle ran.

Interharg saw the blood and couldn't believe so much liquid was in a body. He had killed, now, he realized. He had cut himself off from his kind. Yet the shame was not over.

Doyle ran through the pasture. Tufts of grass twisted at his feet. Twice he nearly stumbled into collapse. He thought clearly enough to zigzag as he ran, but he knew time was short. He heard the shotgun fire again. Crazily, he thought he shouldn't be able to hear the blast—unless the shot had missed him. Then he was hit. The burning began in his back—and he knew how he had been saved. *Rock salt*, he thought. *Mr. Brown always kept one barrel loaded with salt.*

It hurt, it burned—but it wouldn't kill. He could keep running. For a while, he was alive. He ran hard, trying not to think of Meriwether. Tears filled his eyes.

He stumbled blindly. A root caught his foot

and he began to fall forward. He fell and he fell. Everything was black. Everything was very, very black.

"I've lost both of them," Esmerelda said.

"They're still there," Orion said. He lied. He had never before felt the need to lie, but now it seemed to come naturally. Another bad effect of the humans, he supposed.

What next?

Orion was worried. Surely Interharg couldn't have moved so rapidly? It would have required aid, some entree—and Doyle was not dumb. Besides, Meriwether was cagey. To catch the humans on their own turf would surely be difficult.

Perhaps the two had learned some secret of camouflaging themselves? That didn't seem likely, but then nothing about this pair was likely.

"They're in hiding," he said. "That's why we can't see them. It's a clever trick, but it may save them."

This was the time, then. Orion would like to have waited. He would like to savor his world before he lost it—but there was no time.

"You are still attempting to be reasonable,"

he chided himself. "Reason is behind us. We are about to become human."

"I'll need your help," he told Esmerelda.

"Whatever I can do."

Together, they began to breathe life into the dust.

It wasn't squirrel season, but that didn't matter. Not to Jake. Seasons were for people who were scared of the law, not for those who made their own way.

Jake and Cully were climbing up the gully back of the Phillips' place. They were walking and sweating. They'd been talking about knocking the fence down to let Phillips' cows out, but that would only bring out Mr. Brown. Better not let that happen. He'd know; somehow, he'd know. But still they joked about it, even though they knew Phillips was dead. Death was not an important thing to either of them.

"Let him call the sheriff to get his heifers back in," Jake said.

"Yeah. Let him."

"Can you see that pansy-faced Taylor chasing after a young bull? Like a peg-legged man trying to dance."

"Or like he was trying to catch us," Cully said.

They were laughing when they heard the twin booms of the shotgun. The sound came from near the road—from near the white cabin where Phillips used to live.

"What the hell?" Jake said.

"Shotgun," said Cully.

"Yeah, but why?"

"Somebody killing rats," Cully suggested.

"You go up and take a look. I'll go on down and meet you the other side."

Cully found a cut in the gully wall. He scrambled up gracelessly. Without seeming to hurry, Jake picked up speed. He wiped at the band of grease and sweat on his forehead. He came to a pool of water and had to jump. His boots sank deeply into the mud. He cursed.

It had never seemed fair to Jake that others beside himself carried guns. His gun was a part of him, another arm. Other people just carried guns: They didn't love 'em. It was wrong to treat a gun that way, and it led to trouble. Jake suspected trouble now. You just didn't hear guns this time of year and this time of day.

He had come out of the gully and was waiting in the shadows before he ever saw his partner nearing. He thought he saw two other figures far away, but then they seemed to disappear. He rubbed his eyes. He did not see the two anymore.

He listened. The birds were quiet; the cows

were quiet. Tension tightened his skin.

"What you got?" he said to Cully.

"You'll never guess. Old man Brown's up there, laying on his back and drunker than a coot. I smelled the gun. It'd been fired. He must've been celebrating."

"Mr. Brown don't drink. You know that."

"If he ain't drunk, I ain't never been drunk," Cully said.

"You smell liquor on him?"

"No, but he's drunk just the same. Sick drunk, too."

"He seem all right?" Jake said.

"He's sick, like I told you. He needs to sleep."

"C'mon. I want to take a look."

"What about the squirrels?"

"Screw the squirrels."

Jake couldn't figure the trouble. Something was up. Even a gun wouldn't hush the world like this. As the two of them walked, he felt the eerie silence. It seemed to be thicker now. He looked for clouds, but there was no rain coming.

He looked again for the two people he'd seen, but he didn't see them and guessed his eyes were acting up. That, or they were hiding. But who would be hiding from him?

Finally, their shapes held. Sight and sound
and smell and feel combined to rattle Orion.
He felt confused. There was so much to see,
just see. They stood in a woods' edge. Trees
stopped in front of them and green spread
out. The green ran down to a brown strip, that
touched on something shiny. The shininess
was water. The brown was dirt. The green
was grass. Orion breathed deeply. He smiled.

He felt the smile tighten the high flesh of his
face. It was a wonderful thing, to feel a smile.
He smiled again.

"What now?" Esmerelda said.

Orion looked at her. He felt a new sensation
when he saw her. It made him nervous. He
would deal with that later. "We go over there,
I think. That's where we last saw them."

"You lead the way."

Orion walked. The rhythms of the walk
bounced his insides around. It was ticklish,
this walking. He tried hard to focus on what
might be Doyle or Meriwether, but he kept
slipping off into new sensations. When he
finally did make a connection, it was not
happy.

"Wait here," he said. "I want to look this
over by myself."

As he neared, he knew what he was seeing.
It was a body. It was a dark body, and Orion
thought it might be Meriwether. It wasn't. His
stomach tightened as he examined the second

body. This scene was like one he'd culled from Doyle. Blood was everywhere. The scene was similar to Doyle's memory of killing Meriwether. It was murder. He wondered to himself, "Are they that vicious? Have I misunderstood them even worse than I expected?"

He turned toward Esmerelda. "It's okay. They're not our friends. No need for you to look."

"I want to look. I've seen blood."

She probably had, he thought.

Esmerelda swept toward him. Orion could feel himself reacting to her presence as if he were truly human. She was beautiful—bodiless, she was beautiful; once this strange thing called "sex" was added, her beauty was frightening.

She examined the first body briefly. She removed her scarf and rolled it, making a pillow for the old man's head. Then she went to look at the second body. She didn't flinch.

"You're wrong," she said. "This is Meriwether."

"But he's not—"

"I know. But this is his face. I'll never forget his face. This is the second time I've seen his face dead."

Flies were making thick, moving black spots in the blood. It was hot. The world was still. Finally, Esmerelda looked at Orion.

"Is Doyle dead, too?"

"I don't know," he said.

He had oddly mixed feelings. This Meriwether had ceased to be; he knew it, and he knew it was tragic. As of yet, he could not accept the reality. He had one overriding fear: that Doyle had done this. That scared him.

At the same time, he could not help but savor the rich patterns his senses fed into his mind. He watched this woman move, and he envied the patterns of sweat that formed at the small of her back and on her blouse. There was the smell of her sweat and her hair. Touch: He longed to touch.

"Listen," she said. "The old man is talking."

Even as she spoke, she moved toward the other man. It was not until Orion drew even with her that he heard the sounds. The words were strange, disjointed.

"Is this talk common?"

"No."

When they reached the body, the words were clearer—but their rhythm still made them seem incoherent. There were two voices they heard.

"Out, out! Damn you, get out," the body was saying. Then it interrupted itself, with the same voice, but the tone was somehow different. "I have a RIGHT that transcends your petty being. I have a RIGHT—"

"You have garbage."

"You unthinking hull of—"

"I—"

"You—"

"Heat stroke," Esmerelda said. "We must get him in."

"Is it that hot?"

"No, but— "

"I think I know," Orion said. "Wait. Let me listen." As he listened, it became clear. There were two identities here. One of them was familiar. It was Interharg. He had chosen his victim badly, Orion realized. He was now lost in a battle for control of the body he had chosen. Interharg shouldn't have had any problem dominating a body: What had happened?

"Do you understand this?" he asked Esmerelda.

"I don't think so."

"One of those voices belongs to my brother, the brother who seeks Doyle. He has done what I refused to do. To save his energy, he tried to take over a body. Something's gone wrong. He is not in control."

"Then who killed Meriwether?"

"I don't know. It makes no sense—unless, of course, the body was stunned and took a while to begin to fight. That could have happened."

"But you don't believe that."

"I don't know."

"You think it was Doyle," she said.

"I tell you honestly: I don't know."

They examined the body closely. The eyes were open, but they did not focus. The words had stopped. Gurgling came from the throat. An occasional spasm would seize the body. Drool etched itself on the old man's cheek.

There was the smell of excrement, as if even the basic functions were without control.

"He should know what happened to Doyle," Orion said.

"Him? Which him?"

"Good question."

"Who're they?"

"Never seen 'em before."

"Wish I'd seen *her* before," Cully said.

Doyle heard the words through a fog. They didn't make sense. Something about the voices nagged at him. He tried to move and felt a flash of pain. His eyes opened. His surroundings didn't make sense. He was in a pit of some sort. He remembered running and falling. He studied the shape of the pit. He knew what it was, but it had been a long time. When it finally came to him, he almost laughed. He stopped the laugh out of caution.

"Saved by falling into an outhouse pit. Jesus," he thought. It could've been worse: The pit could've been an old pit, in use. One the outhouse had been pulled from.

He had a fleeting image of himself as the first droppings into the pit.

"Appropriate," he thought.

The voices were fainter now. They crystallized. *Cully and Jake. I'll be damned.* He figured both of them would be serving life sentences at Fort Pillow State Farm by now.

And then, then, he remembered why he was running. He remembered the whole sick episode. This time, there was no room for error: Meriwether was dead. There'd been too much blood, and Meriwether had dropped too fast. This was no illusion; this was real. *Everything's dead now. I've killed everything that matters. And I'm left with Cully and Jake.*

One more time the dice had rolled, and one more time he had survived. He'd gotten the rock salt; Answar got the buckshot.

*Why? What keeps me alive?*

He had a feeling he knew: bad luck.

Not for him so much, but for others.

And then he passed out at the bottom of the pit.

Each time Max Gunther passed through Andorra, he felt he had returned to a good dream. Yet Andorra was real—and, now, after Paradise, he could not think of it as a dream anymore. To compare it to a dream was unfair to Andorra. Gunther—clean shaven and

almost embarrassingly fat-faced—sat in the
Casa Andorra. The small cafe outside Saint
Julia was owned by Americans. The cafe was
empty, except for three herdsmen. Outside
the cafe's windows, the Valira River ran clean
and clear with melting snow.

His beer came and Max sipped from it. He
read the International Herald Tribune and
idly puzzled at new developments in France.
*Is that us at work?* Casually, he examined the
herdsmen. All were of stocky Spanish build,
but one in particular seemed out of place. The
one drank tea, not wine.

"That's him," Max thought with disappointment. "Stupid."

It was always stupid to be obvious. That
Fyodor's man could slip so bothered Gunther,
but he supposed there was nothing to fear.
And if there was . . . he lightly touched the
compact Colt, custom-made, that pressed inside his belt.

And he hoped.

Gunther had never had trouble with necessary killing: one death could save many
deaths. Sure, he had killed: he had also felt the
sense of benign justice when he could kill, but
passed the moment by. He wondered, wearily,
how a man like Doyle would handle such de-
cisions. Killing oneself had honor, he
thought—honor of a sort Doyle would not
appreciate and could never understand.

Gunther had enjoyed killing himself. It had
been easy. The Max-who-remained-behind had

deserved it.

He remembered, with a slight shudder, how he'd felt to return to his own body. The other Max had gone soft, had retired from field operations, and had transferred into command of the Thirteen Organization. He had gone to excess weight; his energy, no longer needed for survival, had been spent on internal politics. The other Max had written his own death warrant.

Gunther rubbed his fat cheeks in irritation. Soon, soon, he would be lean again.

His thoughts shifted. There was motion from the herdsmen; instantly, he prepared for action. He enjoyed the adrenalin that surged in his blood. He had seated himself so he could use the window as a mirror. Now he turned, to watch as the herdsmen prepared to leave.

The tea-drinking herdsman lingered, finally leaving last. As he left, he stumbled against Gunther's table.

"Senor," he said in a tinny voice. "I am sorry."

"Por nada," Max said. He motioned for the man to be seated. The man glanced around the cafe nervously before he sat. Bad, Gunther thought.

"I notice your coat, senor. You are one who appreciates finer things, yes?"

Gunther said nothing.

"Perhaps you would be interested in jewelry, some fine gold jewelry?"

"Maybe. Maybe not."

"It is good. A cautious man. Perhaps you would walk with me, and we could talk?"

"Fine."

There was a moment's disorder, until Gunther arranged himself to force the young man through the door first. He envied the youth's innocence—and he hoped the youth was bright enough to learn so that he could someday be old.

They ambled along the cattle path. Max felt electricity inside himself: it was good to be on assignment again. In spite of the breakdowns in the old order that had happened in his absence, he felt renewed. His stint in Paradise had been a vacation, of sorts—but it had done more. It had given him hope. If he was right, a new power was rising up.

If he was right.

Something moved in the shadows ahead. Gunther stopped. He continued to move his feet to make a walking noise, but he did not go forward. His escort moved on.

"Fool," came a voice from the shadows. "Look at you, fool!" The herder had been doing a not-bad imitation of the face-down walk of the local herdsmen: Suddenly, he straightened and looked around. He saw at once the distance at which Gunther stood. He flushed noticeably, even beneath his dark skin.

"Fyodor, you shame me. I could lend you Boy Scouts if you're desperate."

The Russian emerged from the shadows. He was scowling. "What choice have I? This is, what, an unusual situation? I must have those I can trust with me—even if they be trustworthy fools."

"I have come alone," Gunther said.

"You are a free man."

"And not you? The Fyodor Ruthkowski I know has no fear."

The man spat. "You have called me. I have come."

"I wish to speak of Paradise."

"You make jokes."

They spoke in English. Max assumed the youth knew no English. But as he pressed Fyodor, he began to worry: Had he made a mistake? Were his assumptions about Paradise wrong? The Russian, too, was fat; he hadn't the animal power Gunther had expected in Fyodor. There was danger, he thought.

"You have called me to speak of church fantasies?" the Russian said. "Your side must be decaying faster than we believed."

*What is he hiding?* Max wondered. *Have I misjudged? Have I alone found my way back?*

He was answered by the put-ting sound of a gun equipped with a silencer. The Russian looked surprised, then he looked dead. Gunther dived and rolled, and came up to the sound of laughter. He held the Colt loosely in his hand.

"Even with an old body, you move well, my friend," the young herder was saying. He held a clear-glass gun of some sort in his hand.

"Who are you?"

"I am Fyodor. Fyodor the Second, I suppose. I am the one you met in Paradise." He cleared his throat. "I saw no point in taking up my old body, when a young and more serviceable one was available."

"I see," Gunther said. He lowered his gun and smiled. Once again, he had to admire the straightforward ruthlessness of this man—a man he'd never met in the flesh before, but had known as an opponent for years.

"You still carry your Tribune? Did you note the story on Page Three?"

Max turned the front page over and scanned. There was nothing he saw at first. He read more closely, still finding nothing, until he came to a Zaire dateline. He recognized the byline. His smile broadened as he read.

"Well, I'm damned."

"No," Fyodor said. "I think you are saved. I think we are all saved."

The announcement was of a breakthrough a British cyberneticist had made, a breakthrough expected to quadruple the information-processing ability of current software systems. The catch was, the patent was being granted through Zaire—with some very tough restrictions on how the system was to be used.

"I could use a beer myself, Max. Tea disagrees with me."

"On me," Gunther said. "What about . . .?"

He gestured at the body.

"He is not dead. Merely out. He will flee when he wakes and, when he contacts Sergiev, he will be arrested. This was *not* a mission he should have undertaken."

Fyodor smiled broadly. "I hesitate to kill, now," he said.

Gunther thought, watching the teeth, of a monstrous friendly tiger.

"He'll be all right in a little while, don't you think?" the one named Jake asked.

"I'm sure of it," Orion said. "We have another friend we're expecting. This is his house."

They were in the white two-roomed house. Mr. Brown was laid out on the bed. Orion saw the two exchange glances: He had no doubt of the meaning. He felt himself steering into dangerous waters. And, as it was, with the incredible variety of human sentiments that flowed around him, he could probably not expect much help from Esmerelda.

Jake sprawled in a chair. Cully moved casually to the door and rested with his back against it.

"Maybe we ought to call the sheriff," Jake

said. "Better start getting this mess cleaned up."

"Go ahead," Orion said.

"What's your name, mister?"

"Orion."

"That's a funny kind of name. You got a last one?"

"Um, Smith," Orion said.

" 'Orion Smith,' huh. That's good," Jake said. "Real good. The sheriff ought to like that."

Orion shifted uncomfortably. For the first time, he realized how much the physical and the emotional tied together in humans. He felt twinges of sickness now.

"Maybe I should point out something," Jake said. "This man over here's no nigger. Is he, Cully? Is Mr. Brown a nigger?"

"Ain't no nigger 'misters,' " Cully answered solemnly.

"Now that's right," Jake said. "And what I'm thinking is this: If Mr. Brown shot that man out front, there had to be a reason. A good one. Now he can't talk right now, or we'd just let him explain. But it makes me wonder . . ."

Orion said nothing. Esmerelda sat near the old man, listening intently to his odd words.

"The lady don't say much."

"I have nothing to say," Esmerelda answered. She did not look up. Orion heard the strangeness of her accent and cringed.

"May I ask your name, miss?"

"Esmerelda. Esmerelda LaFlore. It's an Italian name, and my accent is Italian."

"You're real pretty, Miss LaFlore. Another Racquel Welch."

Cully snorted from the doorway.

Jake studied Orion and Esmerelda. He offered a cigarette. "Now I'm willing to do nothing, 'cept wait on Mr. Brown. We like to settle our own things our way, when we can. Mr. Brown's affairs are our affairs, you understand? The sheriff isn't going to be in a big hurry anyway."

Again, Cully snorted. He said, "Sheriff has enough problems out here without adding more."

"That he has," Jake agreed. "But that's the lawful way to handle this. What bothers me is, the lawful way isn't always the right way. Begging your pardon, but you're both white. Now I don't care what color your friend is, anymore than I care what color Mr. Brown is—but that can make a difference to the law, even if it shouldn't. I know Mr. Brown wouldn't shoot nobody unless they needed it. You got any ideas what your friend might have done?"

Esmerelda shook her head. Orion glanced at the still mumbling body, and then at Jake.

"I know something that might help," he said.

"Go ahead then."

"I don't know that I can."

"I think you'd better try," Jake said. He

sucked deep on his cigarette and blew out a thick plume of smoke. "I think you'd better try real hard."

Orion's eyes caught movement at the door. Cully had moved the thing he carried. Orion realized, with a dawning despair, that the instruments these men carried were guns. They were what made the huge red place in the man Meriwether's chest.

His mouth and his throat were dry, and it hurt Orion to try to talk. But he tried.

Inside Mr. Brown's head, it was war.

Interharg knew the principles of mental wiring; he knew, not so well as Orion, but pretty well, the strategies needed to control an alien being. He felt he should be able to win easily—but he had not yet won.

Leroy Brown's problem was different. He felt invaded, defiled, angry. He was lost in a dark cave, a cave filled with things of slime and smelling of waste; he felt as if he were walking through fire and then pierced by hot blades. Nausea, violent nausea of the kind that makes you wish for death, flooded through him.

But he did not wish for death. Death was the

enemy; Brown had fought back from the edge of death before, when this Thing had first raped his soul. That he hadn't died then was a victory, he knew. He knew little else except fears—smells and sights and sickness were the clubs this Thing was using to make him give up. But he would not give up.

It was only that he hadn't an idea how to fight.

He felt caught in a web, fighting against ropes and ties that bound him, yet were invisible. He struck out blindly, but his blows had no effect. The pressures, the horrors, continued.

On the bed, the body rolled. It sweated.

Brown sensed that it was his choice, that if he ever gave up, he would be at peace—but would have lost his body. Whatever was in him was growing more and more shrewd in its attacks. Now, he felt, now—the final struggle was beginning.

"I've got you now," a voice said. It was a faraway voice, a voice cool and threatening and confident.

Light flashed around Brown and suddenly he could see and hear again. He was a young boy again. He was playing in the open field behind the shack. Mama had called him twice for supper, but he had hidden. And then the Maples boy appeared, riding a horse that seemed larger than an elephant.

It was a big shining huge white horse.

Brown could feel his heart beginning to

hammer in terror.

"Hey, Leroy! Come see the mess my horse has made. Horse pies, just for you."

Brown stood. He didn't move. He dared not move.

"Not going to make you eat 'em—just want you to play with 'em. Just want you to have a little fun. You going to play?"

Still, he could not move. There was blue sky all around and the green of the field was all around and the air was sweet all around. It had been raining for days, and now the sky was blue. It was a beautiful new summer day —and terror was at the heart of it.

The terror was the Maples boy. They'd thought the Maples boy had something to do with the rash of barn fires last fall; the boy had even put nails in his own father's feed troughs. But those were outside fears, grown-up fears. Brown remembered and knew only one thing himself. He'd been out wandering in the woods when he'd run into little Sammy Maples. Little Sammy had a B-B gun. He was shooting it in a frog. He'd shot that frog again and again. Leroy, curious, had come up to watch. When he got there, the frog was nearly full up with B-B shot. It was trying to crawl away. One of its eyes was out. And little Sammy was just sitting there, shooting, and the B-Bs were going thunk-thunk-thunk into the frog. And the little frog couldn't do *nothin'*. Nothing, but die piece-by-piece.

Leroy'd watched all he could, then he jump-

ed up high and landed hard on the frog's
head—smashing it, killing it. It felt good to
stop its pain, but Sammy hadn't been happy.
He'd swung his gun and clubbed Leroy, who
fell—and when he was down, Sammy started
kicking him. He kicked until his anger was
done.

Now, a different day, a year or two later,
Leroy stood in the open field and looked at the
Maples boy on the horse. He saw his face, and
he remembered the face: It was the face he'd
had shooting the B-Bs into the frog.

"Boy, you going to come here?"

And Leroy didn't move.

The Maples boy popped his horse's flanks
with a switch. The horse began to move. It
moved like a monster, like Goliath, and on its
back was a spiteful hating white demon.

Leroy began to run. He could hear the
hooves pounding behind him, pummeling the
ground; their sound was a tidal wave of
killing horse thunder.

Louder they came, and louder. Leroy's
breath burned and tore raggedly from his
chest. He could feel his blood pumping and
his heart working at breakneck speed. He felt
his blood vessels would burst from the pressure of the exploding blood in them. And the
horse was louder, louder. Above the hooves'
sound there was Maples' crazy laughter. Then
both sounds were on top of him.

The horse veered at the last moment. It was
thirty meters before its rider could slow it.

The laughter did not stop.

"Want me to do it some more—or you want to be a good little burrhead and play with our pies?"

Blue sky and a green wide sea, and terror. Leroy's chest heaved violently in the middle of the calm. *I'm not going to do it*, he thought. Somehow he knew to give in would be to have given in for always. *I'm not going to do it*.

But he also knew Maples would push closer and closer. Today, he was the frog to be killed.

(And the old man, Mr. Brown, was completely and totally the little boy. He begged himself: "Don't give in, don't give up. This is a trap; this isn't real." Deep in himself, he knew his fears of horses and the Maples boy had been resurrected. He could fight those fears. He must. He needed some way to turn the illusion over. Something, somehow.)

In the brilliant, new-perfect day, the horse slowly began to move. It was moving away. Leroy had hope, as he began to let the tears of relief flow. Then, like a destroyer on the green sea, the horse began to turn. It built speed. It galloped. It arced around and was moving faster and faster. Now the arc was complete. Now the horse moved toward him.

"If I stand, he may veer again," Leroy thought. "And if he doesn't, maybe I can jump. But which way? If he veers again, I've got to go the other way."

And the horse thundered closer.

Doyle had a body again. The body was all pain. He remembered waking up before, but now he couldn't move. Now he was alone. He wondered if he'd been left to die.

Emotions rattled around in him. Emptiness, sadness, disgust. "What do I want?" he wondered. "What have I ever wanted?"

He didn't know.

He thought he was making the world a more perfect place, and that was what he had wanted. *But not really.* He had wanted a world where he could be at ease, where enough was enough—where he loved and was loved. *I've killed everything that loved me*, he thought. *I killed Paradise.*

*I killed Paradise—and I killed Janet, and Eskelion, and Meriwether, and Esmerelda. Esmerelda! The one chance I had for Paradise, and I left her behind. Orion? I'll never know. I never gave him a chance, either.*

*And Interharg: Even Interharg, I don't know about. Still he hunts me, and I don't know why. Is he hunting me because he's wise, the way I hunted Meriwether—for a greater good? Perhaps he does know.*

Doyle shook his head dazedly. The confusion was unending. "And maybe he hunts me because he loves me? How would I know? To shuck this off, would that be so bad? Maybe he wants to do me a favor?"

In a way, everything seemed to be coming

together. Now he, Doyle, was a black man in a white world. Finally, a nigger—after years of feeling it, he had arrived. Meriwether had been "whiter" than he was all along; more normal, and better adjusted to the world as it was. The white man was the normal world: The maker of rules, the executioner of the law, the cool and the calm and the unemotional . . . the white man was Interharg, grinding everything away until it was pure and snow white and dust.

White was the annihilating force that had become Interharg, Doyle realized—the stuff of the stuff that had become the Kingdom of the Nothing Makers.

*And the only good nigger is a dead nigger*, he thought.

And Doyle began to let go.

This was the final letting go, he realized. There was nowhere to go after this. He had no energy to go. After this, there was death. He was ready.

*Maybe there's another Paradise, a real one*, he thought.

But he didn't bet on it. More likely, there was a capital-H hell—but he didn't believe that either. Orion and Interharg were greater gods than he'd really expected of this Universe. If there were more, well . . .

He was letting to into death.

This body, the one he had fought for in Paradise and in the Kingdom of the Nothing Makers, this body was not enough.

Having the body was too much.
He could let it go.
He wanted to let it go.

Jake rocked backwards in the cane-bottom-
ed chair. He had one boot heel caught in the
rung of the chair. His other leg sprawled
away from him. He regarded Orion with the
same look of peculiar disgust and fascination
with which he might look upon the Lizard
Man at the county fair.

"You really believe this?" he said. "You do.
Both of you?"

Orion nodded.

Esmerelda said, "Do you think we would expect you to believe it if we didn't?" She looked
hard at Jake, who glanced down. He put his
cigarette under his boot heel and ground it into the linoleum floor. Jake knew he could not
look at the woman and not agree with her—no
matter how much she was lying. He hated
women who made him feel like that. There
was always the attitude that went with that
feeling, that they were better than you. Maybe
they were—he didn't know. He doubted he
would ever have the chance to find out.

"What you say, Cully? You still think Mr. Brown's drunk?"

"Drugged, more like it," Cully said. "Drugs make you think the kind of stuff they're saying. Maybe they forced Mr. Brown into taking something." Cully squatted now, by the door. He was a small dark shadow guarding the door.

"That could be," Jake said. "But you don't think these two are lying?"

"I think they're crazy—crazy like Possum, before he got his leg caught in the grain auger. He used to see blue fairies, but the auger cured him of it. Cured him of his leg, too."

"Possum had the DTs," Jake said drily. "What the auger cured him of was drinking."

He closed his eyes to think, knowing Cully would keep watch. He'd seen Cully sit by a squirrel tree for hours; once he knew a squirrel was in the tree, he'd never move again—not before the squirrel, anyhow. He was a born watcher.

These two ought to be watched—these two, and that other one.

What kind of cock and bull story was this, anyway: Some kind of space ghost had invaded Mr. Brown's body? What kind of story was that? The only thing going for it was that they'd told it as if they expected to be believed—or as if they expected they could put anything over on ninnies in the country. That might be. Maybe he ought to call the sheriff.

"Jake," said Cully. "Something you should see."

Jake's eyes opened. He saw Orion beginning to shift, as if to get up. "Don't move," Jake said.

"But we're— "

"If it's somebody we don't know, we want to make sure they're not your friends. If it's our friends, I don't think you want them to know about you."

Jake rose. Cully had resumed his watch of the two strangers.

"Out where they're digging," Cully said.

Jake looked. He blinked and looked again. A giant yellow boil seemed to be erupting from the spot.

Young Brown felt something twist as he dodged the horse and fell. His side hurt where a stone had bitten into it—but he had chosen right. He had escaped the horse. Twice, now, he had chosen correctly. Three times? Could he bet on three times? He dared not.

Brown rolled over in the deep green grass and watched as the horse grew small. Maybe it was over. Maybe the Maples boy had tired of the game. Brown felt his clothes becoming wet because of water deep in the grass.

The horse began to slow. It began to turn

and amble back. It grew large again. Toward him it came, but not fast. The horse came nearer and nearer. Brown looked up into the shining white freckled face of Sammy Maples. He blinked. Something was wrong with the white boy's eyes. He blinked. The eyes flickered like fireflies, like tinsel on a Christmas tree.

"I'm giving you one more chance to play. One more, and then I'm going to ride right over you. You want to play?"

"No."

"Nigger, you're going to hurt yourself."

"No. You going to be hurt."

The boy on the horse laughed. The laugh was shrill. Brown could feel a thin fresh sheen of sweat breaking out all over him; it was cool in the grass with the sweat, but the covering was like that the barn spider makes over its victim, a silk coffin. The horse and rider turned.

"It's not real," Brown told himself. "Not real." But it was still dangerous, he knew. To give in would be to lose his body; not to give in was to die. There had to be something else he could do: something he knew that he could use.

But first he must run. If he could get to a fence . . . but even as his small legs pumped, he knew the effort was futile. The field was too large.

He remembered forward to a story the young Doyle had told. "What's happened here? Something, something I can use," he thought, running. The sound of the horse's hooves were far away and almost silent, but then their sound began to grow. Deep and low the sound began. The edge of the field was farther away than tomorrow.

The confused words from the old man stopped suddenly. Orion turned, fearing the man had died—that Mr. Brown's battle was lost. As he looked, however, Orion saw the old man's eyelids fluttering. The skin on the face was tight and glowing with sweat. His jaw was working; his teeth made an awful grinding noise. At least he still lived.

Orion turned slightly more to watch Esmerelda. She was watching the broad back of the man Jake. A sharp knife-twist feeling cut into Orion; he smiled ironically. He supposed he had literally felt a twinge of jealousy. That meant he was finally, completely settling into the body. Its hormones and drives were affecting his thoughts. Soon, he would be irrevocably human. Soon, death would become part of his future.

"But not too soon, I hope."

Orion faced the front of the cabin again and

tried to guess what so absorbed the two men.
Cully had positioned himself so he could both
keep an eye on Orion and keep watch outside.
Earlier, Orion had seen the man making almost comic winks at Esmerelda. He had felt a
glib pleasure at the mocking wink she returned.

He wondered if the man had known he was
being mocked. The other one, Jake, would
have known. Cully only seemed to be an ex-
tension of Jake, as if Jake was too complicated for one body.

"Maybe it's some sort of gas," Cully said.

"Maybe. Maybe it has something to do with
their crazy story. I ain't seen nothing like it
before. And it's growing."

"It's, uh, Jesus."

"What?"

"I get the feeling it's feeding on something."
Jake turned. "You. Orion. Come here."
Orion stood and moved to the window.

Friend friend friend friend friend friend
friend friend friend friend friend friend
friend . . .

What had been Eskelion, but was no more,
but still could be considered Eskelion, sang

its message desperately to the hull that was dying. Doyle, its name was. Without this Doyle, there would be no present. And this Doyle was slipping into not-think.

Friend friend friend . . . Eskelion-but-not-Eskelion pressed all its feelings into the word. There were memories it tapped of drinking late into the night and solving all the world's problems; Sunday afternoons, half napping, music playing somewhere; and laughing hard and eating good food. He picked up the feelings and enlarged them. Friend friend friend. He showed the glad feeling that comes of unexpectedly running into a good friend. He repeated his message over and over.

He could not tell if he was getting through.

And then Brown pushed as hard as he could and left the ground. He jumped hard.

He had been running alongside the hidden gasline, all the while letting the horse's hooves sound louder and louder, until the hairs on the back of his neck screamed that it was time. Only then did he veer right, then jump.

He jumped and he began to fall. His soul seemed frozen, as he waited for the verdict.

He fell and he rolled onto his bad arm. He waited for the white huge body to appear over him and for the deeper hurting to begin. To feel the hundreds of pounds of pressure each hoof would bring to his body. To feel smashed like a bug; smashed, thankfully, like the frog. It would be good to end it.

And the thunder stopped.

And a shape flew past, hit the ground, was still. It was the Maples boy.

Shakily, Brown climbed to his feet. He smiled. The horse was mired soundly in the unpacked earth above the gasline. Its belly was flat against the wet earth.

"I win," the boy called loudly. He laughed.

The bright sky peeled back. The wetness went away. The green slipped off into memory. The nightmare ended.

The old cracked lips moved.

"I win," Mr. Brown said.

His eyes opened and he saw a ceiling. Under his back he felt a mattress. He raised himself as high as his strength would allow: He was tired; he was unbelievably tired. He saw a red-haired woman beside him.

"I did win," he told her proudly. Then his tiredness took over. His eyes closed. He slept peacefully.

Not until the illusion had almost completely disintegrated did Interharg realize his failure. It had seemed to be going perfectly, by the book: He had summoned enough of the man's memories and fears to create a perfect box. The man should have died or given up. But it was Interharg, not the man, who had failed. Now it was he who was in danger.

Blackness slammed into him as the bright light of the illusion went out. He reeled desperately and felt himself flickering. He existed now in the physical world: Quickly, he needed a physical shape. Even light would do, but it must be done quickly.

He grasped for something, anything.

He became light. He had no choice. Light was limited, but it would do.

*Limits do not matter*, he told himself. *My will is perfect*.

Shame—shame at having been beaten by a not-worthy creature of flesh—fired his anger. His anger grew and he raged. It made him strong and perfect, he thought. The time of testing was over. The time for decision had come.

Now was the time to find Doyle. Now.

Esmerelda felt her heart skip as Interharg materialized above Mr. Brown's body. She saw him as a swarm of fireflies; he made a chattering like locusts, and he was big. He filled the small cabin with his thousands of starlike bits; his chattering became a chain-saw growl.

Then he swept through the wall and was gone.

Esmerelda bit her lip. "Orion," she said. "I'm afraid." She said it too quietly for any-one to hear.

Orion looked out the window and did not know what to make of what he saw. "I don't know what it is," he said.

Jake looked at him. "You'd better not lie."

"I'm not."

"Shoot it," Jake told Cully. The man moved to the doorway and began to raise his gun.

"Not from here. Closer."

"But I'm— "

"Go," Jake said. "You go with him, Orion."

They moved down the short steps and into the yard. The pink bubble oozed and swayed, changing its shape. Orion could feel no logic to this. At first he'd thought this might be

another member of Interharg's team—but
now doubted it. This made no sense. Dimly, he
could pick up emanations from the spot. All
he could tell was that this had nothing to do
with purging.

He guessed it would do no harm to shoot
the thing.

"I'm scared," Cully said.

"No need to be scared," Orion said.

"Faster!" called Jake from behind.

Who was this bastard with his insane
friendship? Doyle wondered. He'd been almost completely at peace, and then this had
happened. The darkness had almost taken
him. It had been all but over.

And then . . . there had come this. It was thick,
an almost palpable feeling of love. It was
like waves, this feeling of love. Like the touch
of a first kiss—like the way Doyle had felt
when he'd said his "I do's" with Janet. Like
he'd felt when singing bawdy songs with Gentry.

"Gentry? Is that you Gentry?"

Friend friend friend friend friend . . .

"Janet, Answar?"

He was confused now. Who could it be?

Where was he that he could meet with friends?

Doyle was rolled along by the message of love. *Friend, someone still calls me friend. Not me: They couldn't be calling me. And not Gentry. Gentry's long gone—ages gone. And not Janet: Janet is gone, too, in love with her husband—a husband who is not me. And not Answar. Answar was dead. He was dead because he had tried to be Doyle's friend.*

"Go away, just go away."

Friend, I have come. My friend, I have come because of a promise made to the me-before. Friend.

"Eskelion?"

*But Eskelion's dead, too,* he thought. He'd seen Eskelion hit by one of Interharg's bolts —the first warning he and Answar had that judgment had been made. But it felt like Eskelion: How could that be? Doyle felt he couldn't risk betraying another person now. He couldn't have that final sin etched on his soul. There was need here, need for him. He must answer it.

Friend, I need. Friend.

"All right," Doyle said. "Friend: I am here. It's okay. I'm hanging on."

Doyle began to make himself awake, to force himself to see through his body's eyes again. Pain, he felt—but there was promise in the pain. There was something to hang on for, now: He was needed. Meaning. He had meaning.

It was the being needed that was important. Whoever needed him now—whatever—needed him more than life. *If only I can meet the need*, he thought. *If only I can.*

"Okay, buddy. It's all right. I'm not dying anymore, for Christ sake. Let me see you. Let me know what I've promised. Calm down. It's all right."

He felt good, Doyle did.

The words still came. Friend, friend, friend . . . and the words seemed closer, deeper. Then they stopped. Doyle could feel his arms again. He felt his legs. He felt his sprained ankle. His head ached.

But the bad thing was the sudden silence.

"Have I heard it too late?" he wondered. The silence was a gaping emptiness. "Eskelion, I'm here. I'm here!" He saw the world through a red mist. Two figures stood someways off. He must go to them, he thought. Maybe it was they who called.

ENEMY.

The word screeched into him.

ENEMY.

*No, for God's sake, no, not that, God no,* Doyle thought.

Sweat filled Cully's hands. It made them slick and unsure against the stock of his sixteen gauge. He hadn't blinked in minutes, and he could feel the dryness of his eyes. Every time he stopped, Jake urged him forward. Ahead the pink cloud glistened. It wasn't fair, he thought—but he had to do what Jake said.

Without Jake, he was nobody. He must listen to Jake, because Jake always knew. Jake always had it figured. He wouldn't push Cully where Cully shouldn't go. Grudgingly, he moved forward a step. Another step. Another. He stopped, waiting, hoping Jake would be satisfied.

"Just a little more," Jake called.

"Yeah. Right," Cully answered.

The red thing was no more than ten meters away now. It smelled like electricity. It seemed less solid up close, like a mist. He could see something inside the pink cloud. Its outlines were blurred, but it could be a man.

What he wanted now was to shoot. He didn't know that it would do any good: What good was shooting a cloud? It might make it mad, too. He remembered chasing will-o'-the-wisps with Jake years before down in the Hatchie River bottom. He remembered stumbling after the eerie light in the foggy woods. Sometimes they had shot at the wavering light, but it didn't do anything.

Besides, this was no will-o'-the-wisp.

This was in broad daylight.

He stopped again. No word. Maybe he should shoot now. He turned to see what Jake wanted. He turned and saw the swarm of fireflies. He had never seen fireflies like them. Even in the thinning daylight, they shouldn't be so bright. And so many: There must be thousands. And the sound: He'd never heard them sound before.

"Jake?"

"Get down, Cully. Stay down."

Cully collapsed without thinking. As he turned over, he saw the pink thing turning solid and scarlet. It was hardening again. Out of the pink thing was walking a man. The man had his hands stretched out. He was calling something.

"Friend," he was saying. Like he was begging. "Friend. Not enemy. I'm your friend."

The cloud began to move. It began to drift toward the fireflies. The fireflies gleamed brightly. They looked like flashing points of steel.

Cully smelled the electric smell. It was strong, almost overpowering, a smell like you get when lightning hits nearby. The lightning smell. With it was the smell of woods, and a snake smell. Cully recognized it as the smell of a snake nest, half earth and half remains and another something that could make the hair stand up on your arms.

For the first time, he believed the crazy story of the man Orion. This was something out of the late-night horror movies from TV. These were space monsters, and Orion was a space monster, and even the skirt was a space monster. Except, Cully thought, didn't the monsters always land in someplace important like Memphis or New York?

What kind of space monsters would invade Medon, Tennessee?

Good monsters or bad monsters?

But as he watched, he stopped thinking such things. He watched the fireflies-thing try to avoid the red-thing. The red-thing was staying between the fireflies and the man. The man, Cully noticed, was a nigger. Occasionally, the two cloud-monsters would touch and there'd be huge sparkings. The smells would get worse, like burning wire. There was a sulphur smell, too, and Cully could feel a sort of breeze come up when the two things touched. The breeze carried emotions that Cully felt. There were hates he felt, the kind of hate his family had against the Maples—enduring, rich hates. It was a blood hate, something that went on past and future, and ended only in blood.

He forgot the nigger as he watched, until he heard footsteps. The footsteps were close. He looked up and saw the slim figure almost on him. The man was walking stiff-legged. His eyes seemed blank. Still he held out his hands; still he kept calling, "Friend, friend, friend." He'd been saying it so long it was like a drone, a drone Cully had almost tuned out.

Now the man was lurching toward him.

It was a zombie, Cully thought. His sphincter tightened.

The nigger was a zombie.

His stomach knotted and his sweat began to pour out. A zombie. A zombie was a bad monster. He lifted his gun and tried to aim. If the nigger's bad, then the pink-thing's bad, he reasoned. He aimed the gun. The firefly-thing must be good, then. He used both hands to steady the gun. But the zombie lurched again. It was moving slightly away. It was about to pass between Cully and the pink-thing.

"One second, give it both barrels: I can get them both," he thought. He was proud of the idea. Jake would see the logic, sure. He began to tighten his fingers on the twin triggers.

He waited for the gun to boom.

Interharg could feel weakness all through him. This shape was draining and difficult. He hadn't much time, yet he had to face this thing-that-had-been-Eskelion. This child. It was blocking his way.

They parried on some sort of plain. Interharg dimly sensed a nearby presence of water; too, there were multiple hulls in the area. He was losing out on which one was Doyle. His chances for a clean victory were running out:

If this dance with Eskelion lasted much longer, he would have no choice but to enter the body containing Doyle. There, they would fight. And even if he won, he would be doomed to remain there. He did not want that.

"Back, child," he thought, forcing himself

into conflict with Eskelion. "You stand in the way of Council and duty."

Friend friend friend friend.

"I am not your friend," Interharg said.

Orion had stopped moving some time before Cully. He watched the pink mistiness and wondered what he should do. He felt cut off, unable to "feel" the nature of the being. Surely, he thought, it is not Interharg's ally. But if not, what was it doing here?

Then he saw movement inside the cloud. There was a body of some sort in the cloud. The creature could be creating its own body, Orion supposed. Or perhaps this was some Earth being he had yet to learn of?

The body came stumbling out.

"Doyle," Orion said in wonder. It was the man; he didn't doubt it. And yet there was a difference: Something had changed in him. But it was Doyle. "Thank God," he said.

As he thought it, he felt another presence. He turned and saw the flickering fireflies.

For one pure moment, Orion forgot all and admired the two star beings. Never before had he been able to appreciate how elegant his star-brothers looked. Inside himself, he felt sadness at what he had given up.

"This is what I was," he thought. "And now I am not."

Then the two creatures clashed.

"Brothers," he said, but he knew they could not hear.

To himself, he said sadly, "Brothers."

"Orion!" He heard Esmerelda's voice.

"Back in the house, woman," Jake said.

Orion turned. Esmerelda hadn't budged. "Something came out of the body," she said. As she spoke, she saw the flickering cloud. "That," she said.

"Interharg," he said.

*How did he come to the decision to leave the body? Unwise. And the pink cloud? Eskelion —or Eskelion's offspring.* The young one had gone into a spore condition during the purge: It had saved him.

"What's happening?"

"Two of my brothers are fighting," Orion said. "They fight for control of Doyle."

"Of the Wimp?"

"Of him." Orion gestured toward the stumbling figure.

"The nigger?" Jake asked.

"The nigger," Orion said.

Something about the zombie's face was familiar. Cully felt he knew him, somehow—but he couldn't place where. Maybe he shouldn't shoot. Then he worried. "Isn't that one way they get you?" he thought. They took over friends of yours, and then they got you because you trusted them.

The zombie lurched farther away. Now it seemed to be zig-zagging toward the house.

"Let Jake handle him," Cully thought with relief. "I'll get the pink one."

Finally his fingers closed on the trigger. Brief fire appeared at the end of the barrel.

Nothing happened.

The buckshot sailed through the cloud like air.

"Silver buckshot, dammit," Cully thought. "I ought to have silver buckshot."

Or was that for vampires? He couldn't remember.

The noise of the shotgun blast shook Doyle. His head began to clear; his dreamlike trance began to evaporate. He stood groggily and tried to take in his surroundings. Finally, the links between his body and mind closed.

He was standing at dusk near his grandfather's place. He'd heard a shotgun blast.

Three people stood near the house, and one of them was Esmerelda. Esmerelda!

He looked around and saw the two combatant clouds.

"Now what the hell?"

Doyle breathed deeply of the night air. He could see cattle moving around the lake's edge, apparently attracted by the people. They would expect to be fed.

"Esmerelda," he called. "Es!"

She looked at him. Her reaction was odd, he thought. What was the matter?

And then he remembered: He was black.

Will that make a difference? he wondered.

Of course it would, he thought.



Interharg lost his quarry again. He was furious, beating with anger. He must act. Now. He backed away from Eskelion. He shimmered, gathering his energy.

Several hulls moved nearby: Which was correct?

One must be Doyle.

Only Doyle had been moving, he remembered. Only one of these forms now moved. Even if he was mistaken, he could use the last of his energy to crush Doyle even with another body. It would kill him, but death would be a pleasure now. Duty, in fact, demanded his death.

Interharg feinted as if he were once again attempting to get past Eskelion. Eskelion accepted the feint and moved left. Interharg spurted right.

He focused on the moving creature.

"Revenge is mine," he screamed.

Into the body he went.

"Charley?" Esmerelda asked.

"It's me," he said. "I'm a little different than you might remember."

"Charley the Wimp? A nigger?"

"Jake. Well, I'll be damned—but yes. A nigger."

Jake looked from the beautiful woman to the dark man. Instantly, he knew she loved him. But the skin: What had happened to Doyle's skin? He shuddered.

Just then, a cow bellowed down by the pond. It began galloping wildly, its tail raised in the air. The rest of the herd panicked and followed. They thundered over the hilltop and disappeared.

"Cows," Doyle said. "Good riddance."

"The fireflies have gone," Jake said.

The pink cloud drifted toward them. It was changing. It began to appear as an abstract expressionist's portrait of a man. Jake lifted his gun.

"No," Doyle said.

Friend friend friend friend friend . . .

"How did he survive?"

"Spores. Eskelion always was a little odd."

Doyle turned to the speaker. He felt fearful of this man: Fear at how he came to be with Esmerelda. "I don't know you," he said.

"Yes you do. You've just never seen me before. I'm Orion."

"Orion?"

"Yes."

Friend, friend, friend, friend . . .

Even Jake felt the friendliness. He also felt he needed a drink.

Leroy Brown wakened slowly. He felt an exact calmness in his waking, the same way he felt when he awakened after the cotton and beans were in, when the battle before the winter was over. But it's summer, he thought . . . and then he remembered the dream. Even before he opened his eyes, he smiled. He had won in the dream; even though it had only

been a dream, the feeling of victory was
strong.

"Mama," he said. "You shoulda had my
dream last night."

"Easy, Mr. Brown. Easy."

Brown opened his eyes and realized he
wasn't home. He wasn't quite sure where he
was—he remembered it, but not well. But he
knew the man beside him: It was the white
trash, Cully.

"Boy, what you doing here?"

"You been sick. I been watching you."

"Sure, I been sick. Ain't been sick a day in
my life, and I ain't starting now."

"You fell maybe. Anyhow, you've been in
bad shape."

He couldn't remember a fall. A fall? Something clicked. Something had happened, but it
was still foggy—and he'd thought it was the
dream. Somebody had tried to take him over,
and he had fought him—and maybe it wasn't a
dream. Maybe it was real.

But how could that be?

By damn, this wasn't Halloween and he
didn't believe in spooks—but something had
happened. He would have to work at it: He
wouldn't get sense from this boy, he knew.

"You tell Mrs. Brown where I've been?"

"No, sir."

"I better get on then," he said. "And I'm
going to want to talk to you later. You hear?"

Cully heard. The way he heard it made him
regret he'd ever been born white.

First thing in the morning, not half-way through his coffee, Sheriff Clive Taylor got the call from Fanny Lawrence. She called to report strange doings at the old Phillips place. Taylor promised to investigate.

As he drove down the winding Steam Mill Ferry Road, Taylor tried to make some sense of Miss Lawrence's report. If he didn't know her well, he'd suspect she'd been drinking. First was niggers, she said. There was a lot of niggers, she said: maybe a hundred. He discounted that by ninety-nine per cent and decided one or two would be the correct number.

She also reported firefly swarms, a pink cloud and a renegade bull that had gotten loose and ransacked her peonies. That was the major crime.

Taylor would like to have passed this job on to a deputy, but couldn't risk it. Old man Phillips had been regular with his checks to the (perpetual) Re-Elect Clive Taylor campaign treasury. Miss Lawrence chipped in, too. It was important to keep such supporters happy, especially in light of Taylor's recent indictment for shaking down bootleggers.

It was also a beautiful spring morning, though. If Taylor himself didn't have to round up the bull, it could be a nice jaunt. About the only time he got to this end of the county was to arrest Cully and Jake. But not this time.

Those two would have nothing to do with blacks.

As he pulled into the gravel drive, however, he had to rearrange his guess. Cully and Jake were sitting in the yard. *Well, it's at least trespassing*, he thought. *None of the Phillips or the Doyles, for that matter, had any use for those two.*

Taylor smiled to himself in the mirror of the four-cylinder car: Maybe this wouldn't be a wasted trip after all.

Taylor struggled up and out of the low seat. He was a fair-skinned man with bushy yellow hair. He never tanned and he almost always looked pink and boyish. He was fifty. He moved to the aluminum gate, opened it, pulled the car through, then shut the cattle gate. He watched Jake get up and go into the house.

"Lo, Cully," he said as he got out of the car at the house.

"Morning, sheriff. What brings you out this way?" He smiled his thick insolent smile.

"A little bird told me some white trash was messing around out here where it shouldn't. Seems like the little bird was right."

"Now, sheriff. You know better than that."

"You drinking Mr. Phillips' beer?"

Cully shrugged. "Jake'll be out in a minute. He'll explain."

That settled the matter in Taylor's mind: If

Jake was doing the talking, something was up. He leaned against the picket fence and heard it creak. Momentarily, three people came out of the cabin.

"Morning, sheriff."

"Morning, Jake. Who're your friends?"

With Jake were a black man and a woman who looked foreign. Taylor looked carefully at the black man. He was a quadroon, anyhow. The white blood told. It was the black man who extended his hand.

"Remember me, sheriff? Charley Doyle."

"Doyle?" The face did have the Doyle look. The features were more white than black. But the skin was too dark. Still, these city folks and their eternal tans.

"Got a bit of a skin problem since you last saw me. Can you imagine waking up this way one morning?"

"I'd rather not," Taylor said. He laughed a little to put the line over. "Been a while since I've seen you. Eight years, anyhow. You was with your grandfather. You was up here fishing."

"More like fifteen years—and you stopped me speeding. I was doing ninety in a little brown Triumph."

"So it was," Taylor said. He casually took in the place. He didn't see anything that looked peculiar. His eyes fixed on a dark spot on the ground.

"Ya'll got a bull loose? Miss Fanny called to complain," he said.

"One got loose last night. A yearling. We didn't know where it had gone. I'll get on over and round him up," Doyle said.

"You do that," Taylor said. Slowly he lit a cigarette. He puffed it once, twice. "What you been hunting, Jake?"

"Nothing, sheriff. No season's open."

"Ain't stopped you before. And somebody's been cleaning something," he said. He walked over to the dark spot and took his hand and reached down.

"Friend of ours cut himself pretty bad last night," Doyle said. "Real bad. His wife took him on back to Memphis."

"That so? This much blood, you'd done better to take him on into Jackson."

"It wasn't nothing but a lot of blood, sheriff. No arteries. We were away from the house when it happened. He had time to bleed."

"I believe I've heard that story before," Taylor said. "I heard it from this one. Jake said something like it when Sammy Maples disappeared."

"Nobody's going to turn up missing," Jake said.

"That right, Charley?"

The Doyle boy nodded. Skin condition? the sheriff wondered. Something more to it than that—but the Doyles had always been good people, and maybe it was none of his business. The boy was right, too: He had stopped him speeding. Taylor had wanted to look at the little sport car more than anything else—and at the woman in the car.

"What happened to that pretty little woman of yours, Charley?"

"I married her," Doyle said.

"You Doyles always were lucky."

They talked on a while. The sheriff pressed where he thought he could, but the answers he got seemed straight. Something was up, but maybe it wasn't his business. Maybe he could send a deputy by later.

"Well, you get the bull up, you hear? I don't want to have to talk to Miss Fanny anymore. Once a day is too much."

"We'll get right on it," Doyle said.

Taylor nodded, adjusted his hat and scowled briefly at Cully. He smiled at the others and got in his car.

"I'll get the gate," Jake said.

That settled it for Taylor. He would definitely send a deputy by later.

They gathered around the kitchen table. The table had a red-and-white checked vinyl tablecloth. From the other room came snores from Mr. Brown. Orion looked at the four: Doyle, Esmerelda, Cully and Jake. In ways, he felt he understood Cully and Jake more than

his two charges. Those two! He watched dis-
passionately as Doyle's hand slipped under
the table to meet with Esmerelda's. Noon was
outside. The sun ladled a thick heat onto the
world. Sweat still shone on the men's faces
from chasing the bull.

"So Interharg is here," Doyle said.

"Somewhere. Eskelion says he's vanished,
but he doesn't know how. He says the threat is
gone."

"What is it with Interharg?" Doyle asked.

"With any of you," Jake added. He grinned
as Doyle looked at him sourly. Orion ap-
proved.

"The good and the not-good have mixed,"
Orion said. "That would be the judgment of
Council, I think. What has happened is our
age-old rules have broken down. Interharg
has chosen to eliminate the causative agent.
You, in other words. I have chosen another
path. I accept the inevitable; in retrospect, it
is surprising how long our system held. And I
have chosen to give what guidance I can to the
children."

"Us?"

"Yes. You. You have much to learn—and
you will learn it. You have already gone
farther than had been believed possible. I
hope to make your learning less dangerous. I
also hope you will learn from Jake."

"From Jake?"

"Like fishing," Jake said. He said it seriously.

"Fishing?" asked Orion.

"Fishing? I can fish," Doyle said.

"You'll see," said Jake.

Orion considered the Earthman—the true Earthman, he now believed. He didn't know whether it was appropriate to smile. He felt Eskelion's presence pulsing around them. Eskelion had said these woods would do: He would make his home here. If true, Eskelion had become the first to benefit from Doyle's array of disasters.

"I expect Council will judge eventually," Orion said. "With me taking one side and Interharg taking the other, they have no choice but to judge. I envy them not."

"How will they judge?" Doyle demanded. "According to what? If the rules have broken down, what are the rules?"

"There is always the final rule," Orion said. "It is power or strength. Yours against Interharg's, I imagine."

Doyle blinked and Orion watched him. Power, he thought. It would not be world-shaping power anymore. They had tried that, and it was past. It was futile. Unfortunately, there was a power beyond. It was the power of minds and illusions. Doyle had it. Interharg had it. Something had happened to Interharg, but he would return. He would return and it would be up to Doyle to withstand Interharg. No one else would be able to help. Finally, Interharg would not be the enemy: The enemy would be within Doyle. Doyle's sickness was the enemy.

But it was too early to say that, Orion thought. He studied the faces at the table. All were silent; all seemed trapped in their own experiences—all except Doyle and Esmerelda, and they were trapped in something else.

Doyle, Orion thought. He was the man who had killed Paradise, who had upset the careful balance among the Nothing Makers that had existed for star lives. It was not good, but it was not the Not Good, either.

It was life and death.

"I have chosen death," Orion said to himself. He wondered if he had chosen wisely. He looked at Doyle. "And so has he. Over and over, he chooses death above life. Now, finally, he must choose life."

Jake drummed his fingers on the table. "What now?" he said.

Orion shrugged. Again, he appreciated the simple truthfulness of the gesture. "We wait."

"How long?" Jake asked.

"I don't know. Now, soon, a year. I don't know."

"There's nothing we can do?"

"Nothing."

"Then we've got time for fishing," Jake said.

It was hot. The summer had come and all else had stopped. The temperature crawled up and up. Doyle walked in the heat with Esmerelda. They walked through briars, across open fields and crawled under barbed-wire fences. The heat bit through them and warmed them in their gut.

Doyle held out the promise of cool.

"We used to call it an Indian mound, but it's not," he told her. "It's just a hill that rises up out of the middle of nowhere. There's a pine stand at the top, and it's high. There'll be a breeze."

And he thought: There's a carpet of pine needles, soft and thick. God's bed.

They began to walk up the rise. There was a narrow cattle path with blackberries on either side. Esmerelda picked a handful and put them in her mouth one at a time. The juice spilled out and ran in a purple streak on her white cheek. Doyle watched the juice and wanted to lick it off. He didn't know if she would want that. He hadn't pressed her; he had been unable to let himself go much beyond hand-holding and kisses. He felt sure he had killed her desire. Not because he was black, he was sure, but that might be part of it. It was something.

"About here," he said as the path steepened, "a friend and I ran into an owl once. It was broad daylight, and the owl was white. It was an albino owl, I think, and it was sick. It spread its wings and opened its beak. It was fierce. We couldn't get around it. We had to walk back down and come up the other side."

"Was your friend a woman?"

"No. I've never been up here with a woman," he said. "It's been years since I've been up here—back when I still thought this was an Indian mound. We came here looking for arrowheads. Never found any. It was a long, long time ago."

A real long time ago, he thought. He'd been young and it was his first life. He'd had two lives since then, and now he was back to the beginning. It wasn't bad.

For years, he'd refused to come back. There was too much pain here, too much memory. He felt he had outgrown that now and put it behind him. That was in the city, and then he'd left the city for the stars. And he'd left the stars, now, to come home.

He stopped at a likely spot on the crown and dug through the needles. "What're you looking for?"

"Arrowheads," he said.

"You've never found arrowheads here," she pointed out.

"No."

Doyle looked at her. She was a full woman made ghostly by the shadows from the high pine canopy. He remembered the lean women from around here, the women with their hard mouths and eyes of flint. She was not of them. And, so, she was not of him. There were too many gaps between them for it to work. He had chosen correctly not to press her. It was right.

She walked to the shadow edge and sat. She looked over the brown and green patchwork of the fields. He moved closer to her, felt embarrassed, and dug again for arrowheads.

"Sit down," she said. "You're making me nervous."

He sat down. He didn't sit too closely.

"So what did you bring me up here for?"

"It's cool," he said.

"I hadn't complained about the heat," she said.

"No, but I wanted you to be comfortable."

"You didn't bring me up here to make love?" she said.

He was embarrassed. He had thought of it, but had shrugged it off. To be with her was enough. "Well, I knew it was a possibility," he said. "I didn't know if you would want to. I guess if it happened . . ."

She smiled at him. He noticed a hardness to her mouth he hadn't seen before. He noticed it even beyond the berry-stained cheeks and the rich pink of her lips.

"You're a fool," she said.

"What?"

"You don't want to make love?"

"Of course I do. It's just— "

"You're a fool. I don't volunteer to make love. I don't solicit," she said.

"I didn't want to offend you."

She eyed him peculiarly. "I should be offended by being asked? You don't have to rape me."

"I wouldn't."

"I'd break your neck if you tried." She smiled sweetly. He knew she meant it.

"I would like to make love," he said. He could barely hear himself. His voice was scarcely louder than the breeze through the treetops.

"Not good enough," she said. "Do you *want* to? Do you *need* to? Do you want and need to make love to *me*?"

"Yes," he said. "And more."

"Well kiss me and we'll see."

They kissed. It was a long slow kiss. It was too hot for forced closeness. It was too hot for urgency. Everything between them progressed slowly, slowly. He kissed her fingers and sucked them, then bit lightly on the thick flesh at the base of her thumb. He tasted her salt. Accidentally, it seemed, their clothes came off. It was cooler that way. Their sweat mixed into pools. They were both slick with sweat.

"I want to make love to you," he said. This time, he didn't feel fearful in saying it. He felt no shame at his need; the need was a blessing.

She made a low sound. Maybe it was yes.

The pad of needles beneath them turned out not to be as comfortable as Doyle had imagined it would be: The needles jabbed; in the back of his mind, he knew they would both get chiggers. He didn't care. All that was outside.

Inside was her smell, the rose smell and more. Her stomach was white and had laugh lines.

And they made love.

They made love in the heat. The heat made love with them.

And then they were still. The heat of the day was passing or had become irrelevant.

*She made love with me*, he thought.

*Because of my need*.

Inside, he felt something had healed.

They held each other and nuzzled. After a while, he pulled her onto him and they rolled in the needles, laughing. They wrestled, and they laughed. She rolled back under him. "Ouch," she said.

"Did I hurt you?"

"No. I hit something. A rock," she said. Her white hand dug in the brown needles under her back. "Look."

She held it in her hand. He smiled as he looked at the crisp, clean-cut edges of the arrowhead.

Dark came to the Phillips' place slowly, as if the sun were fighting to keep its hold. Deputy Jarrel Tibbs watched the white cabin through field glasses. He watched and wanted a beer.

A beer would be real nice, he thought. Maybe later.

Tibbs' mouth watered. He could smell frying catfish from where he watched. He saw Cully and Jake drinking beer. Those shiftless punks, he thought. It wasn't fair. Here he was, law-abiding and working, and what did he get? Thirsty. Hot. Hungry. But those two, neither having worked a full day in their lives, were eating and drinking and comfortable. They'd spent the day fishing, likely.

"But I got things to be proud of," Tibbs told himself. He was thinking of his bass boat and his Zebco casting rod. There was some justice, after all—but not really enough to satisfy him.

"Maybe I can sneak off. They ain't up to nothing, anybody can see that. Why the sheriff wants me to sit here past midnight is beyond me."

The only problem with sneaking off was the sheriff might catch him, and Sheriff Taylor wouldn't be kind. Better not, not yet. Not yet anyway.

So Tibbs waited and watched, and he got thirstier and thirstier. Jake began singing. It was growing dusk and Tibbs couldn't recognize Jake anymore, but he knew the voice. He must've been watching five hours by now. He checked his watch: 9:18. Less than three hours to go.

And then it started.

Tibbs thought at first a sudden lightning

storm had come up—but there was no thunder after the flashes. He could see the stars,
too. His heart began to beat faster, too, as he
remembered. Six years ago there had been
lights like this, the summer before the
troubles began. There had followed fifteen
months of chaos during which time it seemed
the world had lost direction. Then began the
struggle and the return to normality. It had
been as if the world were robbed of its initiative, then the initiative had been bred back
in.

And now the lights returned.

Tibbs watched the lights with glistening
eyes; his tongue and mouth were dry, too dry.

Zinfaner looked forward to making contact
with Orion. You could depend on Orion for
precise reports and impeccable analyses. Now
in this hub of crisis, such talents would be
welcome. He trembled in the atmosphere and
waited. Where could Orion be? It was long
past time for a resolution. Specious reports
there were that Orion had become an infidel.

Implausible. Zinfaner, the newly chosen
Council speaker, gleamed at the idea.

COUNCIL, he demanded.

Surely Orion would heed the call.

Rainbow lights answered him. The hearing was in readiness. Earth was below, and it was a particular part of Earth. It was the place Orion had said the Decision would be made: His Idea, troublesome as it was, would be rooted in this unnatural setting of lake and trees and air. Interharg, too, would be part of the Decision—and he, too, should answer the call.

Neither had appeared.

COUNCIL, he sang again.

Zinfaner wondered if Not Thinking could possibly have come to either of them, beings who had both been his teachers. It was unlikely. But something had happened. Neither of the two had appeared.

POSITIONS. He flashed out the command. His thoughts spread as light through the evening sky. In his multi-planed "seeing," the lake below was a loudness and the woods prayed to him. Life hosts, hulls with intelligence, were scattered below.

ORION.

No answer.

INTERHARG.

No answer.

ESKELION.

Friend friend friend friend friend . . . came the answer. Zinfaner recoiled at the strength of the emanations. Eskelion was a mere apprentice among the Nothing Makers; his thoughts shouldn't radiate so powerfully—yet

they did. If even Eskelion had gained strength
here, why hadn't Orion and Interharg answered?

"Eskelion, you are welcome at Council. We
are glad at your strength and pleased that you
obey so quickly."

"Obey is not. Eskelion is come as friend."

"Friends and brothers we are," Zinfaner
said.

"Brothers under the skin, yet you have not
skins? It is the Not True you speak. Ask your
brothers Orion and Interharg. They will
understand."

"They do not answer."

"They answer me," Eskelion said pointedly.
"But I have no more time for your games. I
have pecans to attend to."

"Eskelion."

But there was no Eskelion.

ESKELION.

No answer. From far away, however, were
carried the beatings of friend friend friend . . .

"I feel them," Orion said. His voice carried
in the darkness. Doyle and Esmerelda sat on a
cattle blanket some meters away. Except for

the occasional rumblings of cattle, the slap of a hand against a mosquito, the night was quiet.

Above them the sky glowed.

"They have come to make judgment," Orion said.

"What happens next?" Doyle asked.

Orion considered. "They are trying to reach me as a Nothing Maker. They may already have contacted Eskelion and Interharg—but they will have to adjust for my condition, if they wish me to speak. I have lost power to speak to them."

He felt shame at the admission. He must face this which he had not wanted to admit: Interharg had vanished, and it only made sense that he had returned into light. Such would mean he still had vast power; to him, Council would defer.

And what did that mean?

Orion studied the calm countryside, the blue-green night and the stars. He imagined the countryside melting as the sun was made to nova. He imagined the lava cooling among the stars. It would be the sterilization and purification of Earth, if it happened: Orion would have failed. With an effort, he could still comprehend the endless rationalizations of his kind. From their point of view, such an action might seem necessary.

Necessary? Orion couldn't accept that anymore.

*Have I chosen wrong?* He had meant to defend these odd people, but perhaps he had left them defenseless. He had thought Interharg would never retreat once the battle had begun, but Interharg had done just that . . . or so it seemed. At the last, Orion realized, Interharg may have understood that there was no compromise at this level of being. To fight on the physical level was to lose. Grimly, he realized it was a lesson he might never be able to teach.

ORION.

"The message comes," he said. He did not hear the voice with his ears; it was a voice in his bones. "I am here," he said. He said it quietly, humbly. He knew Doyle and Esmerelda would be listening. He thought he felt their eyes upon him. For them it must be terrible, to realize the final action was coming and they were beyond the ability to challenge it.

At the end, as always they had been, they would be victims.

"You have joined the physical?"

"It is noted, Zinfaner. Is that so bad?"

"You have lured a young brother into the physical. That is Not Good."

"I note that, Zinfaner and Council, with objection. It is the Earthmen who were followed, not I."

"A brother followed the word of a non-brother? You say that which we cannot believe."

"You surely know the power of those here. Knowing that, you may believe what you wish," Orion said.

"The Earthmen still think?"

"Think, yes. And feel."

"Is it he who binds Interharg then?"

For the first time, Orion was surprised. So far, the Council was plodding as it always did, and plodding in a direction Orion knew was dangerous. This, though, changed things.

"None here bind the brother. Interharg was here, then he was no longer here."

Silence.

So Interharg had not made it out: Interharg's victory was suddenly less certain. But where was he?

INTERHARG?

The call ached inside Orion.

Orion heard no answer. *What is happening? What has happened*? He looked at Doyle. Doyle had tensed and turned away. The Earthman peered into the darkness, his shoulders hunched. A twig snapped as Orion moved and Doyle jerked back around.

"What is it?" Orion asked.

"He's here."

Orion turned slowly in a full circle. Nothing had changed. He saw the shapes of Cully and Jake. Some cattle drank down by the pond. Birds called their night calls.

"Interharg?" he asked.

"Yes," said Doyle. "He is here. I feel him. He's waiting on something."

"You're over-reacting. I can't feel him; Council can't feel him. How can you?"

"I am stronger than you now—and, in ways, I am stronger than the Council. And I tell you I feel him."

Orion started to argue. It made no sense. How could Interharg be here and yet not-here? It was preposterous.

INTERHARG!!

Orion felt his bones would splinter at the call.

"Tell them," Doyle said. "Warn them."

"Council, I bear warning."

ORION. WE HAVE NO FEAR.

"Interharg has abandoned thinking as his way. He is feel only, now," Orion said. That sounded right. "He is maddened and dangerous."

IF SO, HE HAS SACRIFICED FOR HIS BROTHERS. WE MUST SEEK OUR BROTHER. IT IS DUTY.

"It is not wise," Orion said, but there was no answer. He turned back to Doyle. "They'll sift for the pattern of Interharg now. Since he can't answer, they must find him."

"They're fools," Doyle said bitterly. "He needs them, but he can't come out of hiding." Sweat began to shine on his face. "He is almost ready. It is almost time."

Orion watched the man rock on his feet. He heard the strain in Doyle's voice. There was fear in the voice. Orion watched as Doyle shook his head and turned to Esmerelda.

"I love you," Doyle said. "I have loved you since the time in the fields of Corfu. Since

Paradise, which it was and I was too foolish to know. I wanted to clear something up. The banioxle? There's not such Greek mythical creature. None. I lied. I lied because I was messed up and I was afraid for you to see my weakness."

"Charley," she said. "It doesn't matter."

"It does. My time is come and I wanted no lies between us. I love you, and I wanted you to have no doubts about its truth when I told you that for the last time. I love you, but the time for my loving is over."

"Doyle," Orion said.

"Quiet," Doyle said.

"You don't understand. You're out of your league," Orion said. "Council can still— "

"It's out of their league, too." Doyle grinned a thin line of a grin. "You love Es. You must love her. And Es—you take care of him. He lacks strength and brains."

"What's going on?" It was Jake.

"Listen," said Doyle.

INTERHARG, BROTHER, WE BRING —The words began, then fell off. All heard them this time. Then—COUNCIL! I DEMAND . . . But that stopped, too.

By the lake, a blue glow surrounded one of the cows. Orion saw the glow and suddenly understood. Of course, of course: Interharg, weakened and crazed, had lunged in desperation for Doyle's body—and he had missed. That probably explained the young bull's rampage, for Interharg would have surely entered a body. And had been trapped there. Yes.

Now Council was probing for Interharg, un-suspecting. They were always unsuspecting, so confident were they in their ability to work things out in the long run. They would be open, ready to transfuse power—and Inter-harg would tie into that power. He would be vitalized and liberated.

Liberated for one last go at Doyle.

"Council," Orion screamed. "I demand Council." No answer came. The blue became blue fire. Already, contact was made. The eerie light shone on the surface of the lake. "Council," Orion pleaded, knowing it was futile.

The explosion came and went quickly. Yellow steam erupted from the body of the bull. The bull collapsed. There was a squish-ing sort of whoosh, then a kind of a whine, and suddenly the night was dark again. There was silence.

"I'm coming," Doyle said. "I hear you."

"Charley . . ." It was Esmerelda. Her voice was low and plaintive, without hope.

"He's gone," Orion said stupidly. He thought, He is really gone. He walks open-handedly into the illusions Interharg will set for him. Had he healed enough to survive?

Could he ever be healed enough to survive? Orion wondered.

"Council, I beg intercession. It is a crime." He called loudly to no answer. His voice finally hung in the deep, hot night into which Doyle had vanished.

"Where have you been?" Doyle heard the big man's voice. It boomed out and around him. Inside himself, the terror began. Interharg had chosen brilliantly.

"Reading," the boy said.

"Didn't I tell you to get up the yearlings?"

"No, sir. You— "

"Are you saying I'm lying?"

"No, sir."

"Then why didn't you get up the yearlings?"

Spring became perfect, that weekend in Doyle's youth. He swung his light body from the schoolbus landing. His feet scrunched happily in the gravel. All he had to do was feed the yearlings, that's all he had to do. Then he would be free. He would spend the weekend away from the farm. He could sleep late, watch cartoons and eat peanut-butter-and-jelly sandwiches.

And he would have no calves to feed. Mom had said she would feed them. She would, and he was free.

Charley came out of his sneakers and pulled on his high, black-topped boots. The screen door banged. He headed up the long hill where the ground yellow corn and the cotton-seed hulls waited to be mixed and carried.

While he walked, he imagined himself to be a magician. He carried a stick and pointed it at trees. The trees changed into dragons and princesses. He made up a song to sing about his victories, and he was singing the song as he entered the cool of the barn. He found a suitable tow-sack and began to fill it with the sweet-smelling corn.

"We're high spirited today, aren't we?" Out of the darkness came the voice of his father. The voice sounded happy, and Charley felt good.

"Yes, sir," he said. He looked up at the big man. Now his father was silhouetted in the gaping, sliding door.

"And you didn't dawdle. I saw the bus come in. I heard you coming up the hill not two minutes later. See how much easier it is when you get right to it?"

"Yes, sir," Charley said. He didn't say, "I've got somewhere to go. I've got something to do." Let his father be happy at him; it wouldn't be long before the unhappiness returned.

"You're a good boy, Charley. A good boy." The gentle moment held between them. Charley, even in the dark, felt surrounded by sunshine. Maybe he was learning; after all these years, maybe he was learning.

"I'm glad you're early, because Long John's off. I want you to feed the milk calves, too, and feed the pens."

The brightness wavered in Charley's mind. Quickly he figured: Another hour, maybe. He would run, and it wouldn't even be an hour. He could skip washing up, if he was careful. Everett might have to wait a little, but that was okay. Sure. He wouldn't mind. Charley hoped Everett wouldn't mind.

Everett was Charley's first friend outside family. This was his eighth year, and he had one friend. He'd grown up in the country where there were no people, and where the skills of meeting people weren't known. He didn't understand people. He was a quiet boy and he had no stories to tell on the bus. His stories were silly, about magic and dragons. But Everett seemed to like him, and everybody liked Everett. Everett was Charley's hero.

And Everett had invited Charley to spend the weekend. In an hour, he'd be with his hero.

"Yes, sir. I'll get 'em."

"Good boy. And you'll need to feed them tomorrow and Sunday. Long John will still be off."

Charley tried to listen and comprehend the words. He heard the words, but he couldn't accept them. "No," he said to himself. He did not talk out loud. "No." He looked at the shadow which was his father. "Mom's feeding the calves for me tomorrow," he said. "I'm going away this weekend." He could not tell the expression on his father's face. He was sure the lip had curled slightly and the half-frown had appeared.

"Your mother's not a field hand," his father said.

"No, sir, she's not. She wanted to do it."

"She wanted to? She didn't want to: She's trying to protect you," he said. "You're going to have to stay home this weekend, Charley. I need your help. I know it's disappointing, but we're farm folk. We have our duties."

"But I never get— "

"You get more than I had."

Tears filled Charley's eyes. He couldn't cry, though—crying would make things worse. His father hated tears. "No, sir," he said.

"What?"

"Yes, sir, I mean." His legs were rubbery with misery. He imagined Everett showing up, and his not being there. Or he would be there—and he'd have to explain. He would be stinking of the barns, and Everett would be all clean. It wasn't right. It wasn't right. It wasn't right.

"Now you get on with your chores," his father said.

"Yes, sir," Charley said.

I hate you, he thought. I hate you.

And again Doyle faced his father. In some far away part of his mind, he knew he was dreaming. He knew he was in an illusion that had been set as a trap. He had entered the illusion at his own choice. Now, as a man, he was willing to face his father again. His father had ruled his life from the shadows all these years. Now, they would have it out.

If he could understand, if he could accept —he could win.

Doyle loved his father, yet feared the man's power.

His father's power now flowed according to Interharg's design. Interharg was coloring his dreams, he knew.

Yet Doyle didn't care.

This was his chance to face his father squarely. Not his old father, a ghost wasting in a rest home, but his young father. That was the man he had to face.

For that, he would give up Esmerelda. For that, he would risk his life and his world.

"Where are you?" he called. "C'mon. I'm ready."

The lights faded by the lake. Orion watched the lights disappear and he felt Esmerelda trembling beside him. Carefully, he put his arm around her shoulder.

All was quiet. He heard crickets. Esmerelda's flesh was warm. Gently, he took her hand. Her hand was a cool, white fish in the net of his hand.

The air grew cooler around them. There was a breeze from the lake. Stars came out and moved against the black canopy overhead. The stars had been forever, and they would be there after this, whatever happened. Orion was shocked at the humanness of the thought.

The night passed slowly. Gray appeared in the east. Colors soon streaked the sky, and there were sounds trumpeted in the countryside, the sounds of animals and people.

"I love him, too," Orion said.

"I know you do," she said. "For that, I love you."

COUNCIL! COUNCIL!

"Council is in session. The final battle is drawn. Judgment is out of our hands."

In the darkness, through the thick haze of
his sleepiness, Doyle heard the telephone
ring. Panic and fear twisted through him.
"God, I've done it again," he thought, ter-
rified. He tore himself from the warmth of the
bed.

The phone would be his father calling from
the barn. His father would be waiting. The
milking machines would all be in place. All
that was missing would be the herd, because
Doyle was to have brought in the herd. He had
slipped back into sleep after his father waked
him. He had waited and fallen back to sleep.
Now the telephone was ringing, and his father
was calling, and Doyle had failed again.

He didn't answer the phone. He just ran.
The cattle still had to be gotten up. Doyle
would make up a story, and his father would
believe him. He wouldn't say he had fallen
asleep; that was weakness. Edith, he thought.
He would blame Edith. Edith was the oldest
cow in the herd—a cow that long since had
gone to the stockyards. She was old, arthritic
and cantankerous. She was also what
remained of the two-year-old that had been
his father's only grand champion cow ever at
the local fair. Edith was always getting out:
Charley thought how he would explain, slowly

and precisely, how he had been searching in the gully bottoms for Edith. He would say how he knew he could not bring in the herd until he knew Edith was safe.

Even as he walked the hard earth under the winter-clear skies, as he scurried toward the winter pasture, Doyle knew he would probably not be believed. Somehow, his father would know the truth and he would look at him with eyes of judgment: You have failed me again.

But lying was easier, safer. It would only be another wound between them.

Doyle's mind whirred almost audibly in the 4 a.m. morning. Tears that would not freeze formed rivers of self-pity on his cheeks.

"It's not fair," he said aloud. "It's not fair."

His voice was thin and the wind carried it lightly. He moved into the deep darkness and the hard cold.

Interharg gleefully rode the turbulent passions; he drifted between Being and the realm of the Nothing Makers. He had stolen enough strength from Council, he thought, to do himself justice in the battle with Doyle. He had strength, but still he respected the dark

powers now erupting in the Earthman's mind.
Cautiously, he steered Doyle's dreams. He
must not be noticed, not if he were to wreck
this man. Doyle must return fully to his
dreams and fears. There he would drown in
them.

Thus would the challenge be met. He, Interharg, would return victorious to Council.

To Interharg, the man Doyle existed as a
thin, veiled apparition. A ghost. Interharg
remembered seeing similar terror before, the
terror in the young eyes of his children. The
weak ones must be eaten according to his
people's law, and Interharg had always been
lawful. He remembered, though, the terror
and supplication in those eyes; even now, star
lives later and his planet only a molten glob of
lava spinning about a lifeless sun, he remembered feeling pity.

. The pity welled up at him as he twisted
Doyle's dreams.

Pity, he felt—but also disgust at the weakness.

In his arms, in the summer morning, Esmerelda finally slept. Her weight shifted sig-
nificantly against Orion. He closed his sup-

porting arm a bit more tightly and tenderly against her shoulders. His fingers were pleasantly numb from her weight.

Hours had passed.

How many more?

Orion didn't know. An instant from now or forever from now the battle could end. In the warm sun, the alien also nodded and finally he slept.

Esmerelda dreamed of her island home of Corfu. A sad-faced creature stumbled toward her. It was a banioxle, she realized. She patted its head and it gave her an uncertain smile.

In Poland, the government fell. Max telegraphed Fyodor: GIVE ME A TOUGH ONE NEXT TIME.

"Your game's off, Jake," Cully said. He watched Jake's red puck slide down the wood of the shuffleboard and miss the blue puck. The blue puck was a hanger, a four. Jake didn't miss those shots, not usually. Usually, he didn't even stop to study them. A classic Loretta Lynn tune wailed from the jukebox. It was just turned noon, but Jake had gotten them into the Men's Room early. The bartender owed him, Jake said. It wasn't noon, but Cully already had a buzz on. And Jake's game was off.

Nobody else was in the joint. P.T., black-haired and oozing musk, wiped draft glasses clean at the bar. Cully could feel her watching the two of them with boredom or amusement.

Cully slid his last puck home. It was a two.

"Six points. My game," he said.

Jake walked to the other end of the board as if he questioned Cully's count. His face was screwed up when he looked at Cully. Cully shrugged. "Something the matter, Jake?"

"The Wimp's a nigger," Jake said.

"I know. And he's got space ghosts as friends."

The oddness stayed in Jake's face. His eyes didn't quite focus. Jake was thinking something, and that usually meant trouble. Jake was making up his mind.

"That woman of his doesn't mind," Jake said.

"But he ain't really a nigger, Jake. Just his skin is all. Underneath, he's still the Wimp."

"Hear what you're saying?" Jake demanded.

Cully tried to remember. It wasn't often he said anything worth remembering. He couldn't place it.

"You're saying we're the same under the skin."

It dawned on Cully. He was horrified. "Just the Wimp. Not all niggers. I sure didn't mean that."

"But if him, then why not all of them?"

"Jake, I ain't no nigger lover."

Jake looked stonily at Cully. "But you think it's all right for one nigger to have a white woman?"

What was this all about? Cully wondered. You couldn't really say the Wimp was a nigger, now could you? But that's what Jake seemed to be getting at. Cully clicked his two pucks together out of habit. He looked at Jake. Jake was smiling.

"Then what?"

"Things have changed," Jake said. "Don't you see?"

Cully couldn't see. Jake continued. "I mean, if the Wimp's okay, why not Mr. Brown? We have to let him, too."

Cully couldn't quite see it, but he realized that didn't matter. "We'll have to burn 'em out, I guess," he said.

"Somehow I don't think that would work anymore."

"So what do we do?"

"I don't know," Jake said. He picked up a red puck and it bounced neatly from the right wall one third the way down the board. The puck slowed precisely; Jake's game was returning. Jake was again looking at Cully as the puck halted squarely in the five box.

"Yes I do," Jake said. "We're going to be nigger lovers from here on out." Cully didn't move. He felt a little sick inside. But if Jake said that's the way it was, that's the way it was.

"Your shot," said Jake.

Doyle dreamed again.

In the darkness, the telephone began to ring. He wakened; panic bled in him. It seemed he had spent his entire life waking in terror.

The boy shook his head groggily and stumbled to the window. The world was sheeted in ice. There was a glaze of frost on the window; the mercury lights of the barn burned an unearthly purple against the nightscape. Nothing was inviting about the outside world; somehow, it was not meant for him to go into it.

The telephone hushed.

"Maybe just a minute more, just close my eyes a minute," he said. But no. That would doom him. That would be the end. He drank down a glass of unhomogenized, unpasteurized milk, then he wrapped his scarf tightly and opened the kitchen door.

Cold bit into him, a cold crueler even than it had looked. The sky was clear and black. The stars didn't seem to twinkle, the night was so clear. His breath made thick white bursts; he felt his breath frosting at his lips. The boy tried to hurry, but the hard-packed ground made walking difficult. Once he fell; he felt blood warm at his knee. Long rows of sheds stretched into the night like barracks.

Moving quickly, he entered the near pasture where the cows were herded in the winter. Their dark shapes moved in the night as they broke their rest. Doyle scanned quickly for strays, for laggards, but the herd was a single entity. The cows moved toward the holding pens. Fresh piles of manure steamed.

The gathering took about twenty minutes. By now, Doyle was cold in his bones. His hands were stiff and clawlike. The cattle moved silently, ploddingly, onto the concrete slab of the holding pen. Finally, the last of them moved in and he closed the aluminum gate.

He thought the cattle were wretched, awful beasts. They would already be seeking new manure piles in which to sleep, stealing their own warmth back. By the time they entered for milking, most of them would be caked with their own excrement. The filth would be layered and frozen on them.

His job would be to wash them. He would take the wet cloth and swab the mud and manure from their udders—so the machines could go on to suck out the warm milk.

Then would come barn-cleaning time, then feeding, and then the gathering time would return. As he entered the barn, he was thinking that the summer was no better. The summer was a different kind of misery. The heat was unbearable and the stink would grow until it made you sick to breathe. It was a hellish cycle, a year in which each season was a different kind of horror.

But now he entered the barn and was comforted briefly by the warmth of the space heater.

The morning went slowly. Doyle watched, pumped feed into troughs, and counted. He counted the cows and figured how much time was left until the end. Soon only twenty cows were left, less than half an hour.

Eight at a time, the cows moved through the barn.

Doyle and his father seldom spoke. There were commands, orders, but no communication. "This one needs feed;" "Give me a rag, this one's still filthy," and "Hurry up now. I'm ready on this side."

And then his father said, "Where's Edith?"

Doyle didn't know. "I didn't see her," he said.

"Didn't you look? You took long enough. I thought you were checking the moon."

"I didn't see her," Doyle said again. It was true. He was not perfect and had never said he was. He had done his best. He hadn't seen the old cow. What else was he supposed to say? There was no excuse to be made; he felt he would never be able to make excuses again.

"Go find her. Get her in here."

Doyle nodded and stumbled tiredly into the cold. No telling where Edith was, he thought. She'd always been one to get out; no doubt she'd found shelter from the cold. When Doyle found her, she would rise lazily, but ready to go and be fed the feed that was her due.

That was the way it had always been.

As the cold numbed him, another thought came to Doyle. He had chased the old dilapidated animal too many times. This time he would make it different. He would make this the last time he went looking for Edith.

This time had been coming. He'd hidden a pack and some money in the hay barn. When he could get away from chores, he sometimes held the pack and dreamed of freedom.

The world was growing light.

Doyle picked up a rotted two-by-four. He jerked it free. The board had been frozen into the ground. He carried the board with him as he walked along the fence row, seeking a break where Edith could have gotten free. He came to a hollow, where the fence ran straight across and there was a gap underneath. Water was pooled in the hollow and there was a crust of ice on the water. Hooves had broken the ice. This was it, he thought.

Doyle gripped the two-by-four harder. He imagined what it would be like to bring the board down on Edith's head. He had, in fury, once hit a cow in the head with a hammer. It hadn't bothered the cow. Killing Edith would be hard.

But it wouldn't be impossible.

Doyle smiled.

Interharg cursed the cold bitterly. He could not imagine creatures able to function in such cold—not with the humans' soft skins; not with their soft wills. But here they were, pressing on, their only strength the same perversity that Doyle had used to wreck Paradise. Strength through perversity, Interharg thought wryly. Some virtue.

The only way to manipulate dreams was to enter into the dream. For Interharg to use the dreams against Doyle, he must enter into and feel the dream. He would take the part of the father and amplify it, in order to crush Doyle.

His mind filled with the scene in which Doyle now lived: the wind, the strong smells, the pain of cold feet walking hard earth in unyielding boots. This was Doyle's nightmare, not his—Interharg had read the Earthman's fears truly.

Here, in these hours, Doyle would give in as he had before. This time, however, Interharg would be there to intensify the boy's self-loathing and fear. The emotions would become crippling, incapacitating—and Doyle would stick fast, and die, in the mire of his emotions.

And Interharg would be victorious.

The alien glowed.

He followed the scene as it developed: the ringing of the telephone, the stumbling in the dark, the silent curses of the boy as he moved in the night. Details filtered in: the long cold lagoon into which the barn waste was washed; the gentle, infuriating lowing of the cattle as they rose and began plodding toward the island of light which was the barn; the boy's desperate, anxious anticipation of his father's anger as he slipped and set cattle loose before they had been milked.

All was good; the final scene was developing masterfully.

As Interharg watched and experienced the scene, his only wonder was that the boy had survived his first experience. The boy was a weakling, a coward. On his own planet, right would have been done and the boy would

never have been allowed to grow into warped
adulthood.

The morning progressed. Where he could,
Interharg moved subtly to strengthen the
conflicts between father and son. And he
moved in other ways, too. Boy against the
elements: It became more cold and bitter. Boy
against his father: The man seemed bigger
and more terrible than he actually was. Boy
against himself: The boy's eyes were filled
with a glaze of self-disgust.

Forward the morning moved, perfectly—in-
vincibly.

For all purposes, this memory was better
and more dangerous than the man Brown's
memory. Brown was too healthy; the threat
Interharg had used had been too purely
physical. Physical threats did not seem
terribly effective against any of these people.
"Look at how they take the cold," he marveled
to himself. No, to defeat Doyle, he needed
more. He had it. The physical was here, but
the conflicts with others and within themselves was what made the combination perfect.

And now it was about to climax.

Doyle was about to reach the end of the
dream.

The father had discovered the missing cow.
The boy was commanded to look for it. He
had set out.

And something altered slightly.

Interharg sharpened his attention. What

was it? he wondered as he pressed harder in comparing the memory and the dream.

The memory had changed slightly. Interharg compared it to the original. "Ah. Not so bad," he said to himself.

In this new memory, the dream, it had not yet occurred to the boy that Edith had died. That was his worry originally, in the real scene he remembered. Now he was not worried that the cow was dead; instead, he seemed to want it dead.

Disconcerting, the development was—but it could be handled. When he found the cow dead—as he must, for that was what had really happened—guilt would overcome him. His rebellion would be quashed. This could work better than the original memory, Interharg thought.

But how has he changed it? Interharg wondered. Each time he felt he had finally cornered a human, they changed. They lacked consistency. There was no method to them: no plan.

"All the better," he said to himself. "I have enough method and plan to overcome them."

And then he corrected himself. "Not them. Him. Just him."

But more was at stake here than a single life. It was all these lives. They were dirty, unclean, shambling. Like rotten fruit, they spread their rot. They were a disease, and Interharg was the cure. It was a frightful disease.

Orion has been infected, he thought. And Eskelion. And even Council has its fears. I must show them.

In his hands lay the preservation of the Nothing Makers.

"I must not fail."

He become reabsorbed in the scene:

The boy stumbled along the frozen ground. Interharg watched. There was the tell-tale stump. The boy stopped and looked at it. For years, Interharg knew, the young Doyle had carried the picture of that stump burned into his mind. The stump was gray and iced-over and dead. It was a dead thing in this world of cold dead things. Next, the boy would see the corpse of the cow.

The stump, and the desolation, and the death, and the boy's guilt and hopelessness would fuse.

And that would be that.

Interharg waited. He felt exultant.

Doyle looked at the stump and trembled. He did not think he trembled from the cold. This has happened before: I've been here before, he thought. He stopped in the cold and tried to remember. What does this place mean?

He clenched at the two-by-four in his hand. *I did not have this before.*

His mind worked, and his old wounds bled, and he did not move. *What must I do?* Time froze as thoroughly as the bleak countryside. Doyle did not move. He was one step away from disaster; he knew it. He must not move. Not yet.

Time did not move.

Fall came to the lake beside Steam Mill Ferry Road.

Orion's hands became toughened. He picked cotton; he hauled hay. He waited. He watched as Esmerelda's stomach swelled with Doyle's child. The child wasn't his, he knew—and he regretted that it wasn't.

"How much longer?" he asked her.

"Until the baby comes, or until he returns," she said.

They touched, the two of them, but it was not enough. Orion wanted this woman; he loved her. He loved her better and more truly than Doyle would ever understand, he knew—and he knew that she also knew it.

All that was needed was the proper time.

They waited for the proper time.

Orion did not tell her that the battle was engaged, that somewhere—not in the physical world, and not in the netherworld of the Nothing Makers, but in the twisted world of Interharg and Doyle's mind—the question of time was being decided. Would there be enough time for Orion and Esmerelda?

He didn't know.

Each morning, however, as he woke and the sun was still shining, he had a little more hope. One day more meant one day more. That meant another might follow. As long as the sun rose, Doyle had not lost. Someday the sun wouldn't shine.

Orion's death would come, as would Esmerelda's.

All he wanted was to make love to Esmerelda before that day.

He wished luck for Doyle, but knew luck wouldn't help.

"Soon," Esmerelda told him gently. She squeezed his hand. "Soon."

But soon enough? Orion didn't know.


The world pattern tightened. Esmerelda was not surprised when Max came walking up the gravel path to the cabin. It did not surprise her, when after two days, Max had disappeared without saying goodbye. Jake disappeared with Max.

When Jake returned, he told Esmerelda he would be meeting Max in Praetoria in less than a month. There were some details to be worked out with a fusion mechanic there.

Jake returned with a black wife. At night, Cully slept alone. Jake at least was not alone at night, he thought.

"Your time is coming," Jake said.

Cully grunted. He wasn't sure he trusted Jake anymore.

Restlessness gnawed at Interharg. He had absorbed the details of the scene a thousand times—maybe ten thousand times. Nothing changed in Doyle's scene. Interharg felt himself being drawn deeper and deeper into the scene—but the scene did not change. Now, Interharg had absorbed all of Doyle's pain. He had spewed it back, and he had made it more acid. Still nothing happened.

It was cold; it was cold; it was cold.

Interharg wept with Doyle, and he cursed with him, and he wept again with him. He learned. From learning, he decided what he must do. Obviously Doyle had realized that his next few steps held the outcome to his dream, so he was hedging before he took those steps. His enormous will had halted the flow; now, he would be trying to cut away and change the memory so it would not be crushing.

"So I must bring change," Interharg said.

The most effective way to do it would be to enter into the character of Doyle's father, he thought. That would force Doyle either to move forward or to face his father. The outcome of that was certain. The boy would break.

Interharg came into the memory; he became the father. In the barn, the father grew impatient at waiting. His fool son was loafing again, he knew. He pulled on the quilted coat he had worn for years and stepped to the rear sliding door of the milking parlor. He stood for a moment, peering through the gray dawn. He could not see his son; he did not see Edith.

He stepped quickly down the slick, low steps into the lot. He felt strangely angry and did not realize that the anger was not all his own.

Interharg felt the anger, however. He fed his anger to the man as he watched the world through the man's eyes. Through Doyle's eyes, he had seen the awfulness of the world; now he saw the beauty of it. The ice made crystals along the barn eaves, and even the rich smells were life. Birth, death, eating, purpose: This was a very orderly world to the man, and it was his world.

The man saw only one flaw, his son.

Interharg expected that. He knew that his vision of the father was Doyle's, too. Doyle would feel that way; this man was not the father, really: It was Doyle's vision of his father.

Never mind, he thought. It was another human oddness, an eccentricity—a symptom of the human disease. Interharg could use this character no matter who it really was. Now, for all purposes, he was more Doyle's father than either the father or Doyle.

The man's boots bit firmly into the crusty ground and his eyes scanned the pasture, the trees and the barns.

Doyle stood frozen, but he knew his time was ending. His mind wandered and he remembered what was about to happen—to times that would flow from this, to the other pains that had finally taught him to accept this one.

His fingers loosened. The two-by-four fell with a slight thud. He turned away from the stump and away from whatever revelation it held. He saw, far away, his father moving through the cold toward him. He watched the man and wanted to run, to cry out—but neither would work.

"I have outgrown this," he said to himself.

"I have worked, and married, and I have died and come back. I have been to the stars and I chose to return.

"I have chosen to come back here.

"This is my dream, and I accept it," he said.

He closed his eyes. Another dream burned in him. It was important. It had been a breakthrough, and the breakthrough was what he needed now. It seemed the other dream was far away—years away from this boy, who trembled, and yet years away from this man who lived again as the boy and trembled with him. It had to do with loving.

Loving.

And it was not Esmerelda who held the answer. It was the other love he'd had. The love he'd tried to forget.

"Janet," he said. He stopped feeling the cold.

He remembered the bleakness of Paradise. He had been so empty and so hurt, and she alone had salvaged him—to get him out. He tried desperately to remember.

"I don't want to remember," he said loudly.

He heard his father calling. "Charley! Charley, where are you?"

"I'm over here," the boy said softly. He felt the cold again. He felt tired. He hadn't found

Edith. He must find her before his father
found him. He must go forward. She couldn't
be much farther. Just past the stump, he
thought.

"Charley!"

*But if I go on* . . . He must remember, he
must. Time was beginning to flow again, and
the moment held the decision. There was no
decision to make. Was there? he wondered.

*What have I overlooked?*

Everything was blurry, suddenly. He felt
dizzy. His thoughts short-circuited and he felt
a surge of pain.

"It's too much. It's all too much. I don't care
anymore."

*But you cared once, dammit. Remember. Re-
member.*

"I can't."

His dizziness deepened. He felt nauseous.
Something greasy and indigestible was swelling in his stomach. He tried to open his
eyes to see where his father was. He couldn't be
too far away now. His father would be closing. He would be angry. "What if something
has happened to Edith?" he wailed. It would
be his fault. His father would . . .

The other memory returned. Doyle felt a
flash of longing. He felt warmth, and safety,
and love. He smelled the sweetness of apricot.

"Janet? Janet?"

He was going over the edge, he knew. He
had been to the edge and gone over before. He
had learned something, then, and it was some-

thing he needed now.

The something had to do with Janet—and something to do with his father. He remembered; now, he must tie in what he had learned with himself as a child. Edith and Janet; two females who had shaped his life. Bitches both, the cow and the human. What was it?

"I want to marry you," he said.

That was it. That was close.

*And they moved together again, and she agreed . . . and then . . . and then . . . and then . . .*

"Charley! Answer me, boy."

*And then it was another night. So much like the first when he had proposed. But so different, what she said. That she had miscarried.*

Blackness swarmed around him. The familiar, saving blackness. One of these times it would be death. Maybe it was this time. He hoped not. He didn't know if he really cared.

*She said to him she had miscarried.*

*To him she told: I miscarried.*

*And he believed her absolutely, and they married anyway. It was good. It was damn good. Damn good.*

*Only he knew she had not miscarried. She had had an abortion.*

Doyle remembered, in the cold, beneath skin not yet broken with puberty, what had put him over. His eyes opened and he saw his father coming toward him across the ice-locked barnyard. His father moved with an awful sureness. He moved as the opposite of Doyle's uncertain walk.

Time flowed again.

Doyle closed his eyes and listened to the rest of the words:

*She killed my son, and I love her, and I don't care. Father! Hear me: She has killed my son. And I love her. Father, Father . . . forgive me for the son you never had.*

It was all in place now.

Time moved toward its conclusion.



Interharg wore the old man's body and feelings loosely: They didn't fit well. His eyes scanned again and again, finally catching sight of the goofy-looking hat his son wore. Interharg monitored the man's emotions:

Cold, too cold. Son hates it, my son . . . Necessity. No choice. Boy must learn. Responsibility, that's it. He must learn responsibility . . . Cold night, cold. Edith's hidden . . . Died, maybe? Maybe died . . . The summer of the grand championship, maybe the last time I felt young . . . My father died. Had to work. Had to . . . and then came this boy . . . He'll never be young either, he won't. Yet his skin's soft. He'll never be hard . . . Never a rock . . . Not of the church . . . not of me . . .

The cold misted his eyes.

"Charley," he called.

The boy's name bit into him like an insult, a curse.

Doyle opened his eyes and saw his father.

"Father, I forgive you. I understand."

Everything cleared rapidly. He saw the cold, barren landscape—and he saw that it was real. He saw that his father had no more choice in this than he, a boy, had. They were both in battle against an unrelenting world. This was real.

He was blameless. His father was blameless.

There was no blame.

The hardness, and the cold, and the misery: They were things that existed. They were without malice.

"Over here," the boy called to his father. He turned and saw the stump. He took another step. He could see there was a gully beyond the stump, with a grove of skeleton trees. He didn't have to look in the gully to know. Edith was in there.

He took another step forward and saw.

The animal was bloated and stiff. Her four

legs splayed out from her body. Her face was frosted. Doyle looked at the body and felt pity, a pity not unlike that he felt for his father and himself. And for Meriwether. For Janet. For Interharg.

"It's all right," he said. He knew it was. Edith was dead, as he would one day be dead, and there was no malice in it. The whole thing was an accident; you accepted that, and you did what you could. You went on. "But you were a champion once, old girl. You were my father's champion."

Boots crunched in the ice. Doyle turned. "She's dead," he told his father. He felt no fear.

The father stepped closer and looked. His shoulders shook slightly and he didn't move. He just stood, staring at the bloated corpse in the gully.

"Dad . . . It's all right," the boy said. The big man didn't answer. "It's not your fault."

And light began to dance around him.

The cold fell away. The ice disappeared. The gully was long gone.

COUNCIL: Doyle heard the word.

COUNCIL!

Interharg wept.

The alien was trapped in the body of this man, a man who existed only in a dream. It was not Interharg's dream; it had never been his illusion. Interharg was the man, and the pieces were all in place. He knew it was over.

*I am here, and my prize is lost. I am nothing.*

It was the father thinking.

It was Interharg who thought.

It was neither. The dream was ending; the dreamer had wakened. The illusion had been swept away by the real.

Winter had captured the lake, the cabin and the farm. Orion didn't mind. When the wind died, he picked up the rickety fly-rod he'd gotten from Jake. It was too cold for good fishing, but Orion didn't mind. It was the process of trying to fish that was important. You didn't fish *for* fish, but *to* fish.

He'd learned that from Jake.

"So you like Max?"

Jake grunted. "I don't know if you can like him—but I respect him." Jake flipped a spinner into the dark lake waters. Orion, caught in a breeze, untangled his green floating line.

"But you're still signed on with him?"

"Of course."

Orion smiled to himself. Humans were so damn busy. They had fishing, yet they wanted the stars. He'd had the stars: He'd stick to fishing, thank you.

He put his line out in the water, then lifted it for a perfect backcast. The line was arrow straight behind him, then moved forward. His black bream popper landed gently on the lake surface. He was pleased with the cast.

He also admitted he was pleased by Max's work. In a way, it validated Orion's plan. His Paradise program had worked: Earth seemed to be shaping up. It had not worked how Orion had wanted, but it had worked. His choices for the Egg had now returned. They were without limits now, yet they insisted on testing their limits. They would stretch until they were stretched thin—if there was time.

Orion glanced at the sky. It was dead-man gray. The early moon was behind a veil of snow clouds. There had at least been time enough for him to learn to bounce jigs across the pond bottom; he'd almost had time to learn to use a fly-rod. Maybe he'd had more time than he deserved.

Maybe they all had.

And, maybe, the battle between Doyle and Interharg would go on until this universe wound down.

It was out of his hands now.

"You see Es on the way down?"

"Yeah," said Jake. "She's making a hot rum punch."

"Sounds good."

"Max sent her his love, by the way."

"Figures. Everybody loves Esmerelda, and nobody loves Max. You call that fair?"

Jake glanced at him. He grimaced. Orion went on. "You'd have her in a minute, too—nigger baby in her stomach and all."

"I don't like that word," Jake said.

"You taught it to me, for God's sake. And I'm right?"

"Well . . ."

"So you want her, and I want her, and Max wants her—and she's saving herself for a nigger space ghost."

"Don't use that word."

"All right," Orion said obligingly. "The point is that she loves one of the pre-eminent lunatics of all time—a man so crazy he's walked off from her. Our problem is we're too sane."

Something splashed in the water. The popper disappeared. The end of the green floating line dipped into the water. The line made tight little circles.

"I'm damned. I got one."

"In this weather? You're crazy."

Orion was using a one-pound test leader. He was cautious. The fish came close, touched the surface, and then began to pull away. Jake whistled. "Two pounds. It'll go two pounds." Orion laughed. He was very gentle with the play.

He was still playing the fish, fifteen minutes later, when he heard the call. The call came in his bones.

ORION.

He stopped retrieving.

"Careful, Orion. You'll lose it."

COUNCIL DECIDES.

Orion felt his heart stop. He trembled. The rod and reel dropped from his hands. He took in the sky, the trees, the white cabin. They were beautiful. *So this is it*, he thought. *This is where it ends*.

JUDGMENT IS MADE.

"You're losing the fish!" Jake grabbed for the rod. The line was slack. He tightened the line and felt the strong pull at the end. "You okay?" he said to Orion, but his attention was on the tight circling at the end of the line.

Orion didn't answer. Words wouldn't come.

COUNCIL AWARDS YOU JUSTICE, HONORED ORION. YOU HAVE THOUGHT WISELY AND ACTED DUTIFULLY.

"How about that?" Orion said.

"It's one hell of a fish all right," said Jake.

PLEASURE IS OURS TO OFFER YOU AGAIN YOUR COUNCIL PLACE.

"I'll pass," Orion said. "I'm doing fine—but thanks."

There was silence. Orion again took in the world, his world. Tears burned in his eyes. The wind picked up. Far away, Jake seemed to be shouting. Orion smiled through his tears.

Inside him came the voice he expected. "I envy you," the voice said. "This saving the Universe isn't all it's cracked up to be. I envy you Esmerelda's love."

Orion answered. "Good luck, Charley Doyle." He waited, but no more words came. He wondered what had happened to Interharg —and he was glad he didn't know. The pain that must have come as the battle ended: Interharg had never deserved that.

"Eskelion, did you hear?"

For once, something had happened that was important enough to divert Eskelion from his devotion to pecans. "I hear. We live."

"We do indeed," Orion said.

"You've lost your mind," Jake was screaming. "The last bolt has fallen out and you've gone beserk. One fish all day—a record fish— and you break off in the middle to talk to your tree friend."

"The fish?"

"I lost it. You lost it."

Earth was saved and Orion had missed catching his record fish. *Life isn't fair*, he thought.

Orion found that his angling skill increased as he aged. In the spring that followed, Esmerelda gave birth to a son. They named the child Answar. Orion and Esmerelda married. When Answar's half-brother arrived, they named him Charley.

Sometimes the sky above their farm glowed. No voices came, however. Orion imagined Doyle hovering above, regretting, wondering, but still afraid to make human contact. Somewhere Doyle would be fighting. Orion was glad it was somewhere else.

The same spring that Answar was born, Orion bought a bass boat.

He got a hell of a deal.

# Best-Selling Science Fiction from TOR

# Best-Selling Science Fiction from TOR

# Philip José Farmer

| | | | |
|---|---|---|---|
| ☐ | 48-511-5 | The Cache | $2.50 |
| ☐ | 48-508-5 | The Other Log of Phileas Fogg | $2.50 |
| ☐ | 48-504-2 | Father to the Stars | $2.75 |
| ☐ | 48-535-2 | Greatheart Silver | $2.75 |
| ☐ | 48-522-0 | Stations of the Nightmare | $2.75 |
| ☐ | 48-529-8 | The Purple Book | $2.95 |

# Fred Saberhagen

| | | | |
|---|---|---|---|
| ☐ | 48-501-8 | The Water of Thought | $2.50 |
| ☐ | 48-564-6 | Earth Descended | $2.95 |
| ☐ | 48-520-4 | The Berserker Wars | $2.95 |
| ☐ | 48-536-0 | Dominion | $2.95 |
| ☐ | 48-539-5 | Coils *with Roger Zelazny* | $2.95 |
| ☐ | 48-560-3 | **The Sword Game** *The First Book of Swords* March 83 | $5.95 |
| ☐ | 48-568-9 | **A Century of Progress** *May 83* | $2.95 |
| ☐ | 48-573-5 | **Berserker's Throne** *July 83* | $2.95 |

# Keith Laumer

# DAVID DRAKE

● ● ● ● ● ● ● ● ● ● ● ● ● ● ● ●

# C.M. Kornbluth